"Are you okay?" Armstrong asked, his voice a loud whisper. "How is your head?"

Cradled in the curve of his arm, Danni nodded. "I'm good," she answered. "I just needed to be near you."

He gave her a gentle squeeze and shifted his body against her as he placed a damp kiss against her forehead. Danni eased her body up and over his. She captured his mouth, kissing him eagerly, her lips dancing easily with his lips.

Danni winced, a hint of pain shooting through her.

"Sorry! Baby, I'm so sorry. I didn't mean to hurt you," he said as he snatched his hands from her.

She shook her head. "Just not so tight. I'm a little more banged up than I realized."

Armstrong nodded as he resumed his ministrations. His hands gently caressed her, sliding beneath her T-shirt so that his fingers heated her skin.

"You know what you're doing to me, right?" Armstrong whispered.

She gave him a seductive smile. "I know. I'm doing it on purpose."

* * *

Don't miss future installments in the To Serve and Seduce miniseries, coming soon...

* * *

If you're on Twitter, tell us what you think of Harlequin Romantic Suspense! #harlequinromsuspense

Dear Reader,

SUSPENSE! Fast-paced, heart-wrenching, nail-biting SUSPENSE! I can't begin to tell you how excited I am about all of this. It has been such an amazing journey! And, it brings me much pleasure to introduce you to the family of Jerome and Judith Black. This family embraces every value I hold near and dear to my heart. I hope you'll grow to love them as much as I do.

I had a wonderful time writing Armstrong Black and Danni Winstead's story. These two together just make my heart sing! Detective Black is all kinds of delicious! He is flawed perfection with his serious demeanor, slight arrogance and passion for the law. When he falls head over heels for Danni, he falls hard, his heart landing on everything good about the petite beauty. Danni challenges his sensibilities, and her fierce independence and take-charge personality make them a pairing of magnanimous proportions!

I really love this story! I hope you will, too!

Thank you so much for your support. I am humbled by all the love you keep showing me, my characters and our stories. I know that none of this would be possible without you.

Until the next time, please take care and may God's blessings be with you always.

With much love,

Deborah Fletcher Mello

www.deborahmello.blogspot.com

SEDUCED BY THE BADGE

Deborah Fletcher Mello

HARLEQUIN® ROMANTIC SUSPENSE

Recycling programs
for this product may
not exist in your area.

ISBN-13: 978-1-335-45645-8

Seduced by the Badge

Copyright © 2018 by Deborah Fletcher Mello

Printed in U.S.A.

Writing since forever, **Deborah Fletcher Mello** can't imagine herself doing anything else. Her first novel, *Take Me to Heart*, earned her a 2004 Romance Slam Jam nomination for Best New Author. In 2008, Deborah won the RT Reviewers' Choice Best Book Award for Best Series Romance for her ninth novel, *Tame a Wild Stallion*. Deborah received a BRAB 2015 Reading Warrior Award for Best Series for her Stallion family series. Deborah was also named the 2016 Romance Slam Jam Author of the Year. She has also received accolades from several publications, including *Publishers Weekly*, *Library Journal* and *RT Book Reviews*. With each new book, Deborah continues to create unique story lines and memorable characters. Born and raised in Connecticut, Deborah now considers home to be wherever the moment moves her.

Books by Deborah Fletcher Mello

Harlequin Romantic Suspense

To Serve and Seduce
Seduced by the Badge

Harlequin Kimani Romance

Visit the Author Page at Harlequin.com for more titles.

To Nanette Kelley

Thank you for your kindness!

Your buoyant spirit is absolutely everything!

I value your opinion and trust your intuition.

You are much loved and

It is an honor to call you my friend.

Chapter 1

Chicago Detective Armstrong Black pulled his car into an empty parking spot behind police headquarters. It was early, the new day just getting started. The morning sun sat hidden behind a cluster of thick clouds, and the smell of rain was in the air. Shutting down the vehicle, he took a deep breath and then a second before throwing open the door and pulling his large frame out of the black-on-black Ford Expedition. He slammed the car door closed, set the alarm and headed toward the employee entrance.

Inside, the West Harrison Street building was bustling with activity. He was reporting for duty on what should have been his day off and he wasn't happy about it. Working a case that was taking all his energy had him needing all the rest he could get to clear his head. The criminals hadn't gotten the memo. The early-morning call commanding his presence had set the tone for his not-so-good mood, and he noticed the scowl on his face had others eyeing him warily.

Despite his disposition, the Bureau of Detectives was like his second home and a place he liked. He was comfortable there. As he moved through the narrow halls, past his own office and desk, toward the other end of the building, he felt his bad mood beginning to lighten, despite knowing that whatever had necessitated his presence couldn't be good. A commotion at another desk stalled his steps and pulled at his attention. A young man in ill-fitting jeans that hung too low on his narrow hips and an army green military jacket had become combative, thrashing about angrily. Armstrong felt his body tense as three other officers reacted swiftly. He stood staring until he was satisfied that everything was under control, the man in handcuffs now behaving like he had some sense.

Resuming his trek, he came to a stop at the end of the hallway and the corner office with a perfect view of the I-290 highway. Armstrong knocked on the door of his lieutenant's office. There was just a brief moment of pause before the other man's voice beckoned him inside. Pushing the door open, Armstrong stepped through the entrance and closed it behind him. He greeted his older brother warmly.

"Good morning, Lieutenant."

Parker Black lifted his eyes from the papers he was reviewing. He gave his brother a nod. "Detective. How goes it?"

Armstrong shrugged his broad shoulders. "I'm tired and I was supposed to sleep in. Until you called bright and early. So, what's this emergency?"

Parker stood and moved from behind his large oak desk. He grabbed a manila folder from the desktop as he gestured for his brother to take a seat. He joined him in the leather wingback chairs that decorated his office. Armstrong knew that side by side they looked like bookends, their familial resemblance marked by chiseled features and solid frames. Both wore meticulously tailored wool suits, one in black and the other in navy blue, with bright white dress shirts and complementing neckties. Black dress shoes polished to high shines completed both their looks.

"Last night the body of a young woman was discovered in a Dumpster down by Montrose Beach. Her name was Crystal Moore. She was a student at DePaul University, and then her parents reported her missing after she didn't show for classes. That was about six months ago. It appears she flew back from the Czech Republic just a few days ago. However, we can't find where she exited the country. According to Interpol, she was in the company of a known Czech gang member who has ties to a European prostitution ring. We believe he also has ties to the Balducci crime family here in Chicago. We have him in custody, but it looks like he has an airtight alibi. We can only hold him for a few more hours, and then he'll be back on a plane before the week is out."

Armstrong nodded. "Who picked up the case?"

"The Forty-First Precinct. Every indication says it's related to the others you've been investigating, so the commander dropped it on my desk for your joint task force. They want you to solve these murders and shut down this trafficking ring, and they want it done now. The press is starting to run with this story, and we're not looking good." He passed him the folder he'd been holding. "Do what you do best, please."

"I appreciate the trust, big brother!" And Armstrong

did. Theirs was the First Family of law enforcement in Chicago, he and his siblings following their parents into law enforcement. They had big shoes to fill and failure wasn't an option. He had worked hard to earn his spot in the Detectives Bureau, nothing but an opportunity given to him. Most assumed his family name had made things easier, but such had hardly been the case. He and Parker both had been made to fight twice as hard for their respective positions; needing to do far more than their counterparts to prove themselves capable. This case was proving to be a thorn in both their sides and despite his best efforts, Armstrong was no closer to solving it than when the first few bodies had landed on their doorstep and he'd been tasked with the case.

Parker seemed to read his mind. "I know you won't embarrass your parents."

Armstrong laughed.

Parker moved back to his desk and tore the top sheet from a notepad. He passed the page, and his scribblings, to his brother as he continued. "They're expecting you down at the Twenty-Fifth Precinct to meet up with the newest addition to your team. You're being partnered with a Detective Daniel Winstead from Atlanta, who's joining the task force this morning. They call him Danny or Dan. I think that's what they said. He's meeting you there. I'm still waiting for his paperwork to come over, so I can't tell you anything about him. I'll send you his file when I get my hands on it."

"Partner?" Armstrong came to an abrupt halt. "I don't do partners, you know that." His gaze narrowed, his stance tensing. Even as a child Armstrong hadn't played well with others. He was a loner by nature and didn't trust anyone easily. His last partner, a rookie trans-

ferred from another division, had almost gotten him shot,
the guy's smart mouth pissing off the wrong person. He
preferred to do things on his own and this was no exception. The look on his face expressed his displeasure but
his brother wasn't moved.

"You'll do this one. They say this guy's a bit of a wild
card, but that's all I know. The commander wants someone who can keep him in line. We can't risk his becoming a casualty on these streets. You're the best man for
the job, and you know it."

Armstrong blew a heavy sigh, warm breath blowing
hotly over his lips. His first instinct was to balk at the
request, but he would never challenge his brother's authority, nor did he want to be a disappointment to him.
His success or failure reflected back on his family, so
he bit back the snarky comment on the tip of his tongue.
He moved toward the door, shaking his head from side
to side. "You owe me," he said instead.

"Put it on my tab."

As Armstrong made his exit, his brother called after
him. He paused, turning around to look directly at his
family member.

"Make us proud," Parker said. "And keep your head
down, please. Our mother will hurt me if anything happens to you. That's an order, Detective."

Armstrong nodded. "Yes, sir, Lieutenant!"

Danni Winstead paced the conference room floor.
She'd spent the last hour studying the images pasted to
the wall. Pictures of young girls and women who'd either disappeared and were still missing, or had not been
found alive. One woman was one too many lost to a
black-market business that traded bodies like children

used to trade Pokémon cards. Blowing a soft sigh, she trailed a finger across one of the glossy images. It infuriated her and she was anxious to get to work, desperate to be busy with the case.

Her eyes darted back and forth at the flood of activity on the other side of the large glass wall. It had taken collecting on a half dozen favors and promising a dozen more to get assigned to this task force. Her superiors in Atlanta hadn't been overly supportive, but then that was her own fault. Although great at her job, Danni was known to sometimes ignore procedure to accomplish her tasks. She knew she had a brilliant analytical mind, and people often underestimated her. She brought a skill set to the table that intimidated most men, and her brash mannerisms sometimes threw people off guard. When their expectations didn't mesh with her actions, they were surprised more times than not. Even though her tactics most always got the criminals, they had also gotten her in trouble more times than she cared to count. When people looked at her, they saw sugar and spice, her petite frame and youthful appearance belying her strength. But she couldn't afford to not be taken seriously. Sometimes nice wasn't an option, so she didn't waste her time. She was a black woman in a field dominated by white males, so she was forever proving herself worthy of the badge she'd earned.

Her commanding officer had sent her off with a lengthy lecture, reminding her of protocols and admonishing her not to embarrass the Atlanta Police Department. Now all she wanted was to get to work, to bring down the cartel that was responsible for all those pictures being posted on the wall. She paced to the other side of the room and then to the door to peer out for the umpteenth time.

A uniformed police officer tossed her a look, gesturing with his head. He moved to where she stood.

"Detective, is everything okay?" the man asked.

"I'm sorry, you are?"

"Officer Lankford."

"Officer Lankford, do you know what's taking so long?" she questioned, her arms crossed over her chest in frustration. An air of attitude simmered just beneath her skin, and she took a breath to stall the wave of emotion that threatened to spew.

"Your partner hasn't gotten here yet. He's expected any minute now."

"Partner?"

"Yeah, they've partnered you with one of our senior detectives. He'll hold your hand until you get acclimated."

Danni felt herself bristle. "I don't need *hand-holding!*" she snapped, that attitude weighing down every word. Her emotions were running slightly high. Knowing that many questioned her abilities because she was a woman had her feeling a tad sensitive. That, and a lack of serious sleep.

"He's just going to show you the ropes until you get acclimated."

Danni suddenly felt bad about the outburst. She apologized. "Sorry. I didn't mean to snap."

The man shrugged. "Whatever. Do you want coffee?"

She shook her head, gesturing toward the empty foam cups that littered the tabletop. She didn't need coffee. She needed to get to work. She was just about to snap a second time when there was a rumble from the other side of the room, the noise level rising a decibel. She and the officer both turned to stare at the same time.

Across the way a new face had moved room center. Looking through the glass, Danni eyed the handsome man curiously. The stranger was clearly popular, everyone greeting him warmly. He had a dynamic presence, and it had nothing at all to do with his good looks. Because he was extremely handsome, a delectable version of tall, dark and delicious. Although he wasn't dark, his complexion more of a coffee and cream, with much cream and barely a hint of coffee. His eyes were round and bright, expressive orbs the color of warm honey. And his mouth was sheer perfection, full lips that stretched into the most beautiful smile.

He wore a tailored suit that fit his broad shoulders and large frame nicely. His *GQ* styling was polished and his tastes clearly expensive. The dark blue fabric complemented his warm complexion and the hint of facial hair made him look quite distinguished. Danni had no doubt that he was a fan favorite among the women, the few in the room fawning over him. But he commanded attention that was more about how he took full and total control without any effort at all. He was tall in stature, with a very majestic air, and it was totally captivating. It was obvious from everyone's reactions that others readily deferred to him. He was all that, the chips and the dip.

"Who is that?" Danni asked, the words slipping past her lips before she could catch them. She felt herself blush, color heating her cheeks as if she'd been caught with her hands in the cookie jar. But it was only a question, she thought to herself, purposely ignoring the smug look the other man was giving her.

"That's Detective Black. Detective Armstrong Black. I should go see if he needs anything. I'll be right back."

The man left her standing there, still staring. She watched as he moved in Detective Black's direction, his hand extended in greeting. There was a brief exchange between the two, and then both turned to look toward where she stood, the officer pointing in her direction. Her breath caught deep in her chest as she and the detective locked gazes. And then his expression dropped, a deep scowl filling his face.

Chapter 2

Armstrong knew there was no masking the shock that painted his expression. He felt surprise seep past his narrowed stare and pull the edges of his mouth into a deep frown. He dropped his gaze to the manila folder in his hand, shifted through the papers inside and then returned his eyes to hers. Danny Winstead wasn't a Dan. Danny with a *y* was actually Danni with an *i*, short for Danielle, not Daniel. Danny was female. Very female. He couldn't wait to call his brother to update him with that piece of information. He eyed the stunning woman from head to toe, his surprise registering in the muscles that pulled taut through his southern quadrant. He inhaled swiftly, a deep gasp of air that caught deep in his broad chest. He held it, fighting to stall the quiver of energy that shot heat through every fiber of his being.

The woman named Danni looked too soft and too

pretty to be a decorated officer of any police force. Her petite frame was lean with just enough curve to capture a man's attention. She had delicate facial features, killer cheekbones, and even from where he stood he could feel himself getting lost in her ocean-blue eyes. If he'd been made to guess, he would have said she was a kindergarten teacher, her bright smile so endearing that he found himself feeling like a kid again. The emotion was deeply disturbing.

The rookie officer intruded on his thoughts as the young man leaned close to mutter under his breath, "I'd hit that if she wasn't such a…" he started, his tone as if the two were old college buddies.

"Show some respect, rookie. This isn't a frat house," Armstrong quipped, cutting him off. The comment had been inappropriate and had hit a nerve. He bristled with indignation. "Get me a cup of coffee," he commanded, and then after a brief pause, he added, "please."

Officer Lankford nodded. "Yes, sir. Sorry, sir. It won't happen again, Detective."

Armstrong cut an eye in the man's direction as he watched him scurry off toward the break room. He paused for another quick minute to gather himself, and then he sauntered slowly in Detective Danni Winstead's direction.

Meeting him halfway, Danni extended her hand to shake his. "Detective Black? I'm Danni Winstead. I look forward to working with you."

"Detective Winstead, it's a pleasure to meet you," Armstrong said as he met her palm with his own, flesh gliding like silk on silk. The handshake was quick and abrupt, both of them snatching the appendages away after the initial contact, a wave of heat surging between them.

The moment suddenly turned awkward as the two stood staring at each other, neither saying a word.

Danni turned swiftly on her low heels, heading back into the conference room. Following behind her, Armstrong found himself staring at her backside. She had a lush, apple-shaped bottom nestled in slightly snug black slacks that she'd partnered with a tailored white blouse that was buttoned to the collar. Despite his best efforts, he couldn't stop himself from staring, or imagining what each cheek might feel like in the palms of his hands. He shook the sensation away, turning his focus to the business at hand.

"I'm told you've met most of the team?"

Danni nodded. "Yes. Briefly. Officer Lankford said you would bring me up to speed."

He pointed to the photo gallery that decorated the wall. "All the women here have been tied to a local crime family here in Chicago."

"The Balduccis. I'm familiar with them. We know they're running drugs through Atlanta but haven't been able to tie them directly to any of our big busts."

"They have their hands in a lot of dirt." He pointed a second time. "Maureen Winters, Priscilla Montgomery, Gina Torres and Faith Becker were all connected to the Balduccis. Maureen, Priscilla and Faith worked in one of their nightclubs. Gina was the family's personal masseuse for a year before returning to school. All four were murdered after traveling abroad with a known Balducci associate and returning here to the United States. Bethany Brooks and Alice Mumford were known prostitutes with connections to the sex trade in Atlanta, and Jane, Erica and Felicity had ties to an escort service based in New York. Another body was found this morning. A young woman named Crystal Moore. She was a student who went missing about six months ago. We know she flew back from the Czech Republic earlier this week, but we don't have any record of her ever leaving the country." He shifted his weight from one side to the other, pushing his hands deep into his pants pockets as he continued.

"After we leave here you and I are headed over to talk to the man who flew back into the United States with her. He's a low-level criminal with a long list of misdemeanors—petty theft, check fraud, shoplifting. He came on Interpol's radar a few months ago, but they don't have enough to charge him with anything, either. We know he's well connected, though. His attorney's one of the top litigators in the state. He can't afford that kind of legal counsel without some serious backing. Bottom line, though, we can only hold him for a few more hours before we'll have to cut him loose."

Danni turned her eyes back to the wall to stare one last time, watching as Armstrong added Crystal Moore's photo to the collage. She moved to get a closer look at the image. She tossed him a quick glance. The comment that came was filled with an air of awe and the sincerest appreciation. "You know all their names," she said, her tone just a decibel above a loud whisper.

Armstrong met the look she was giving him with one of his own, contemplating her remark. He didn't bother to tell her that he'd attended all their funerals and had made it his mission to speak to each woman's family personally. He blew out the breath he'd been holding. "Yeah," he said finally. "I do."

The ride to county lockup was quiet. Armstrong made small talk about the city, the weather and the best places to grab good coffee and fresh pastry. Danni said little, responding politely as they crossed town, fighting morning traffic. When they fell into silence, enjoying the quiet and the light chatter of the police radio in the background, she was surprised by how comfortable they felt in each other's company. Neither evidently had any need for words, focused on the tasks that lay ahead of them. When he broke the silence, his question startled her from her own thoughts.

"So why are you doing this? Why is this task force so important to you? In Atlanta, you investigate drug cases, correct?" He cut a quick eye in her direction.

She pondered his question for a split second before she answered. "Six months ago, my sister befriended a man she met while working at Emory University Hospital. She fell in love. He became someone she thought she could trust. One day he invited her to his home to meet his parents, and instead she was drugged and kidnapped. She was able to get away, to get help that saved her life. There were two other young women being held with her, but we weren't able to find them after he realized Shannon had escaped. Long story short, the investigation led us here. Alice Mumford was one of the women held with my sister. I can't let this rest until I find her killer and take down the monsters that are trafficking these women."

Armstrong nodded, understanding wafting over his expression. The slightest smile pulled at his full lips. "I like your passion," he said as Danni felt a glimmer mist her eyes.

Danni shrugged ever so slightly. She shifted her gaze to the view outside the window. She was taken aback by the current of emotion that fluttered in her midsection. It reminded her of the fear she'd felt when her sister had disappeared. Her anxiety had been corporeal. Thick and abundant, its viselike grip so intense she could barely breathe. The fright of not knowing where Shannon had disappeared to, or if she would ever be found, had been devastating.

She and her sister had been each other's lifelines after the death of their mother. Their father, an over the road trucker, had mourned the loss in the cab of his tractor trailer, disappearing when they'd needed him most. Their paternal grandmother had taken up the slack as best she could, but her age and failing health hadn't served them well. The wealth of their childhood had revolved around the old woman's dementia and unruly behavior. They had found moments of solace only with each other. She couldn't begin to explain how the prospect of losing her sister scared her, the very thought-provoking anxiety attacks that regular visits to a therapist still hadn't healed. She closed her eyes and took two deep breaths.

After pulling into a parking space down at the county jail, Armstrong shut down the engine and exited the car. As Danni took another breath to collect her thoughts, she was suddenly surprised when he opened the door, the chivalrous gesture unexpected.

"Thank you," she said softly.

His smile was brighter, filling his handsome face. "My mother raised me well," he said teasingly.

Danni chuckled. "I'm sure she'd be proud."

After passing through the security checkpoint and signing in with the officer on duty, the duo was led down a lengthy hallway to the interrogation area. They stood on one side of a two-way mirror, staring at a small wooden table and an empty chair. Minutes later the door swung open and Josef Havel was led into the room, handcuffed and in leg irons. The officer gestured for him to take a seat, then moved to stand in the corner of the small room.

Danni's eyes widened in recognition. "That's him!" she said, her voice rising slightly. "That's the bastard that took my sister!"

Armstrong looked from her to their suspect and back again. "Are you sure?"

Danni narrowed her gaze. She felt the color drain from her face, and she clenched her hands in tight fists by her side. When she spoke, she bit back the emotion, her words edged in an icy chill. "I met him once when he came to pick Shannon up. It's him."

He nodded. "Let's go nail him."

"I'll take lead," she said as she pushed past the man and stormed out the door.

Entering the interrogation room, Danni said nothing, her gaze meeting Josef Havel's evenly. The man eyed her with disdain, his arrogant expression meant to be dismissive.

"Why am I being held?" he sniped, his eyes shifting toward Armstrong. "I have done nothing. Where is my attorney?"

Neither responded as they took the seats on the opposite side of the table. Danni suddenly thought about Shannon and the fear that still followed her sister. The memory of what her sibling had been made to endure still haunted her. It made her angry, rage rising like morning mist on a new day. She clenched her teeth, her jaw tight as she slowly opened the manila file folder she'd been holding, scanning its contents briefly before she spoke.

"Mr. Havel, you are not obligated to speak with us without your attorney. But you are going to be arraigned on kidnapping and assault charges. It would probably be in your best interest to be as cooperative as possible. We have a few questions that you might be able to answer."

He interrupted her, snapping sharply. "I did nothing! You have no proof. I do not know anything about that girl!"

Danni paused as he narrowed his gaze on her, his eyes thin slits in his flushed face. Gone was the air of confidence that had edged Havel's runway-model looks. The haughtiness that her sister had once found so attractive was diminished substantially. His left brow twitched and spittle clung to his thin lips. She leaned back in her seat, her arms crossing easily over her chest. "We're not talking about the young woman you flew into town with. That's not your problem right now. Do you remember Shannon Winstead? Or Alice Mumford?"

The man bristled noticeably, that twitch over his eye suddenly intensifying with a vengeance. He didn't respond, his expression hardening even more.

Danni shifted forward in her seat. Her eyes narrowed as she glared at him. "Do you remember me, Mr. Havel? We met in Atlanta. When you were wining and dining my sister, and making her promises you had no intention of keeping. When you took her hostage, and held her against her will. Does that bring back any memories for you?"

The man met her stare and held it. Danni stared back, not at all intimidated. His gaze dropped to the tabletop, and then his eyes shifted back and forth between them. "I want my attorney," he snapped.

"We'd like your attorney, too," Danni interjected. "Because we're really not interested in you. We want the people you work for. So why don't you help yourself by helping us?"

The man snarled, suddenly leaping from his seat, the

table between them shifting. Armstrong stood abruptly, his stance defensive. The other officer in the room took two steps forward, his hand braced against the weapon at his waistband. Danni didn't flinch, her eyes locked tight with the suspect's.

"Sit down!" she snapped, her tone low and even.

The quiet in the room was suddenly thick and tense, everyone waiting to see who might jump first. Havel took a breath and then slowly eased himself back into his seat. He closed and then opened his eyes, turning to stare at Armstrong.

"You'll be sent back to Atlanta to face charges," Danni said. "And I'll be there personally to see that you get the maximum. This is your last chance to help yourself."

The moment was interrupted as the door swung open, a well-dressed woman stepping into the room. She smiled sweetly, her head shaking from side to side. "Detectives, you do know this is a violation of my client's rights. How dare you interrogate him without my being present?"

"Your client was here voluntarily, Ms. Harper," Armstrong said. "He wanted to cooperate."

"I'm sure he did," she said, her eyes never leaving Armstrong's face. "I'm sure I should be asking what you did to be so persuasive, Detective Black."

Danni felt something like jealousy waft through her spirit, the sensation unexpected and unnerving. It was obvious Armstrong and the other woman had history, and her awareness of such suddenly made her uncomfortable. She came to her feet as she cleared her throat. "The state of Georgia is pressing charges against your client. He'll be extradited back to Atlanta as soon as we can get him processed."

The other woman shifted her gaze toward Danni, eyeing her from head to toe. "And what has my client been charged with doing in Atlanta?"

Danni smiled at the woman. "Didn't he tell you? One of his victims got away. He left a witness behind."

The man suddenly said something in his native Czech, a wave of anxiety crossing his expression. The other woman hissed back in response, her reply terse and heated. She regained her composure as quickly as she'd lost it.

Armstrong chuckled. "We'll give you and your client some privacy. Let us know when you're ready to talk about that deal," he said.

Danni led them toward the exit, Armstrong on her heels. As she passed Havel, she swept his chair leg with her foot, the aggressive gesture sending the chair and the man tumbling to the floor.

"Oops! Sorry about that," Danni said, her tone dull. "I don't know how that happened."

The man and his attorney both glared as Armstrong reached out to pull him to his feet, pushing him back into his seat. "Accidents happen," he said, shrugging his broad shoulders. "It's good to see you again, Leslie," he said, dispensing with the formalities. He winked an eye at the woman.

"I'm filing a formal complaint against her, Armstrong," the woman snapped as they reached the door.

Armstrong nodded. "I'm sure you will," he responded before the door closed tightly behind them. On the other side, he shot Danni a look. "Nice work," he said sarcastically.

Danni ignored him. "Who's Pius?"

"Excuse me?"

"Pius. His attorney told him Pius wasn't going to be

happy. Do you know whom she might have been referring to?"

"You speak Czech?" Surprise wafted across his expression.

"I speak twelve languages."

"I'm impressed."

"Are you on a first-name basis with all the women
around here?" she quipped, completely off topic.

Armstrong smiled. "Only the ones who matter."

Danni turned. "I'm not impressed."

He laughed, the wealth of it searing as Danni tried
to stall the quiver of heat that suddenly surged through
her feminine spirit. He pushed past her as they headed
back to his car.

As he opened her door for her, he met her gaze, his
own stare intense. "Leslie Harper and my sister were in
law school together."

"You don't owe me any explanation."

"I don't, but I believe in full disclosure."

Her eyes dropped to the concrete beneath her feet,
unable to hold the look he was giving her a minute longer. There was something about the way he stared at
her. Seeming to inhale every line of her profile as if he
were casting it in memory, painting the best of her in
his mind's eye. She couldn't remember any man looking at her so intensely. There was something seductive
about his gaze and she knew if she wasn't careful she
could easily lose herself in the wealth of it. She shook
her head, desperate to wave the rising emotion away.
"You have a sister?"

"I have two sisters and four brothers."

"Wow!" She stole a quick glance in his direction.

"I take it you don't come from a big family?"

Danni thought about her family. Hers had been a happy home when her mother had been there to give them balance. Laughter had been abundant, and she had felt safe. Being a little girl had been all about tea parties and playdates and dress-up, with her and Shannon the pretty princesses of their own fairy tales. That disappeared with the aftermath of a car crash that no one had survived. It had devastated their family, their father barely able to handle his own hurt. Holidays passed without celebration, home-cooked meals were a rarity and two little girls were left to keep their crazy grandmother from running through the neighborhood naked. She shook her head.

"No. It was just me and my sister, Shannon. Our mother died when we were in grade school, and our father and grandmother raised us. He was a trucker and always on the road, and my grandmother was…well…she was special. I always thought it would be cool to have a big family like yours."

He chuckled. "It can be interesting, but I confess there have been moments I wished I was an only child."

"Really?"

"When you meet my family, you'll understand."

"I look forward to it," she said, more out of politeness than actually thinking she would meet his family.

"Good. Then you'll join us for Sunday dinner."

"What? No… I can't… I…" she suddenly stammered.

"Do you have plans?"

"No, but…"

"Then it's a date. My mother would kill me if she found out you were new in town and I didn't welcome you properly. Sunday dinner with my parents is mandatory for half the neighborhood. I can pick you up at your hotel at two o'clock."

"I can drive myself…"

"I'll pick you up," he said, an air of finality in his tone.

Her first instinct was to balk. Arguing the point would have been second nature, Danni not accustomed to any man telling her what to do on her personal time. She was quite capable of finding her way around and more than able to decide for herself about her plans. But she held her tongue, accepting his directive in a way that was completely out of character.

Armstrong gestured for her to get into the car, then closed the door. She watched as he rounded the front of the vehicle and slid into the driver's seat. There was a moment of hesitation before he engaged the engine.

"What?" Danni questioned.

"We need to go change our clothes. We look like cops, and where we need to go, we'll need to blend in if we're going to get any answers."

"Where are we going?"

"To find a man named Pius!"

Chapter 3

Danni did not realize how exhausted she was until she stepped into the shower. The day had been longer than she'd anticipated, and it was only when Armstrong had asked her to change and be ready by the time he returned that she questioned if she had the stamina for round two. As she eased her naked body into the mist of hot water, every muscle from her head to her toes seemed to convulse, constricting and then relaxing before she felt as if a wealth of weight had suddenly been lifted off her shoulders. Taking a deep breath and then a second to steady herself, she found herself feeling lazy and tired and ready for a long nap. She had an hour before Armstrong would be back to get her, so a nap was out of the question. She needed to make the most out of the downtime that she could.

The task force had put her up at the Chicago Lake

Shore Hotel. Located in the Hyde Park neighborhood, it was clean, cozy, convenient to the downtown area, and the staff was pleasant. She had six weeks before she would have to return to Atlanta or find her own place to lay her head. Six weeks was at least four weeks too long, Danni thought, determined to bring down someone named Pius and anyone else involved in their case before then.

Thoughts of Armstrong Black suddenly pitched through her thoughts, a cavalcade of energy shooting through her body. The palm of her hand trailed a soapy path from her shoulder, down her arm, to rest against her abdomen just below her belly button. A quiver of energy rippled through her midsection. The man was as intense as she was, and there was no mistaking how seriously he took his job. As he had dropped her off at her hotel, he'd given her a list of directives, his tone brusque and commanding. Clearly, he expected that she would follow orders and do what she was told. Danni had never been one to take direction well, but she was determined not to rock the boat when he could be the help she needed to finish her task.

Stepping from the flow of water, she turned off the faucet with one hand and reached for a stark white towel with the other. Moving naked into the other room, she dropped onto the corner of the bed as she dug into her luggage, looking for a jar of Cetaphil lotion, a clean pair of panties and something to wear.

Minutes late she was moisturized from head to toe, spritzed with the light scent of lavender and dressed in a pair of frayed and torn denim jeans, a cotton T-shirt and black, steel-toed work boots. Taking a quick glance at herself, she pondered whether or not to put on makeup and then decided against it. She pulled her fingers through her hair, twisting the strands up into a high knot atop her head. Satisfied with the reflection staring back at her, she moved to the window to stare out to the parking lot and wait.

She looked like a grade-schooler, Armstrong thought as Danni sauntered out of the hotel toward his car. He would have been lying if he said he hadn't been excited to get back to her. Because he had. Overly excited, and it surprised him. He'd been thinking about her since they'd parted ways, him headed home to shower and change while she returned to her hotel room to do the same.

She'd become an irritation, a prickly thorn in his side determined to have his attention. Despite his best efforts he was finding it difficult to get her out of his head. He hadn't expected to like her, but he did. He liked her gumption and the fire in her spirit that would probably prove to be a challenge for any man. She had managed to do what few women ever had before and that was to hold his full and undivided attention. Now she was walking toward him looking like a twelve-year-old and not the stunning woman who'd been with him most of the day. Well, maybe not twelve, but definitely younger than she had hours earlier. It was unnerving, and he didn't mind saying so.

"How old are you?" he asked as he moved to open the car door for the woman.

Danni laughed. "Old enough. Why?"

He shook his head, a slight smile pulling at his mouth. "You look like you're just starting puberty. It's scary."

"Starting puberty? Really?"

He shrugged.

Her rich laugh echoed in the early-evening air. "As long as I don't look like a cop!" She pulled the seat belt across her lap and engaged it. "And I'm thirty-four, so puberty has surely come and gone."

Armstrong shot her a look, surprise creasing his brow. "Thirty-four? You're kidding, right?"

"No. I'm very serious. How old are you?"

"Thirty-six."

"Oh." Danni turned to stare out the window. A smile pulled gently at the corners of her mouth.

"Oh? Why did you say it like that?"

"I thought you might have been in your forties," she answered, turning back to stare at him.

Armstrong bristled. "I do not look that old."

She shrugged, feigning indifference. "If you say so."

"Do I look like I'm forty?"

She laughed heartily. "You look like you're well past puberty."

Armstrong laughed with her. "Touché! At least I don't look like I need my mommy's permission to come outside and play."

Danni rolled her eyes skyward. "So where are we going?" she asked as he pulled his car out of the hotel parking lot.

"We need to stop by a house party not far from here. No time like the present to introduce you to some of the South Side's criminal element."

"So does it live up to its reputation?"

"If you're asking me whether or not the South Side of Chicago is the dregs of hell like the media has made it out to be, then the answer is no. Those of us who live here actually love it. The diverse neighborhoods that make up our side of town are one of our city's best-kept secrets. And trust me, Lincoln Park and Wicker Park are a hell of a lot scarier between the hours of midnight and six. We also have Harold's, and they have the best fried chicken around."

Danni smiled. "How's the shopping?"

"You'll get your best deals on Eighty-Seventh and Dan Ryan. White socks and T-shirts, candy, soda pop and bootleg movies are all cheap."

"Good to know!"

Stalled in traffic, they fell into a quiet reverie. Armstrong gave her a look as she sat staring out the window. He *really* liked her. Despite his best efforts not to feel anything at all for her. He found himself drawn to her spirit. She had an energy that he rarely found in the women he dealt with. She wasn't fawning over him like he was the biggest prize at the state fair. She didn't wear an air of desperation like some women, wanting a husband and kids before plucking the first strand of gray hair. She had a keen sense of humor, and in their line of work one was necessary. He also appreciated that she didn't seem to be easily frazzled, her nerves seeming as steady as a rock. If he was going to have a partner, he needed to trust that she had his back, that he didn't have to worry about a crash and burn when he least expected one. Danni seemed up to the task, and he was willing to give her a chance. Clearly, they had made significant progress since that morning and their first meeting.

Danni interrupted his thoughts. "So, tell me more about this house party."

"It's at the home of Miss Nanette Perry. She's a fixture in the neighborhood, the community mother. Everybody knows and loves her. When she needs to pay her mortgage, she'll cook, throw a party and sell plates. And the woman can cook! She'll also feed the hungry if they come through and don't have any money. Her home is considered neutral ground for the gangs, and at any given time you don't know who you might run into. The lowest of the city's downtrodden and Chicago's most elite have dined together at her table. If there is anyone who knows who Pius is, Miss Perry will know."

Danni nodded. "I look forward to meeting her."

A series of turns and two traffic lights later, Armstrong pulled into an open space at the end of West Twenty-First Place. The homes were older brick row houses lining the length of the street. Parking came at a premium, and it was by the luck of the draw that the space became empty as they turned the corner.

Danni paused for a split second as he exited the driver's side, and then she pushed open her own door and stepped out. Armstrong gave her a look, his eyebrows raised.

"In case anyone is watching," she muttered, her head tilted toward the men gathered on the front porch a few doors down. "I assume someone may know you're a cop, but they don't need to know that I am."

Armstrong nodded. As he sauntered past her, she noticed his attire for the first time. He wore denim jeans that fit him snugly through the hips, accentuating his backside. Beneath a wool and leather varsity jacket he wore a long-sleeved hooded T-shirt. The newest Jordan sneakers adorned his feet.

As he passed her, he pulled the hood up over his head and moved toward the home, where a crowd was coming and going through the front doors. Some carried foil-covered paper plates out, while others were bringing bottles in brown paper bags in. There were a few individuals who seemed to be moving with a sense of urgency. But most seemed glad to just relax in the moment.

Danni followed Armstrong, who moved swiftly up the flight of stairs to the front porch. He gave the men gathered there a nod as he pounded fists with one or two of them. Their gazes skated over her briefly, then the men returned to the conversation they were having. No one spoke, so neither did she. Danni pushed her hands into her pants pockets, painting her expression with indifference.

Inside, the noise level rose substantially, a wealth of chatter vibrating off the walls of the small home. Music played out of an old stereo, the deep bass of some old-school R&B song ringing through the air. Standing in the doorway between the kitchen and the living room, an older woman called out Armstrong's name.

"Detective Black, what brings you to my neck of the woods?" Miss Nanette Perry asked.

It looked like she was floating on air as she moved toward them, Danni thought. She was tall, with a copper complexion, hazel eyes and a blond buzz cut. She brought to mind what Danni imagined an Amazonian queen might look like. She was beautiful, and there was something very romantic about the air around her. She made people smile, and her gregarious personality served to punctuate her sharp intuition and razor-sharp tongue. She reached Armstrong's side, throwing her arms around him in a deep bear hug as she kissed his cheek.

"I heard you had some fried chicken," he answered as he hugged her back.

"Fried chicken, collards, mac and cheese, potato salad and some candied yams, baby! You plan to eat it here, or you want it to go?"

"I actually need two plates," he said, gesturing over his shoulder toward Danni. "And we'll have a seat so you and I can catch up."

"That sounds like you want something, sunshine!"

"Something," he answered.

Miss Nanette nodded. For a brief moment it seemed as if she were sizing him up, as if such was necessary. "How is that handsome father of yours?" she suddenly asked.

Armstrong smiled. Amusement danced across his face, and Danni sensed there was something in the older woman's question that only they understood. Armstrong finally answered. "He's doing very well. And so is my mother. She's good, too!"

Miss Nanette laughed heartily and winked an eye at the man. She shifted her attention toward Danni. "What have I told you about picking up strays? Whose child is this?"

Armstrong shrugged. "Don't let her fool you, Miss Nanette. She's not as young as she looks."

Miss Nanette's eyes narrowed as she studied Danni intently. Her head bobbed ever so slightly before she spoke. "She's too skinny. We'll need to put some weight on her. Looks like she might blow away if the wind picked up."

Danni smiled, a slight bend to her lips that Armstrong found beguiling. "I like your music," she said, her voice soft like spun cotton.

Miss Nanette smiled back. "You'll like my cooking more." She led them to the dining room, shooing three boys out of their seats. "Sit down and make yourselves comfortable. You want corn bread or a yeast roll?"

"Corn bread," Danni said.

"Yeast roll," Armstrong answered.

Miss Nanette chuckled. "Sweet tea, baby girl?" she asked.

Danni nodded.

"Baby girl has some Southern roots. I heard it in that accent. The tea just confirmed it for me."

"I'll have a glass of..." Armstrong started.

"Boy, I know what you drink. Sit on down!"

Armstrong grinned. "Yes, ma'am!"

Armstrong pulled out a seat for Danni and then took the one beside her. There was an elderly man and a couple still seated at the table with them. The old man had drifted off to sleep, leaning so far forward that he looked like he might fall face-first into his empty plate. The couple were focused on their meal and each other, barely giving Armstrong, or Danni, a look.

Armstrong spoke anyway. "How's everyone doing this evening?"

The younger man gave him a quick stare and a nod. "Good. How about yourself?"

He nodded. "I'm good. Glad for a hot meal."

"Miss Nanette put her foot in this here supper!" the woman exclaimed. "Best potato salad this side of town!"

"I'm a fan of her fried chicken," Armstrong responded. "I come at least once a month to get me some."

The man shifted his gaze from Armstrong to Danni. "Your daughter doesn't look like she gon' eat much," he said teasingly.

Danni laughed as Armstrong rolled his eyes at her. Before he could respond, Miss Nanette swept back into the room with an oversize tray that held two plates loaded with food and two red plastic cups filled with drink. She placed both down in front of them, completing the setting with yellow paper napkins.

"Eat up, baby girl. There's seconds for you if you want," Miss Nanette said as she placed a warm hand against Danni's shoulder. "And I have some banana pudding for dessert, too."

"Thank you," Danni said as she reached for the plastic fork. As the decadent aroma of the home cooking wafted up her nostrils, she suddenly realized she hadn't eaten since breakfast and she was starved.

The first taste of macaroni and cheese was orgasmic, the creamy cheddar thick and rich and loaded with flavor. It was an explosion of flavor against her tongue, and it was only when everyone around the table burst out laughing that Danni realized she'd moaned, a low purr escaping past her lips. She blushed profusely but kept eating. The fried chicken instantly became a favorite and, Danni and Armstrong both agreed, part of a necessary food group, as they licked the seasonings from their fingers. Minutes later there wasn't anything left on either's plate.

Armstrong was amazed at the amount of food the petite woman had been able to consume. She had a healthy appetite and clearly had no interest in hiding it. He found himself watching her, staring in anticipation of her saying or doing something that he didn't want to miss. His response to the nearness of her had him feeling slightly out of sorts, and he found it disturbing. He shook his head, trying to wave the sensation away, and then he realized Miss Nanette was staring at them both. He smiled as the woman narrowed her gaze then shifted her attention back toward Danni.

"You should own a restaurant," Danni said as she finished her last spoonful of banana pudding. "This was wonderful!"

Miss Nanette smiled. "This suits me just fine. I feed folks once, maybe twice each month. I get something out of it. They get something, and everyone's happy." She turned to face Armstrong. "So why don't you tell me what you came here to get."

Armstrong looked over his shoulder. The crowd had thinned substantially. The old man was still sleeping soundly, having laid his head down onto the table, his plate pushed to the side. The couple was long gone. His voice dropped an octave. "We're looking for someone. They call him Pius. I was hoping you might be able to give me a name or point me in his direction."

"Pius?"

Armstrong nodded. "Do you know him?"

Miss Nanette smiled. She rose from her seat and reached for all the empty plates. "Come help me in the kitchen. Bring your friend."

In the other room, she dropped the plates into a sink filled with soapy water. She extended a pair of rubber gloves toward Danni and pointed her index finger. "Earn your keep, baby," she said. She spun to the other side of the room and pulled a plastic container from an upper cabinet. She moved back to the counter and filled it with what was left in a pan of banana pudding.

Danni took a deep breath, shot Armstrong a look and then moved to wash the dishes that cluttered the sink.

Armstrong laughed, stopping when Miss Nanette slapped him in the chest with a drying towel. He sputtered as the two women both giggled heartily. Minutes later, with the dishes washed and dried, Miss Nanette handed him the container of dessert. In return, he pulled a hundred-dollar bill from his wallet and pressed it into the older woman's palm. "So, do you know this Pius?"

"Alexander Balducci has a grandson. Paul Balducci. He's been bad news since preschool. He's coming up fast in the family business and fancies himself to be quite the kingpin. His mother used to call him her little priest. But that was wishful thinking on her part. In her mind, he was a good Catholic kid. The truth was his grandfather bailed him out every time he got into trouble—and he got into trouble a lot."

"Do you know who he runs with?" Armstrong asked.

Miss Nanette shrugged. "If it helps, there's a coffee shop on California Avenue that he and his associates are known to frequent," she concluded. "They say he's quite the Renaissance man. You might find him there."

"Thank you," Armstrong said.

"We really appreciate everything," Danni added.

Miss Nanette winked an eye at the young woman. "Be careful out there," she said, staring directly at Danni. "Pius and his kind chew up pretty girls like you and spit them out like they're sucking all the salt off some sunflower seeds."

Chapter 4

Armstrong stepped into the shower, anxious for the cool spray of water that rained down from the shower-head. Nothing about his day had been what he had expected. He wasn't accustomed to having anyone in his space as he worked a case, and Danni's presence had been completely disquieting. There was something about the young detective that had him feeling out of sorts, and he couldn't begin to understand it. Explaining it would have been virtually impossible, so he was grateful to keep the unsettled feelings to himself.

Despite his best efforts to put the day and the woman behind him, there were too many thoughts lingering in his head. He pressed his hands against the tiled wall and leaned his face beneath the warming flow. Water rained over his brow and down his cheeks, droplets lingering in the strands of his beard.

He needed to run by the barbershop for a trim and edge, he thought to himself. There was also laundry in the trunk of his car that he needed to drop off, the errand deterred by the impromptu dinner plans with the queen of the neighborhood watch. He smiled as he thought back to their meal with Miss Nanette.

Danni had been ready to head over to the coffee shop to search out Pius the minute they stepped back out onto the front porch. But he'd called an end to their day instead, knowing Pius would still be there when they picked back up in the morning. He had wanted to pull the career criminal's file first, hoping to discover a lengthy rap sheet and at least two outstanding warrants for failures to appear in court. When they finally did cross paths, he wanted to ensure they'd have reason to cuff and arrest him.

Armstrong could tell by the shift in her mood and the expression on her face that Danni hadn't liked the idea, but she didn't say so out loud. She'd been exceptionally polite, and dismissive, when he'd returned her to her hotel. She'd wished him a good night, and then she'd stomped into the building.

Danni was fire and ice, intensely calculating with a quick fuse. She was not an easy woman to read. She intrigued him, and he found himself wanting to know more about her. Needing to understand what drove her. Unlike women he'd been known to date, she reminded him instead of his mother and his sisters, her staid demeanor marked by a piercing stare and terse tongue. There was a moment with Miss Nanette where she'd finally relaxed, her smile fueling the light in her eyes. Her laugh had been airy and her brow had smoothed, no longer furrowed with emotion. That woman had made his heart skip a beat, and he couldn't help but hope that he'd get a chance to know that side of her better.

Stepping from the shower, he grabbed an oversize towel and tucked it around his waist. Minutes later he'd slipped on a pair of sweats and sat alone in his living room. Settling himself comfortably against the chenille sofa, he sipped on a cup of hot coffee laced with Irish whiskey. The file on the Balducci family wasn't quite light reading to send him off to sleep, but it was necessary. He needed to learn everything he could about the kid, because he had no doubts that Junior already knew everything there was to know about him.

The coffee shop on California Avenue would have been easy to find if she hadn't been looking for it, Danni thought as she pushed her way inside and looked around. There was a late-night crowd of regulars who all seemed to turn and stare as she entered. Her gaze swept quickly around the room as she moved swiftly to the counter to order an iced chai latte and a brownie.

"You new around here?" the young man who took her order asked.

She nodded. "Yeah, I just got into town." She pushed her hands and the change he'd passed her into her pants pockets.

He nodded. "My name's Carlo," he said as he extended his hand to shake hers.

"Danielle, but my friends call me Danni."

He smiled, flashing bright white teeth with a center gap and dimpled cheeks. His eyes were black against an ivory complexion, his hair cropped just low enough to define wavy curls.

"Do you have somewhere to stay, Danni?"

There was a moment of pause as Danni pondered her response. Carlo continued before she could respond.

"It's not safe out here. Especially for a young girl. I don't know what your story is, but if you need some help…"

Danni smiled sweetly. "Thanks, but I'm good. I'm staying with a cousin. She doesn't live far from here. She works late and I just wanted to get out and do some exploring." The lie rolled effortlessly out of her mouth.

Carlo nodded. "Okay. But if you ever need help, there's a shelter close by and people you can turn to."

"Why are you so nice? You don't even know me."

"My sister was a runaway. She didn't make it home. I want to think that had she ever asked someone for help they would have been there for her."

"I'm so sorry."

Carlo shrugged. "Grab a seat and I'll bring your coffee to the table."

"Thank you," Danni said, offering him one last smile.

Grabbing a table by the window, Danni positioned herself so that she could see most of the room, anyone coming through the door and the sidewalk outside. The sun had set hours earlier, and a full moon shone through the windows, illuminating the dark sky and the street outside. There were more people inside than Danni would have imagined. Most looked like college students. There was a couple out on a date and the occasional single with a laptop and headphones pretending not to be paying attention to the conversation at the next table.

But what drew her attention and held it was the table way in the back where three young women sat, silent. There was barely the hint of a conversation between them, each staring off into the distance. A man with bad skin and a too-small suit sat with them, his demeanor and presence seeming everything but protective. When one girl rose to go to the restroom, he grabbed her wrist abruptly and held it a tad too tightly for comfort as he hissed something under his breath.

Danni bristled, her hand falling to the waistband of her jeans and the small pistol tucked beneath her shirt and jacket. She clenched her fingers into a tight fist as she watched the girl continue on her way, her companion dropping back into his seat. The moment was interrupted when Carlo moved to her side, setting her drink and dessert down onto the table. He turned to see where she stared.

"Everything okay?"

Danni shifted her gaze to meet his. "Everything's fine."

He stole another quick glance over his shoulder. "That's the kind of trouble you don't need. Trust me. Nothing good can come from hanging with that crew."

She nodded. "I was just being nosy," she said softly.

Carlo smiled. "You ever hear about curiosity and that cat? The cat died." His deadpan expression moved her to laugh.

"I get it," she said.

He winked an eye at her. "I have to get back to the counter, but if you need anything else, just let me know."

"Thanks, Carlo."

As the man moved to help another customer, Danni shifted her attention back to the other side of the room. The girl had returned to the table, looking disinterested as she and the other two young women finished off sandwiches and mugs of drinks covered with whipped cream. The man with them studied a copy of the *Chicago Tribune*, ignoring what little chatter there was between his companions. And then the front door swung open, a mini storm moving into the space.

Everyone in the room turned to stare as a couple in heated conversation swept past the counter, moving directly toward the back table. He was tall and lanky with thick black locks pulled into a loose man bun at the back of his head. Dressed in a black, collarless jacket, black slacks and just the hint of a white turtleneck peeking past the jacket's neckline, he carried himself with an air of irrefutable arrogance. The girl with him wore a gold lamé dress that dipped low in the front and even lower in the back, barely covering her assets. A white fake fur coat was slung over one shoulder, and she stomped in strappy gold high-heeled shoes. She was strikingly beautiful, with a porcelain complexion and raging red hair that fell to the middle of her back.

The young woman was angry, cursing profusely as she slammed her purse onto the table and her backside into a chair. She crossed her arms over her chest and pouted, then shouted again as a fresh irritation crossed her mind. Anger painted her companion's expression. Infuriated by her outbursts, he slammed a flat palm down against the table, the harsh gesture silencing the entire room.

The couple on that date rose from their seats, waved a hand at the barista and hurried out the door. Everyone else went back to minding their own business, not interested in getting caught up in any fray. Danni's eyes widened as she eavesdropped, her head hung low over her plate as she pretended to pick at her brownie.

"I'm done, Pius! Do you hear me? I'm not going back to any of those parties ever again," she screamed before the pout returned to her heavily made-up face.

Carlo moved from behind the counter, his hands resting on his hips as he stared at the table.

Danni turned swiftly to look. The woman's companion stood with his back to her, seeming to hover over the table. He snapped a finger, and the other man sitting with the women moved onto his feet, moving to give up his chair. As he sat down, his arm flew from his side, backhanding the woman he'd arrived with. Her head snapped back and then her hand flew to the side of her face, tears raining from her eyes.

"Shut up," he snapped gruffly. "No one said 'speak.'"

The woman swallowed a sob, and then she stood slowly. She hesitated when the man Danni assumed was a bodyguard took a step in her direction. The quiet in the space was eerily disconcerting.

Carlo's voice suddenly rose above the silence. "Pie!"

The other man turned in his seat, acknowledging their familiarity with an exaggerated eye roll. "What?" he snapped back.

"You're scaring my customers," Carlo quipped.

The other's man's gaze swept around the room. He paused for a swift second as Danni met his stare briefly before dropping her eyes back to the table.

"Sorry about that. Coffee's on me," the man nicknamed Pie finally said. He turned back around and gestured toward his companion. The bodyguard stepped aside as the woman resumed her trek to the restrooms, still holding on to the side of her face.

"Are you having your regular, Pie?" Carlo questioned. His tone was edged, just shy of being abrasive. Frustration rounded his shoulders and tightened his jaw. He was clearly pissed and fighting not to let it show.

Pie didn't answer, his attention shifting to a cell phone

that vibrated in his breast pocket. He moved to answer the call, ignoring whatever else was happening around him.

"That's what I thought," Carlo muttered. He tossed Danni a look, the young woman on the edge of her seat, her body tense. He turned an about-face. "We close soon," he said loudly, the comment meant for the entire room. "Last call for refills."

Danni guzzled the last of her coffee, then stood up and headed to the bathroom. Inside, the space was tight, with two stalls and a single sink. The tile wore its age, and new fixtures would have been an improvement. But a fresh coat of pale yellow paint made a pleasant difference, and someone had gone to great lengths to make the space feel comfortable.

The young woman dressed in gold stood looking in the only mirror, fixing her makeup. Ire furrowed her brow as she hid the rising bruise on her cheek beneath a layer of powder foundation. She wasn't a happy camper, and her anger seeped from her dark eyes past her lashes.

Standing beside her, Danni realized the girl wasn't nearly as old as she'd initially thought. She stared, realizing the young lady might have been in her late teens or early twenties. She took a deep breath and one step closer. "Hey. Are you okay?" Danni asked. "I saw what your boyfriend did."

The young woman tossed her a look, a moment of silence shifting between them before she responded. "That prick's not my boyfriend. I just work for him."

Danni nodded. "Do you want to call the police or anything?"

The other woman's incredulous expression gave Danni pause. "Are you stupid?" she snapped.

"I was just trying to help."

"I don't need your help. And I definitely don't need no cops."

Danni nodded again. "Sorry."

The girl turned to stare at her. Her gaze swept from Danni's head to her feet and back. "How old are you?"

"Old enough."

She laughed. "At least you lie quick. It'll come in handy." She extended her hand. "Everyone calls me Ginny. Short for Ginger. Because of the red hair." She swept her hand through her thick locks.

"Danni. Short for Danielle."

"You're new. I've never seen you here before."

"I just got into town. I got into some trouble back home in Georgia, and my folks sent me here to stay with my cousin."

"Shouldn't you be home or something? You look like the curfew type."

Danni shrugged, a slight grin on her face. "My cousin's a stripper and she works late."

Ginny laughed. "I bet your old people don't know that!"

"My parents think she's going to school. I don't tell and she lets me do what I want to do."

The bathroom door suddenly swung open, one of the other young women in Ginny's party of friends searching her out.

"Pie said to move your ass. He's ready to go."

"Are you going to be okay?" Danni asked.

Ginny nodded as she dropped a tube of bright red lipstick back into her purse and snapped the latch closed. She pushed her way past Danni. She paused at the door, turning back to face the woman. "Thanks," she said, "maybe I'll see you around," and then she turned, exiting the room.

Danni suddenly realized she'd been holding her breath and her knees were shaking. She inhaled and leaned back against the tiled wall to stall the rush of adrenaline that had moved her to follow behind the girl.

Despite the occasional infraction, some of which had gotten her a solid slap on the wrist, Danni was good at what she did. But it had taken every ounce of fortitude she possessed not to throw herself across the room to slap the taste out of Pie's mouth for putting his hands on Ginny. It infuriated her that no one else had stepped up to defend the young woman. Knowing Pius was possibly the ring leader behind everything that had happened to her sister and the women who'd lost their lives only further fueled her wrath. But blowing her cover before she could prove his guilt wouldn't have served any of them well.

She moved to the sink and stuck her hands beneath a flow of warm water, splashing her face before reaching for a brown paper towel. When she'd counted to one hundred, she made her way back outside.

Ginger and her friends were gone. There was no one else left in the coffee shop, and Carlo was busing the last table. He smiled as she moved to grab her coat.

"Sorry," she said. "I didn't mean to stay past closing. I'll get right out of your way."

"It's not a problem. Do you have a way home? Because I can give you a ride."

She nodded. "I'm good."

"It was sweet of you to check on Ginny. She's a nice girl. Unfortunately, my brother isn't a very nice guy."

Danni's eyes widened in surprise. "That was your brother?"

Carlo nodded. "Technically, my half-brother. Pie and I have the same mother, different fathers."

"Pie?"

"One of his many nicknames."

"Why Pie?"

"Because he eats it all the time. Breakfast, lunch and dinner, if he could. Preferably apple, although he's been known to devour a good chocolate pie by his lonesome!"

She laughed. "Do you have one?"

The slightest smile lifted his mouth. "Don't we all?"

Danni shrugged, her shoulders lifting ever so slightly "Does *Pie* always beat up on his girlfriends?" she questioned, more emphasis on that nickname than she would have liked.

"Like I said, he's not a very nice guy."

"Ginny said she works for him."

The man took a deep breath, wiping down the table before turning his attention back to her. He shifted the conversation. "I need to lock up. If you don't need help getting home, then I need to throw you out. Sorry."

Danni pulled her coat on, shoving her hands deep into her pockets. "Thanks again for everything," she said.

"I hope to see you again, Danni. And next time bring that cousin of yours. I'd like to meet her."

Danni nodded. "You never did tell me what your nickname was."

He laughed heartily. "It's Carlo!"

As he locked the door behind her, Danni pulled her coat tight to ward off the Chicago wind. She would definitely be back, she thought. Her new friend didn't need to worry about that at all.

The next morning Danni couldn't miss that Detective Armstrong Black wasn't happy with her. Although he hadn't, she could tell that he had wanted to yell when she'd told him of her late-night visit to the coffee shop.

Instead, he had bitten back the snarky condemnation, storming out of the conference room to distance himself from her. When she'd shown up for her shift, she'd been anxious to recap her evening and her experience in the coffee shop. She'd spent most of the night believing that she had made a significant stride in their case in getting a step closer to Pius, but clearly her new partner hadn't agreed. In fact, he was clearly pissed, she thought as she watched him storm through the space barking orders at other officers. It was a good thing she hadn't shared her intentions to go back again, alone, she mused. Not that she cared whether he liked the idea or not, because Danni was doing it, with or without his permission.

Her thoughts were interrupted when Armstrong moved back into the room, his gaze meeting hers evenly. His jaw was still tight, and his body was tense. He closed the door behind himself, then sauntered to the other side of the room, his arms crossed over his broad chest.

"What if something had happened, Detective? You didn't have any backup." His tone was brusque.

"I am perfectly capable of handling myself."

"I didn't say you weren't."

"It's what you're implying."

"I wasn't implying anything. I said it wasn't a smart move, and it wasn't."

"I saw an opportunity and I took it. And granted, it wasn't the brightest thing for me to do but you would have done the same thing if the shoe had been on the other foot."

"You don't know that."

Her brow lifted slightly. "You're saying you would have waited and come back to coordinate with every-one and hope that when you went back, the door would still have been open? Because I might not know you that well, Detective, but I know enough to bet that you will always do whatever it takes to get your bad guy. Whatever it takes!"

Armstrong paused, a moment of hesitation that neither denied nor endorsed her statement. She was right, but he didn't need to admit to it. "I'm saying that these lone-wolf antics of yours will get people hurt and that's not what we're here for. I told you not to go to the coffee shop and you ignored a direct order."

Danni took a breath and held it, reflecting on his comments. She nodded her head slowly. "I'm sorry, but hopefully, it will help us find our killer and shut down this trafficking ring."

There was a moment's pause as he seemed to ponder her statement. When he finally responded, he surprised her. "You might be right."

"Excuse me?" Her eyes widened.

He gave her a look that moved her to smile ever so slightly. "You got your foot in the door. We should take full advantage of that. But we need to be smart, so I can't have you going off half-cocked on your own."

"So, you're going to let me go undercover?"

"I'm going to let this play out and see where it takes us."

Danni grinned. "Thank you."

"Don't thank me yet. There are rules, and you will follow them. Is that understood?"

"What kind of rules?"

"For one, I need to know where you are at all times. And you're going to wear a wire."

"No wire."

"Then I'm shutting you down now."

"No wire!" Her voice was raised, her hands clutching

the line of her hips. "If I can get in I won't risk blowing my cover."

"I wasn't asking you nicely, Detective."

"And I meant what I said," Danni countered.

Armstrong sighed, a deep gust of air that hinted at his wanting to rage back at her. It suddenly felt like they'd come to an impasse. He knew he needed to shift the conversation before spewing something they would both regret. He gestured for her to take a seat as he moved to the chair on the other side of the table. He slid two manila folders across the polished wood toward her.

"What's this?" she asked as she opened one folder and found nothing inside.

"It's the file we *don't* have on Paul Balducci. Everything prior to his eighteenth birthday is sealed. We can't get our hands on it. Not even the petty, juvenile stuff, like shoplifting, or vandalism, that we know about. The other is his father's file. And make no mistakes, Leonard Balduccci was a career criminal."

Danni flipped quickly through the documents inside, one piece of paper grabbing her attention. She read it once and then a second time before lifting her eyes to his. "You killed his father?"

"Ten years ago. Junior would have been a kid. Barely out of grade school. His father was running the family business. He and his crew were hijacking trailer shipments and sending the cargo overseas. We caught them after they took down a truck full of TVs and electronics. The security guard was able to signal the alarm before they killed him. There was a shootout at the docks, and Senior took a bullet. It was one of my first cases and the first time I ever had to discharge my weapon. He died three days later."

Armstrong's gaze suddenly shifted into thought. Despite his best efforts, he often thought about the night he'd killed Leonard Balducci. Taking fire, he'd had no other option but to shoot back. His bullet had hit its target. He'd been blessed that those meant for him had missed. The shooting had almost derailed his career in law enforcement. He'd been grounded, confined to a desk and the shuffling of papers. There had been months of scrutiny from Internal Affairs and strangers who knew nothing of him. The media had questioned his integrity and others had a field day, calling him a monster. He'd felt boxed in and had been ready to give it all up. Despite everyone's assurances that it hadn't been his fault, the guilt he still carried was immense.

"I'm sorry," Danni said softly.

Armstrong shrugged. "It didn't have to end that way, but we weren't given a lot of choices."

Danni nodded. "So how would you like me to play this?"

"Trust your instincts. You got yourself further than I would have anticipated, so play it how you think best. When you're undercover I can only support you from a distance. Although Pius would have been a kid and might not know who I am, the family definitely knows me, so the best I'm going to be able to do is my good-cop or my bad-cop routine, if needed."

"I think I made a connection with the girl Ginny. And then there's his brother."

"Pius's brother?"

"Well, half-brother. His name is Carlo. He said they have the same mother but different fathers. He runs the coffee shop. I didn't even notice the family resemblance until he said something, it's so slight."

Armstrong's brow creased as he seemed to search for something in his memory. He reached for the file, flipping through it briefly before slapping it back against the table. "From everything I know, Paul was an only child. He doesn't have any siblings."

"Not according to Carlo. He also said something about a sister. Allegedly, she was a runaway."

He gestured back toward the file folder. "Find out what you can about him. And before you leave, head upstairs to the tech guys."

"The tech guys?"

"I'm putting in a request for that surveillance wire. They'll get you hooked up."

Danni laughed. "I told you I'm not wearing a damn wire, and I mean that."

"Don't try me, Detective," Armstrong said, amusement dancing in his eyes as he stood and moved back out the door. "I've been a very nice guy up till now!"

Armstrong watched her as she made herself comfortable with the other members of the task force. Danni had a relaxed disposition, and people were at ease with her. For most of the morning she'd been researching the files to ensure she was up-to-date with the investigations, asking pertinent questions when needed. She seemed to enjoy engaging each person individually, her dry humor winning her a number of fans. Her likability factor was extraordinary, and he instinctively understood how she managed to integrate herself into other people's spaces so effortlessly. She was a force to be reckoned with, a quiet storm that seemed to sneak up unnoticed before raging gallantly and then dissipating like a sweet summer rain.

He rocked back in his seat, the front legs of the wooden chair he sat in rising off the vinyl-tiled floor. His hands were folded together in his lap. His expression was reflective as he sat in quiet deliberation. The faintest smile ever pulled at his lips. She amused him as much as she infuriated him, digging her heels in when she wanted to prove a point. She challenged his intellect and seemed comfortable with testing his authority; doing her job as she ignored protocol. And she made him smile. She was not the detective he had expected, but she was one his intuition told him he was going to enjoy working with immensely.

Sitting forward in the chair, he called for her, his deep baritone voice bellowing through the space. "Detective Winstead!"

From where he sat he saw her toss him a look, her gaze narrowing. She shifted her eyes back to the conversation she was in the middle of, seeming to ignore him. He glanced to his wristwatch, taking mental notes as he continued to observe her. After six minutes passed, he debated whether to call out a second time, and then she turned, sauntering easily in his direction.

"Yes, sir?" she said as she moved into the conference room to stand before him. Her arms were crossed over her chest. "You called?" Her expression was nonchalant, barely curious. Her lips were pursed ever so slightly, and her eyes were focused on him intently. She gave him reason to pause as he stared back, suddenly wondering what it might be like to kiss the soft curve of her bottom lip.

He shook the thought away, ignoring the sensation

that suddenly swept through his southern quadrant. "Is there a reason you haven't been upstairs yet, Detective?"

"Yes, sir, there is."

His brow shifted upward, his expression questioning.

Danni continued. "I am not wearing a wire. I won't risk blowing my cover before I figure out if I can even infiltrate Pius's crew. You need to trust me on this one. Sir."

There was a moment of hesitation as they continued to stare at each other. Armstrong finally nodded. As he did, he pushed a small white box across the table in her direction and gestured for her to take it.

Danni's eyes shifted from his face to the box and back. "What's this?" she questioned as she took the container and lifted the lid. Inside lay a silver cross embedded with marcasite jewels and an inlay of red coral. It was about the size of a small plum and fit nicely in the palm of her hand. An extended length of silver chain was threaded through the charm's silver loop. She lifted her eyes a second time, curiosity seeping past her lashes.

"My extremely savvy tech guys call it wearable technology. If you find yourself in a situation, you push the large jewel in the center to trigger the alarm. The device then starts recording audio and calls your emergency contacts to let them know your location. The team and I are your emergency contacts. It's also waterproof, so once you put it on you don't need to take it off. And if you activate the sensor by accident, you just deactivate it with your smartphone."

Danni turned the piece of jewelry from one side to the other, eyeing the details.

He continued. "The tech guys…upstairs…can explain it to you in greater detail. Go up and talk to them," he said, his tone commanding. "Now, wear the damn wire!

And the next time I give you an order, either follow it, or take your ass back to Atlanta. Is that understood?"

Danni nodded. "Yes, sir!"

Chapter 5

Danni had deserved the tongue-lashing she'd gotten from Armstrong. She knew she'd been pushing his buttons, and she'd done so willfully, testing the boundaries. Asserting her authority hadn't always been easy, others dismissive because she was a woman who looked too soft to be effective. Experience had taught her that a strong start usually gave her necessary leverage until she could earn a partner's trust. She pushed, knowing there were risks, but willing to accept the consequences if she failed to prove her worth. If he had sent her packing there wouldn't have been anything she could have done, the punishment deserved. But he hadn't, and she took that as a positive sign.

She took a sip of her coffee, settling down at the same table she'd occupied the previous night. Despite having a line of customers in want of attention, Carlo had greeted her warmly when she'd come through the door. Then he'd filled a large mug with hot coffee, cutting the line of orders to deliver her a drink. After promising to come back to the table to chat once things quieted down, he'd gone back to the counter. He seemed genuinely excited to see her again, his contagious smile heartwarming. Danni had been slightly flattered, the gesture unexpected and catching her off guard.

In the back of the shop, Pie and family—two other men and the female brigade from the night before—sat like stone. They were dressed all in black, dark suits and dresses that had them looking like an *Addams Family* reunion gone awry. The space they occupied felt like it had been reserved especially for them, the other customers seeming to have gotten the memo that they were to sit anywhere but there. Danni couldn't help but wonder what was going on with the morbid attire and their less-than-pleasant demeanors.

She and Ginger exchanged a look, the other woman nodding in her direction. The smile she gave Danni was bright, but there was something else in her eyes. There was an air of sadness that seemed to rise to the surface of her stare before being replaced by a look of ambivalence. Danni tossed her a slight wave, debating if she should go say hello or not. Ginger made the decision for her, rising and moving in her direction after a brief exchange with the man in charge. The two men turned to stare at them both, but Pius barely raised his eyebrow in concern.

"Hey! You came back," Ginger said, dropping into the seat beside her.

"Hi," Danni greeted. "I didn't have anything else to do."

"No homework? Your cousin didn't make you go to school today?"

Danni laughed. "She doesn't care. If she had her way, I'd be dancing in the clubs to help earn extra money. But my dad sends her a check every month, so I don't have to."

"So, would you? Dance?"

Shaking her head, Danni blushed profusely, feeling color rise to her cheeks. She shrugged her shoulders slightly.

Ginger nodded. "I get it. We do what we have to do until we have to do something else."

Wanting to deflect, Danni pointed across the way. "You said you work for him?" she asked, tossing a glance toward Pie. "What do you do?"

Ginger stared at her for a split second before rolling her large eyes skyward. "I do a little more than dancing," she said, her tone rife with sarcasm.

Danni's gaze widened with understanding. "Oh. Sorry."

The young woman pushed her narrow shoulders toward the ceiling. "Nothing for you to be sorry about. It can be good money and Pius…well, Pius is cool most of the time. And he takes care of us."

"And when he's not cool he hits you?"

An awkward silence wafted between them. For a split second it looked like Ginger wanted to say something about that slap, and then just like that she didn't. She seemed to be studying her, and her stare made Danni slightly nervous, like maybe she'd pushed too hard and Ginger had figured out who she was.

"Sorry. It's none of my business," she said as she dropped her gaze to her coffee cup and took a sip.

"You're so green! I bet you still fawn over Justin Bieber," Ginger said with a hearty laugh.

Danni smiled. "I fawn over Chance the Rapper."

"There's a party tomorrow. At Pie's house. Are you interested?"

Danni grinned. "Yeah!"

"Meet me here at nine o'clock. And don't dress like you're homeless," Ginger quipped.

Danni glanced down to the oversize sweats she wore. The jersey was emblazoned with a North Carolina State University logo, the pants a dingy shade of dirt and gray. She had to admit her undercover wardrobe wasn't the most flattering, but it served its purpose. Practical, cheap and nondescript. Nothing that would make her stand out and definitely not provocative. "What should I wear?"

"Doesn't your cousin have something you can borrow?"

Danni blinked, trying to make herself look even younger and completely lost. She shook her head. "My cousin's nickname is Juicy. She's got curves and I don't. Lots of curves."

Ginger chuckled softly. "Don't worry about it. I'll bring something. Be here at eight thirty instead."

Their conversation was suddenly interrupted by Carlo. He gave them both a bright smile. "Everything okay, Ginger?"

The young woman nodded and winked an eye at him. "No complaints," she answered as she stood up, easing the chair she'd occupied back beneath the table.

"I'll see you tomorrow," she said, her eyes shifting toward Danni.

Danni tossed up her hand in a slight wave. "Tomorrow," she echoed.

"What's tomorrow?" Carlo asked as they both watched Ginger return to her seat beside Pie.

"She invited me to a party at your brother's house."

He shook his head. "That might not be a good idea."

"Why?"

"Because that's not the kind of crowd you want to get mixed up with."

"It can't be that bad, right?"

"Stay away from them, Danni. You seem like a really nice girl. I'd hate to see you get caught up in something you can't handle."

"I'm a big girl."

"Exactly how old are you?" Carlo questioned, a hand falling to his hip as he eyed her curiously.

She threw up her hands in frustration. "Why do people keep asking me that? I'm old enough—that's how old I am!"

"You look very young, and I don't need that kind of trouble here."

"Trust me, I'm not nearly as much trouble as some of your other customers," she said, gesturing toward the gang in the corner with her eyes.

He stared at her, neither saying anything, and then he asked again, "So are you going to tell me how old you are or what?"

Danni rolled her eyes. "I'm eighteen. I'll be nineteen in August. I swear. Do you want to see my driver's license?" She shoved a hand into her pocket, pretending to dig for her ID.

Carlo held up a hand, his head shaking from side to side. "That's not necessary. I didn't mean to upset you."

She took a deep breath. "I'm not upset."

"You still need to be careful, though. You can't trust everybody out here."

"I can take care of myself," Danni answered, a hint of indignation in her voice.

He hesitated, his eyes sweeping around the room. "Just

take my advice, please." Carlo turned easily back to the counter and a customer waving for his attention.

As she watched Carlo return to his business, Danni hated that she was deceiving him, because she thought he seemed like a really nice guy. But she couldn't heed his advice and she had to do the job she was there to do. The nice guy would lose out if she had to choose between him and her job. But then nice guys always did, she mused.

She suddenly found herself thinking about the men who'd tripped into and out of her life. Men she'd shared space and time with. Most were still sweet memories that made her smile. A few had simply been horrific nightmares she was glad to be done with. There had been a lot of nice guys in the bunch. Men who attended church regularly, adored their mothers and who had even liked her cat. But every one of them had given her an ultimatum at one time or another: them or her job. The job had won out each and every time.

Daniel Tabrizi had been the only one who'd truly had her reexamining her choices. He'd been as close to perfection as she'd ever fathomed any man being. Their relationship had left her imagining life with a husband, kids and a minivan. Then Shannon had been taken, the abduction of her sister and those other women changing the trajectory of her life. Her badge and the need to chase after the bad guys had won again. Now Daniel was engaged to a former beauty queen turned newscaster who was excited with the prospect of being a stay-at-home mother who baked fresh bread and ironed her husband's shirts by hand.

Danni suddenly wondered what kind of man Armstrong Black was. Pondering if he was a nice guy who liked his mother and cats and could make a woman smile and think about things that had nothing to do with chasing bad guys. If he could love a woman without being unreasonable in his demands and support her dreams as much as she might support his.

The door to the coffee shop swung open, the sound of the chimes drifting through the air. As if she'd somehow conjured him up, Armstrong stepped into the space. He wore his dress uniform, making no effort to hide what he did for a living. He'd also been the third or fourth police officer who'd passed through since Danni had gotten there. She was suddenly wondering if something was going on that she didn't know about and if it was going to piss her off and threaten what she was hoping to accomplish.

Armstrong's gaze moved around the room as he stepped into line to place an order. Danni watched him intently, her breath suddenly catching in her chest.

"Good evening, Detective. What can I get for you?" Carlo asked, his professional tone ringing through the air.

"I'll take a large Earl Grey tea, please."

"Cream and sugar?"

"Just sugar and a wedge of lemon if you have it. And I need that to go, please."

"Coming right up."

Danni watched as Carlo grabbed a foam cup and filled it with hot water. As he did, Armstrong looked around the room a second time, his gaze meeting hers and then sweeping nonchalantly away.

There was a rumble of noise coming from the gallery across the room, and Danni turned in time to see Pie and Ginger rising from their seats and moving toward the door. The others followed like obedient puppies. As they passed Danni's table, Ginger gave her a nod but said nothing, and then just like that they were all gone.

"Thank you," Armstrong said as Carlo handed him his order.

"No, thank you, sir. It's on the house." Danni watched as Carlo gave her partner a generous smile.

Armstrong smiled back. "I appreciate that." He slid a hand into his jacket, pulled out his wallet and pushed a five-dollar bill into the tip jar. As he exited the space, he paused, taking one last glance in her direction before disappearing through the door.

It was only when he was out of sight that Danni realized she'd been toying with the jeweled cross around her neck. She tucked the trinket back down under her sweat-shirt. Carlo moved to join her at the table, both watching as the crowd in the room suddenly thinned. He carried a pot of hot coffee, refilled her cup, then moved to fill one other. Just as she thought he might be able to take a break, two more uniformed officers stepped inside, made quick purchases and exited. It was eerily quiet when he finally moved back to her table and dropped down into the seat across from her.

"You've been busy," Danni said, a warm smile lifting easily.

"Just our regular crowd."

"Really? That's interesting."

He chuckled. "You mean all the law enforcement officers?"

"I didn't get the impression that this was where the cops hung out."

"It's not. Tonight's the annual Police Recognition Ceremony at the Hyatt Regency down the road. I'm sure most of those guys who came through just need to be there early to prep."

"Oh."

"It's a pretty big deal. This year especially. They're honoring the superintendent of police, Jerome Black, and his forty-five plus years of public service."

"Jerome Black?"

"The Black family is a big deal here in Chicago. I think all of them are in law enforcement or politics." Carlo leaned forward, clasping his hands together atop the table as he continued. "Pick up any newspaper, on any given day, and one of them is being honored for something."

"They can't all be that perfect."

"No. One of them is definitely dirty, and another got hemmed up in a shooting a while back that left a man dead."

His expression darkened, something Danni couldn't quite read crossing his face. She knew he was referring to the death of Pius's father, and she wondered why he didn't just say so. She was also curious to know who among the Black family was thought to be a dirty cop. She suddenly had questions that were concerning. What did she really know about Armstrong, a man who'd shown her nothing but respect and kindness? She enjoyed their conversations and he seemed like the nicest guy, but he didn't ever talk about himself or his family and avoided her questions when she asked. And now, based on what Armstrong did talk about, she found herself also questioning what she knew about her new partner.

Danni pretended to be shocked, widening her eyes. "So this police officer killed someone?"

"They said it was a justified shooting, but you never know about those things."

Danni nodded. "You know a lot about what's going on around here."

"It's my civic duty to be informed," he said. "And I'm also the neighborhood watch leader!"

Danni giggled. She was just about to ask another question when the door swung open and Pie entered. Carlo didn't seem surprised to see him back. The two men locked gazes as he moved toward Carlo, coming to stand by the table.

"Hey," Pie said, turning to stare at her as he greeted the other man. "You got a minute?" His eyes swept her slight frame from head to toe before he turned to meet Carlo's stare.

Carlo moved onto his feet. "Yeah," he answered. He turned his attention to Danni. "Sorry, I need to talk to my brother for a minute. Do you need me to call you a ride home?"

She shook her head. "No, thanks. I'm good."

He suddenly dropped a warm hand to her forearm. "Be careful out there, please. I wouldn't want anything to happen to you," he said. He turned, moving toward the office door behind the counter.

Pie stood staring at her for another quick second before he spun on his heels to follow behind his brother. The look he gave her made Danni's skin crawl, a sensation so uncomfortable that she felt like she needed to stand fully clothed in a hot shower with strong disinfectant. Reaching for her jacket, she pushed her arms through the sleeves, tightened the garment around her torso and practically ran out the door.

* * *

Armstrong saw her before she saw him. Stopping back at the office had not been in his plans, but something about the case and Danni had him feeling out of sorts. He couldn't put his finger on what had him so discombobulated, and he was hoping that reviewing the files one more time might help him figure it out.

He was only slightly surprised to find her in the conference room, papers strewn across the tabletop as she sat deep in thought. There was no denying the dedication she brought to the assignment. But it was the start of the weekend, and the late hour should have found her someplace other than work. She jumped, startled out of contemplation, when he entered the room and called her by name.

"Detective Winstead. I'm surprised to find you here."

Danni turned abruptly toward the door, her breath catching ever so slightly. "Detective Black! Hey, I wasn't expecting you back."

He smiled, sliding into the seat beside her. "I wasn't expecting to come back, but there's something about this case that's bothering me."

"Something in particular?"

"Something I can't put my finger on."

"I know the feeling. I've been trying to put the pieces together for the last three hours, but we seem to be going nowhere and getting nothing fast."

Armstrong's brows lifted slightly. "You really should get some rest. No one expects twenty-hour days out of you."

Danni smiled sweetly. "I know. I just want to make sure I earn my keep."

He nodded. "Anything happen tonight that we need to know about?"

"Not really. I did get an invitation to a party tomorrow night, though."

"Do you think that's wise?"

"I think it'll help me get even closer to Pius. Who, by the way, is one really sketchy guy. He really gives me the creeps!"

"Have you even talked to him yet?"

"He's not really the talkative type, but I'm hoping to make some headway at tomorrow's party."

Armstrong nodded again. "What's your take on the brother?"

Danni's gaze dropped to the table. She clenched a fist and bit down against her bottom lip.

Something in her tone changed as she answered. "He seems like a really nice guy. And he doesn't have any priors, so he's kept himself on the right side of the law. I'm not sure if he plays into this at all."

The shift in her disposition didn't go unnoticed as Armstrong eyed her intently. Nor did he miss when she changed the subject.

"How was your evening? Did you have a good time at your policeman thing?"

Armstrong chuckled. "You say that like I went to party or something."

Danni smiled. "Or something. So did you? Have a good time?"

"I did my duty and stood beside my family as my father was honored for his service."

"You never told me your father was the superintendent of police."

"I didn't?"

"No."

"I guess I didn't tell you that my mother is a federal court judge, either. Or that my brother Parker is a lieutenant and we report to him."

"I did know about your brother."

"Well, the whole family is employed by the city of Chicago, or the state of Illinois, or the federal government, in some capacity." He paused for a split second and then corrected himself. "Take that back. Two of them are in private practice. Mingus is a former police officer turned private investigator and Ellington has his own law firm. My sister, the state's prosecutor, is the only lawyer in the family who gets a paycheck from the commonwealth."

Danni chuckled. "Are you all named after jazz musicians?"

He grinned. "After God, each other and their children, the only thing my parents love and agree on is jazz. They thrive on it! It's all I heard growing up. I didn't know there was any other kind of music until I was in my teens. My mother says naming us after all the greats was a necessity."

"That's actually pretty cool."

Armstrong shrugged his broad shoulders, and the gesture focused Danni's attention on how handsome he looked in his uniform. His tall stature was imposing, and his presence was commanding. His good looks presented more model-like than pedestrian, and he could have easily graced the cover of any fashion magazine. He was a beautiful specimen of masculinity. Danni realized she was holding her breath and staring. She snapped her gaze back to the files she'd been studying, hoping against all odds that he hadn't noticed.

* * *

But Armstrong had been eyeing her just as intently. Her brow was furrowed as she suddenly turned back to the documents in a file folder on the table. Her cheeks were flushed, and her thick lashes were batting fervently as if something suddenly had her nervous.

"Detective, you are officially off duty. You need to relax and get some rest. That's an order," he said.

Danni nodded. "I guess you're right."

"Have you eaten anything?"

"I grabbed a sandwich at the coffee shop."

"Well, a few of us were headed out to grab a beer. We're headed over to a little club called Andy's. The food's pretty good, and the music is always on point. Why don't you join us?"

She pondered the invitation and then declined. "I appreciate the offer, but I think I'm just going to head back to the hotel and go to bed. I really could use some rest."

Armstrong eyed her for a minute longer. Finally, he said, "All right, then. I'll see you tomorrow." And then he left her, disappearing as quickly as he'd arrived.

The crooner Sam Smith was playing out of the club's massive speakers, the sound system reverberating around the room. Like many of the men and a few of the women in the room, Sam was begging someone to stay with him. The lights in the club were dim. Couples gyrated in slow rotations against each other on the dance floor, and the ambience was easy and casual.

Armstrong glanced around the space until he caught sight of his brother waving a large hand in the air for his attention. He sauntered easily down a short flight of stairs and pushed his way through the crowd until he reached the table across the way.

They were all there. His brothers, Ellington, Parker, Davis and Mingus, and his sisters, Simone and Vaughan. They were not only his family, but his best friends, the bond between them impenetrable.

They each greeted him warmly.

"We didn't think you were coming," Simone said, kissing his cheek.

"Obviously, you don't know your brother," Mingus countered. "Because we knew he was coming!" He and Parker slapped palms.

Armstrong dropped into the empty seat they'd been holding for him. He apologized. "Sorry, I made the mistake of running back to the office."

"Sometimes you need to let the work go," Vaughan said.

Armstrong nodded in agreement. "That's what I was just telling my new partner," he said as he gestured toward the waitress and ordered a beer.

"So, how's that working out?" Parker questioned, sipping his own drink.

Armstrong pushed his shoulders toward the ceiling. "I actually like her," he said, trying to keep his tone as nonchalant as he could manage.

Simone shifted forward in her chair. "Your new partner is a woman?"

"You have a new partner?" Vaughan interjected.

"Yes, and yes!" Armstrong quipped.

"If you like her, that can't be good," his sisters chimed in unison.

The brothers all laughed.

"Seriously," Simone continued. "That would surely be a lawsuit waiting to happen!"

"Give me some credit, Simone," Armstrong muttered.

A look swept around the table, the siblings all breaking out in laughter.

"What?" Armstrong said, feeling genuinely confused.

"You know what?" Vaughan asked. "I think Simone's referring to that last lawsuit against you. What was her name? Kandi Kane?"

Armstrong rolled his eyes. "*Kandyce* was an informant. And nothing happened between me and that girl. Nothing."

"It's your lie," Simone countered. "Tell it any way you want."

"I think the paternity test proved my innocence."

"That paternity test proved Kandi Kane got around and you were not her baby's daddy. The rest has yet to be disproved."

"Whatever!" Armstrong snipped. He shook his head. Despite his continued protests that he hadn't slept with that woman, rumors about them persisted. His sisters were champing at the bit for a hint of spilled tea and it annoyed them to no end that he refused to give them anything. They pushed, hoping to trip him up, and he rarely, if ever, fell for their antics. He pulled a chilled mug of Heineken to his lips and slowly savored the drink.

Davis changed the subject. "So what's she like?"

"Who?"

"Your new partner. What's her name?"

There was a pause as Armstrong collected his thoughts. The question was simple, but he instinctively knew more were coming and he had to decide just how much he intended to share. "Her name's Danni," he finally answered. "Danni Winstead."

"She has quite the reputation," Parker said, filling them in on the highlights of Danni's résumé.

Armstrong picked up where his brother left off. "She's smart and quick. So far, I'm really impressed."

"So when do we get to meet her?" Vaughan asked.

"Why do you people need to meet her?" Armstrong asked.

The two sisters both shot him a look, their expressions practically identical. His brothers laughed, also turning their gazes on Armstrong.

He shook his head. "She's joining us for family dinner on Sunday."

Simone and Vaughan exchanged a glance. "You're bringing her to meet the parents?" they asked in unison.

Mingus tossed his hands up. "Pop the popcorn now," he quipped as he rubbed his palms together.

Armstrong laughed. "Don't scare this woman away, please. I do have to work with her."

Davis chuckled. "Is that what they call it now? Work?"

"What are you implying?"

Another round of looks passed between them all.

"He's not implying anything," Ellington said. "He's saying you've had partners before, but this is the first time you've ever invited one to meet the parents at Sunday dinner."

"In his defense," Mingus said, "he has had people he's worked with who have come to family events."

"But it was Mom or Dad who actually extended the invitation," Simone countered.

"That's true," Davis added. He chuckled. "Sounds

to me like this Danni Winstead might be a very special lady."

Armstrong gulped down the last of his beer and gestured for a second round. He didn't bother to comment, seeing no need to add that Danni Winstead was in a class by herself. *Special* didn't begin to describe her.

After a quick shower, Armstrong settled down on his chenille sofa with a James Patterson book and a bag of his favorite Jelly Belly jelly beans. The late-night news played softly on the television set, the weatherman updating the audience on the threat of a potential storm. There was a slight chill in the air, and he pulled a wool blanket up around his chest. He'd had a great time with his siblings, and the good-natured ribbing he'd taken reminded him once again of those things that were most important to him. He loved his family, and they loved him back.

He'd been disappointed when Danni had declined his invitation, but being with his brothers and his sisters had moved him well past the pinch to his ego. Despite his best efforts to keep his mind distracted, he still wondered about her, curiosity questioning what she might be doing. There was much he didn't know about Danni, and his wanting to discover what moved her heart and motivated her spirit compelled him to want to spend time with her to learn everything he could.

What he did know was that she took what she was doing seriously. She had done her research, asking the right questions of people in the know, and it had taught her that human traffickers preyed on women and girls who were vulnerable or easily impressed and manipulated. Young girls in tenuous family situations or who were rebelliously defiant were often targeted. Innocence and naïveté were desirable traits. She'd taken that knowledge and created a persona that she could easily wear when necessary. Undercover, she was Danni, a girl who was barely eighteen and not particularly savvy to the ways of the world. Innocent and curious, even slightly desperate for friendship and acceptance. And just as swiftly, she could become Danni the cop, highly decorated, well respected and determined to be the best police officer possible.

Armstrong shifted his body lower against the sofa pillows. He was curious to know more about her personal life. Was there someone back in Atlanta waiting for her to return? Someone she might be missing? Had she wanted to return to the hotel to spend time sharing the story of what she was going through with someone special to her? To maybe complain about him and his management skills? There was much he didn't know about her, and he looked forward to the opportunity to ask about those things that made her who she was.

He popped a handful of the sugary candy into his mouth as he turned the page on the bestseller in his lap. Two chapters in he realized he couldn't remember a word he'd read, thoughts of Danni Winstead still on his mind.

Chapter 6

The next morning Armstrong met Danni at the conference room door. "Good morning."

"Good morning," she said, once again surprised to see him at the station, particularly since she wasn't expecting him so early.

"Drop your stuff and meet me in the basement," he said.

"The basement?"

"Yeah, it's on the bottom floor of the building," he said sarcastically as he swept past her. "Just push the down button on the elevator."

Danni rolled her eyes skyward as he laughed. "Do I have time to grab a cup of coffee?" she asked, her eyes following him down the hallway.

He nodded. "Make it a small cup," he answered before disappearing around the corner.

Minutes later Danni stood with him in the police station's shooting range. There were ten pistol lanes in the sound-insulated space. He passed her a pair of tactical shooting glasses and a set of Howard Leight earmuffs. "You're past due on your recertification," he said. "How often do you train?"

"At least twice per month with my personal weapon. Maybe once per month with my duty gun."

"That's a lot. Is that a state mandate in Georgia?"

"We're required to attend a one-hour training class for firearm recertification each year and a one-hour class for the use of deadly force."

"That's the norm for most states. I tend to train more also. I think it's necessary to help an officer make proper deadly-force decisions on the job."

Danni gave him a slight smile as he led her into one of the classrooms toward the back of the large space.

"Let's get started," Armstrong said. "This will more than fulfill all of your state requirements."

For the next two hours the duo and three other officers were retrained on their firearms. The instructor, a large man with a Grizzly Adams beard, took them through the usual range topics. They discussed low light and judgmental or decision-making shooting, shooting while moving to cover, one-hand firing, giving verbal challenges, firing from an officer-down position and engaging multiple targets. He also took them through the paces of clearing weapon stoppages with either hand, drills that simulated weapon malfunctions, emergency tactical reloading and the manipulation of safeties.

When they were done in the classroom they moved to the firing lane for target practice. Armstrong was impressed with her expertise. She was a skilled shooter, leaving a perfect half-inch grouping of holes in the center mast of the target practice silhouette.

"Nice job," he said as he sent a second target sheet down to the other end of the lane. "Tighten your stance a bit more, though," he offered. "But don't lock your knees. You need the flexibility."

Danni nodded. "Okay," she said as she prepped her gun and aimed.

He stepped in behind her, so close that she could feel the heat from his body mingling sweetly with her own. The moment suddenly had her anxious, her next shot missing its mark.

"You okay?" he questioned.

Her head bobbed fervently. "I'm fine."

He slipped a large hand beneath her elbow. "You need to raise your arm just a fraction, then aim and fire. You'll hit him in the heart every time," he said, stepping back out of her space.

Danni took a deep breath and closed her eyes for a split second to regain her composure. When she reopened them she focused on her target, took aim and emptied the clip in her weapon.

When they were done, Armstrong lauded her skills. "Very nice shooting, Detective."

"Thank you."

"How are you going to arm yourself tonight?" he asked. "Have you thought about it?"

Danni nodded. "It'll all depend on the dress Ginger wants me to wear. I hope to wear a thigh holster. But if that doesn't work, I have other options."

For a split second Armstrong found himself imagining where those options might be found on her body. He shook the thoughts from his head and continued. "You'll have two teams trailing you tonight. One will leave with you from the coffee shop. The other will already be in place outside the Balducci home when you get there. I'll be there, too. If you get into any trouble, you push the button," he said, a hand reaching out to toy with the necklace around her neck.

Danni nodded as she took a step back to widen the gap between them. "Any other advice?"

"Yeah," he said as he stared directly into her eyes. "Don't get into any trouble."

"What the hell are you wearing?" Ginger asked, eyeing Danni with amusement.

Danni looked down to see what her new friend was seeing. Her undergarments looked like they were government issued: oversize, stark white cotton that loosely fit her petite frame. She'd bought them earlier that morning, not wanting her personal wardrobe of satin and lace to deflect from the cover story she'd created.

"What?" Her eyes graced the length of her body down to the floor and back. "What's wrong with what I'm wearing?"

"Have you ever heard of Victoria's Secret? It looks like you're wearing my sister's clothes, and she's only eight."

"No one is going to see my underwear."

"You sure about that?"

Danni's eyes widened. "I'm positive!"

She stepped into the dress Ginger was holding out for her. It was a simple shift dress with split sleeves in a vibrant shade of green that complemented her warm complexion nicely. It stopped just at her knees and was nothing like she'd anticipated. The look was cute and fresh and gave her a girl-next-door appearance. She'd been expecting short, tight and inappropriate and was pleasantly surprised.

The other woman shook her head. "You're going to have to lose the bra. The straps show, and that's not cute."

"I don't think this is a good idea," Danni said.

"Don't be a baby. It's going to be fine."

Danni took a deep breath as she undid the straps to her brassiere and slipped her arms out of it. Ginger reached behind her to zip the dress closed. "Now, that is so cute on you!"

Danni smiled. "It's not bad."

"And it matches your necklace," Ginger said, trailing a finger across the jeweled cross. "That's pretty. Where'd you get it?"

Danni instinctively drew a protective hand to the charm. "My grandmother gave it to me before she died."

"Well, it works, so I don't have to loan you anything."

Ginger pulled at the scrunchie that held Danni's hair in a loose ponytail. She brushed the thick strands loose and reached for the curling iron she'd plugged into the electrical outlet.

Minutes later Danni didn't recognize herself. Her hair was full and lush with loose waves, and Ginger had applied the barest layer of foundation and a light coat of mascara to her face.

"Pius said you were a beauty," Ginger muttered, admiring her handiwork. "I see why he likes you. That's a good thing."

"Really? He did?"

Ginger shrugged, her expression shifting. "We should go. Stay close to me tonight. It'll be fun."

Danni grabbed the woman's arm. "He doesn't expect

me to…well…" She deliberately hesitated, her eyes dancing back and forth.

Ginger stared at her. "It's a party! No one expects you to do anything but have a good time. What's wrong with you?"

"Sorry. I wasn't sure if he expected me to work or something."

"That's not how Pius operates his business."

Danni pretended to blow a sigh of relief, relaxing so that the tension eased from her face. Staying in character sometimes required her to feign emotion she didn't necessarily feel. The challenge came with balancing how she truly felt with the lie she needed to tell and making it all appear natural. She reached for her bra and the clothes she'd discarded, rolling them up to fit into her backpack. As she tucked them inside her fingers grazed her service weapon, hidden in a bottom compartment.

"Are you a virgin?" Ginger suddenly asked, the question throwing Danni off guard.

She felt her cheeks tint a deep shade of red. "What? Why?"

"Are you?"

Danni swallowed hard before nodding. Another lie rolled easily out of her mouth. "Yes."

Ginger paused before responding. "That makes you a prime catch," she finally said, a slight smile lifting the corners of her mouth. "You're going to have to make the boys work for it. There are men who will pay a premium to be your first."

"I wish I had your confidence."

"What I have are survival skills. They will take you farther than confidence ever will."

* * *

Stepping out of the restroom, Danni felt a wave of anxiety wash over her. The list of things that could go wrong was lengthy, and she'd been playing a game of what-if in her head. The most pressing were what if she messed up and blew her cover? What if she blew the case, destroying months of hard work and effort? If that happened, would she be able to recover and come back from that? Would Detective Black be disappointed that he had trusted her?

She took a deep breath, hoping that everyone else saw that anxiety as her just being nervous about going to a party. As she moved into the space, Pie and his brother were in a deep discussion, Carlo waving his index finger to make a point. Their voices were hushed, and the conversation was cut short as everyone seemed to suddenly be staring at her. Danni's gaze skated around the room before focusing back on Carlo. She forced a smile onto her face as he turned to stare.

"Wow!" he exclaimed, moving toward her.

"Is it too much?" she whispered.

"You're gorgeous," he said softly.

"Thank you," Ginger said, grinning broadly. "I do really good work!"

Danni laughed. "Ginny works miracles!"

He reached for her hand, his warm palm caressing the back of her fingers. "No miracles were needed here. You're a true beauty!"

Danni's smile widened. She took a deep breath. "Will you be coming to your brother's party?"

Carlo shook his head. "I may stop by after I finish up here, but like I told you, this isn't a crowd you really want to get caught up with. Why don't you let me take you to dinner instead?"

Ginger rolled her eyes skyward as she grabbed Danni's arm and tugged. "He's a party pooper. Let's go have some fun!" she exclaimed as she positioned her body between the two of them. "Don't let him scare you off!"

Danni laughed again. "Who's scared?"

Carlo shook his head. "One day all of you are going to figure out I know what I'm talking about," he said. He shifted his stance so that he stood facing her. They locked gazes. "Ginny has my number. If things get out of hand and you need a friend, you call me."

"She'll be fine," Ginger interjected. "I'll take good care of her."

Carlo gave her a look. "You better," he said, the teasing in his tone suddenly turning serious. "If anything happens to her, I'm not going to be happy," he stated.

Danni grinned. "Thank you," she said. "But I'll be fine."

"Let's go," Pie snapped, seeming annoyed with their conversation.

"Happy birthday, Pie," Carlo said as the other man stomped toward the door.

"Yeah," Pie answered before disappearing out the entrance.

"It's his birthday?" Danni exclaimed, her eyes darting from Ginger to Carlo and back. "He doesn't seem happy about it."

Ginger nodded. "He's never happy about anything," she said. She and Carlo exchanged a look. "Let's go," she said.

With one last glance toward Carlo, Danni smiled and followed after the woman.

* * *

The sprawling Wicker Park estate was not at all what Danni was expecting. From the back seat of the BMW, she tried not to let her expression show her surprise. She wanted to say something, but neither Pie nor Ginger had spoken during their ride. She had tried unsuccessfully to draw them both into conversation, only to have him glare at her with annoyance. To say the moment was uncomfortable was an understatement. As they pulled up in front of the fenced property, she found herself glad for the loud music and noisy chatter that emanated out of the brick-front home.

Danni hesitated as the other two exited the luxury vehicle. Pie tossed them both a look over his shoulder, he and Ginger seeming to have a conversation only they were privy to. He tossed Danni one last look, then hurried up the front steps and into the home. When he was out of sight, Ginger seemed to breathe a sigh of relief, everything about her stance relaxing.

"Sorry about that," Ginger said, her voice a loud whisper. "He can be a bit overbearing sometimes."

"Does he ever talk?" Danni asked as she smoothed the sides of her dress with her palms.

Ginger shrugged. "Trust me. The less he says, the better."

Danni took a deep breath. "This is Pius's home?" she queried.

Ginger tossed her a look. "Pius? No, their grandfather owns this place. He's throwing Pie this birthday celebration."

Danni nodded. "It's very nice."

"Yeah," Ginger said, her tone dismissive. She gestured

for Danni to follow as she took the short flight of steps up to the front door and then entered the home.

There was a sizable crowd gathered inside, and the mood was cheerful. Laughter vibrated off the pale gray walls, and there didn't seem to be anything unsavory about what was going on. It was a birthday party with balloons, a banner, an oversize cake and a variety of food and drink. Alexander Balducci was front and center, a heavy arm wrapped around his grandson's shoulders. It was the first time Danni had ever seen the young man smile, picture-perfect teeth in his usual scowling face. Pie actually looked happy and not nearly as ominous.

Ginger was saying something, but Danni hadn't been paying any attention, too focused on taking in her surroundings. The young woman called her name again.

"I'm sorry. What did you say?"

There was an air of attitude in Ginger's tone. "I said, let me introduce you and please do not say anything stupid!"

"For real, Ginny? I wasn't raised by animals."

Ginger laughed. "I didn't say you were. It's just that the Balducci family can be very…well…particular." She shrugged her shoulders. "You'll see," she said.

Alexander Balducci locked his gaze on her as they crossed the room to where he stood. He was a big bear of a man, tall and wide with a tight beer gut beneath an expensive wool suit. He looked as if he spent considerable time tanning, his complexion a strange shade of orange-brown. His eyes were a bright blue, crystal pools of water that felt like they could easily swallow you whole. He was nicely polished and carried himself with an air of authority that could be intimidating.

Ginger pulled a bright smile across her face as she

extended a manicured hand in greeting. "Hello, Mr. B. How are you, sir?"

"I'm very well, thank you. So glad that you could join us, Miss Taylor." His eyes swept past her to Danni. "And who do we have here?"

"This is Danni...Danielle. Danielle, this is Mr. Balducci."

"It's a pleasure to meet you, Danielle."

"Thank you, sir. Please, call me Danni."

"Danielle is more appropriate," he said matter-of-factly. "Do you have a surname, Danielle?"

"It's Porter. Danielle Porter," she said, claiming her mother's maiden name.

"Your reputation precedes you, Ms. Porter. I've heard wonderful things about you from my grandson. It seems Pius is quite fond of you."

Pie grunted, his eyes skating skyward. He suddenly walked off, disappearing from the room.

His reaction was unexpected and confusing. Danni forced her own smile, trying not to let her face show any emotion. "Thank you. You have a beautiful home, sir."

"Well, consider my home, your home, Ms. Porter. You are always welcome."

"Thank you, sir. That's very nice of you."

He winked at her. "I hope you enjoy yourself this evening."

Danni had questions, but she knew better than to ask. Instead, she nodded, thanked the man and took a step back out of his space.

"You two head downstairs with the other young people," Balducci said, the suggestion clearly an order. "Danielle, I'm sure we'll see each other again soon." He turned to shake hands with another guest, and the two women knew they'd been dismissed.

"Come on," Ginger said, grabbing her hand and pulling her along. "Let's go have some fun!"

Chapter 7

The basement of the Balducci home had been transformed into a 1970s disco party. Strobe lights, mirrored
disco balls, a DJ with a turntable and the multicolored
tiled floor made the space look like it had come out of a
retro photo of Studio 54. One side of the room had been
set up with tables and board games, and there were a few
younger kids playing Twister on the floor. Pie sat on the
sofa in front of the television set, playing Pac-Man on an
old Atari gaming system.

About thirty teens were dancing to a playlist that
included Michael Jackson's "Don't Stop 'til You Get
Enough," Wild Cherry's "Play That Funky Music" and
Queen's "Bohemian Rhapsody." The music was loud,
the bass throbbing and the laughter abundant. Almost
instantly, Ginger left her standing alone, moving into

the center of the mix as she tossed her hands above her head and gyrated to the music.

Danni stood watching for a moment before she moved to the bar where the food and beverages were located. A hired server dished her up a plate of chips and a hot dog and bun and handed her a chilled bottle of generic cola.

"Thank you," she said as she moved to sit on the sofa beside Pie.

She sat quietly and watched, nibbling on the chips and gulping the soda. The dance crowd was lost in the music, and it didn't appear that anyone was paying any attention to her or him. Pie pretended to ignore her, continuing to play, but when he cut an eye in her direction, she saw that as an opportunity.

"You're really good at that, Pie," she said, tilting her head toward the monitor.

He shot her another look but didn't bother to respond.

Danni continued. "Your grandfather is pretty cool and I really like your brother. He's been really nice to me."

Pie grunted and shifted his body ever so slightly.

She took a breath, reaching to drop her glass onto the coffee table. "Ginger's been really good to me, too. And I know she works for you. I was wondering…"

Pie stood up abruptly. He glared, clearly not happy. He threw his game controller down to the sofa. "Why are you bothering me?" he said with a scowl, his fists clenched tightly at his sides.

Danni bristled. She stood slowly and took a step back. "Sorry, I was just trying to make conversation."

He suddenly bellowed, his deep baritone silencing everyone in the room. "Get out of my space," he snapped sharply. "If I want you in my space I will call for you!"

"I really am sorry. I didn't mean to…"

"Danni!" Ginger was moving swiftly in their direction, coming to stand between them. It was as if the alarm on her radar had gone off. "Sorry, Pie," she said. Something like fear pained her expression.

He raised his hand, his index finger wagging as if it were unhinged in front of her face. "Check her!" he snapped.

"I will, Pie. It won't happen again," Ginger said, her soft tone consoling. She drew her hand over his chest, tapping him lightly. "Play your game. We won't bother you anymore," she said. "I promise! Don't be mad, Pie."

There was an awkward moment as he continued to glare in Danni's direction, and then just like that he sat back down, resuming his game play.

Danni felt herself exhale a sigh of relief. Ginger snatched her arm and pulled her to the other side of the room.

"What do you think you were doing?"

"I wasn't doing anything. I just wanted to…"

"You don't talk to him unless he wants to speak to you. And you definitely don't ask him questions about his family or his business."

"I was just trying to be friendly."

"Pie doesn't need you to be his friend. Stay out of his way."

"Sorry," Danni said, her eyes wafting back toward the man for just a brief moment.

Ginger took her own deep breath. "Come on," she said, "let's dance. I'll introduce you to a few people. I brought you so you could have some fun. Don't pay Pie any attention."

"Are these people your friends?"

"Something like that."

"Do some of them work for Pius, too?"

Ginger laughed. "We all work for Pius."

The party was still going strong when Danni called herself an Uber and climbed the stairs back to the home's main floor. As she moved through the hallway past the living room, she caught the eye of Grandpa Alexander the patriarch standing in conversation with two suited men. It was a brief second before she realized they were the same suited men who were always following on Pie's heels. He gestured for her attention, stopping her in her tracks before she could reach the front door.

"Ms. Porter, a moment, please."

Danni smiled, pausing as he moved to where she stood. The two men swept past them, headed for the back stairwell and the room downstairs. She followed them briefly with her eyes before turning her attention to Mr. Balducci. "Yes, sir?"

"I hear there was a slight misunderstanding between you and my grandson?"

"I apologize, sir. Apparently I said something to upset him."

The old man smiled. "Pie can be a little temperamental. I'm sure he didn't mean anything by it."

Danni smiled. "I'm sure he didn't," she echoed.

"Were you leaving us? The party sounds like it's still going strong downstairs."

"I promised my cousin that I wouldn't stay out too late. She'll be looking for me."

The old man nodded. "I can have my driver take you home. I know you drove over with my grandson and Ms. Taylor."

"Thank you, sir, but that's not necessary. My cousin

gave me money for an Uber and I've already called them." She stole a quick glance to her smartphone. "It says they'll be pulling up in three minutes."

"Technology is quite the thing, isn't it?" he mused.

She nodded. "Yes, sir."

The front door of his home suddenly opened and Carlo stepped through the entrance. His arrival took her by surprise. She felt a grin pull across her face, her eyes widening with an air of excitement to see a friendly face. She waved her hand, trying to contain her energy.

"Danni, hi!" he exclaimed. "I didn't expect you to still be here," he said as he moved to her side. He leaned to press a quick kiss to her cheek, the gesture unexpected. Her breath caught deep in her chest as he shifted his attention, extending his hand to shake the older man's.

"Let's talk in my office when you're done here, son," Alexander said. "I hope you'll visit with us again, Danielle."

"Thank you again for welcoming me into your home, sir," she responded.

Danni's phone suddenly vibrated. "That would be my ride," she said, feeling nervous. She had hoped to slip out unnoticed but now the attention from both men had her slightly on edge.

Carlo looked confused. "Your ride?"

"My Uber. It's out front."

He nodded. "Did you have fun?"

She shrugged. "It was okay."

He chuckled. "Not what you expected, was it?"

She shook her head. "Not really."

"But you looked cute. That's all that's important," he said teasingly.

Danni laughed. "I need to be going. It was good to see you again," she said.

He trailed a gentle finger across her cheek. "Be safe, Danni!"

Just before making her exit, Danni took one last glance over her shoulder. She watched as Carlo and Alexander walked side by side toward the opposite end of the home. After making her way to the Uber, she climbed into the back seat of the four-door vehicle. When the driver turned around to greet her, she felt the safest she'd felt since her evening had started, his familiar face a welcome sight.

Once they'd pulled out of the parking space and turned from the Balducci home, Armstrong grabbed the brim of his baseball cap and tossed the headpiece into the empty passenger seat. He drove the Toyota Avalon until he was certain no one was tailing them, and then they both relaxed, heaving a collective sigh.

"I could really use a drink," Danni said as Armstrong steered the sedan. "That was truly painful!"

"You didn't drink enough at your party?"

"Cola was the only beverage of choice. That party was very kid-friendly."

Armstrong tossed her a glance in his rearview mirror. "I'm confused."

"You're confused! Not nearly as much as I am," she countered as she took him step-by-step through her experience in the Balducci home. "It was very PG," she concluded, "and there was absolutely nothing illicit going on. It was just a kid's birthday party for a crime lord with anger management issues."

"And you didn't learn anything else about him or his business?"

"Talking to Pius was like talking to a toddler having a tantrum. The rest of the time he practically sucked his thumb and literally played games. It was crazy!"

The quiet in the car rose to a deafening level as they both reflected on the events. Danni sank back against the leather seats, closing her eyes and pulling her arms above her head. The vehicle hit a bump and then turned sharply.

"Sorry about that," Armstrong said.

"No problem. Are we close to the hotel?"

He shook his head. "No. I figured I'd buy you that drink. It sounds like it's well deserved."

"I was really just kidding," she said as she sat back up, pulling herself straight in her seat.

"I know," he replied. "But it was a great idea. Besides, you've had my nerves frazzled for most of the night. I could use a drink myself."

"Why were your nerves frazzled?"

"My partner was undercover. I was worried. As I should be."

"I'm a big girl, Detective. I really wish you would trust that."

"I do. It's the villains I don't trust."

Any other time or place, or with any other man, Danni might have been concerned about where he was taking her. But there was something about Armstrong Black that had her comfort level at an all-time high. She followed behind him as he led her through the door of an old brick building on what appeared to be a deserted street. They headed down a flight of well-worn steps to a second door, this one painted a vibrant shade of glossy red. Armstrong lifted the heavy gold knocker and waited for someone on the other side to welcome them inside.

The doorman greeted Armstrong by name, the two men slapping palms and doing some strange thumb-twisting fist bump. The look he gave Danni was part curious and part salacious, his eyes narrowing as his tongue trailed across his lips. She felt herself take a step closer to her partner, her stance tensing just enough for him to notice.

"Why are you leering at the woman, Tank? Didn't your mother raise you better?" Armstrong quipped.

The other man laughed. "Sorry about that. How are you tonight, beautiful?"

Armstrong's jaw was tight as he gave the other man a look. "The lady has a name. But she's Miss to you. Act like you've had some home-training, please."

"No disrespect intended, my friend."

"None taken," Danni answered. The sweetest smile pulled at her lips.

He extended his arm in greeting. "Everyone here calls me Tank."

As she went to shake the man's hand, she couldn't miss that two of his fingers were missing.

Armstrong's gaze shifted skyward. "Danni, this is retired detective Marshall Bryant. Tank, this is my new partner, Danni Winstead."

"Nice to meet you, Tank."

"They didn't make partners like you when I was on the job!" the man teased.

Danni giggled.

"Is my table available?" Armstrong asked, interrupting their moment.

Tank laughed. "Isn't it always?"

Armstrong grabbed her hand, entwining his fingers between hers as he pulled her along. The gesture was almost protective, and it made Danni toss one last glance over her shoulder. Tank grinned, gestured at her with his hand and winked an eye. She could feel him still staring until they disappeared behind another door at the end of a short corridor.

As the third door closed behind them, Danni felt as if she'd been transported to another time and place. The lighting was low and slightly seductive. The walls were oak-paneled, polished to a high shine and looking like an expensive old library. Round tables were neatly arranged around a dance floor and full bar. The room was close to capacity, an eclectic mix of middle-aged men and women, some senior citizens and a few youngsters. Armstrong was clearly well-known and much beloved by the crowd of regulars who greeted him warmly.

"What is this place?" Danni asked when they finally came to a corner table near the dance floor.

Armstrong pulled out a chair for her and then took his own seat.

"Welcome to Peace Row," he answered. "It's a membership-only establishment for law enforcement officers. It's owned by a cop, specifically for cops."

"Sweet!" Danni exclaimed as she took another look around. The ambience was grown and sexy, the music a far cry from the earlier disco playlist. It was comfortable and almost instantly relaxing.

"We think so."

A waitress dressed in black slacks and a black turtleneck moved to the table and dropped a tumbler of amber-colored fluid to the tabletop. "It's nice to see you again, Detective Armstrong."

"You, too, Angela."

"Ma'am, what can I get for you?"

Danni pointed to his glass. "I'll have what he's having," she answered.

The young woman nodded. "One scotch, neat, coming right up," she said as she started to turn.

"I'll have a beer chaser with mine," Danni added. "Whatever you have on tap."

"Yes, ma'am."

Danni grimaced. "Scotch? Really?"

"My father use to say a good scotch would put some hair on your chest."

She laughed. "That might work for you," she said.

He laughed with her. "You're right. I don't think it would be all that flattering on you."

She settled back in her seat, allowing herself to relax fully for the first time that day. The waitress delivered her order and promptly excused herself. Danni took a sip and suddenly leaned forward in her seat.

"I think we need to approach this from a different angle. Clearly, something is off with Pius, so I need to work Ginger and the rest of that crew. I need to understand how he operates. How the business functions. How he's connected domestically and internationally. And Ginger might have those answers. And if that doesn't work, there is always Alexander Balducci."

"You're right, but you also need to step away from it for a minute. Approach it with fresh eyes. So, let it go for tonight and come back to it in the morning with a new perspective. You can't keep going over the same details and not miss something. You've been trying to tie it up quick and fast, and that's not working. I think it's why we're stumped."

She nodded. "You might be right."

"I know I'm right, so no shop talk tonight. Just enjoy the music," he said as he gestured toward the stage and the dance floor.

The evening's entertainment was a jazz and blues guitarist who was older than dirt. He was a pretty man with skin the color of black licorice, and lush, snow-white curls. A quiet reverie had settled over the whole room as he played one blues tune after another. Danni fell into the wealth of tranquility, her eyes closed and every one of her senses heightened. By the second drink she was feeling all kinds of warm and fuzzy, not an ounce of tension pinching any nerve.

The conversation between them was easy and comfortable. She talked about her family, and he talked about his. She discovered he had a love for chocolate chip cookies and ice cream, and she shared that cheese puffs and barbecue potato chips were her go-to snacks. He was well traveled, detailing how he and his brother had trekked through Europe the summer between high school and college. She bemoaned the fact that the extent of her international travel was one cruise to the Caribbean by her lonesome after a bad breakup.

As the alcohol began to simmer through her bloodstream, everything starting to feel distorted, Armstrong ordered food from the kitchen. The cook, a robust Jamaican woman with waist-length dreads, personally delivered platters of curry goat, jerk chicken, peas and rice, fried plantains and coco bread. Danni ate heartily, savoring every forkful until she was stuffed and ready to be rolled home.

"This was so good!" she exclaimed, her hands resting atop a slight bulge in her abdomen. "I couldn't eat another bite!"

"That's not good," Armstrong said as he licked jerk sauce from his fingers and then swiped them across a yellow paper napkin.

Danni slid an antibacterial hand wipe across the table toward him. "You look like you need this," she said, eyeing him smugly.

He tore the small packet open and swiped his fingers. "Thank you."

"Thank you for suggesting this. I've had a really good time."

"You're very welcome, but you say that like we're done."

She blinked, her lashes batting fervently. "What else are you planning?" she questioned.

He pushed his empty plate forward. "We need to burn this food off," he said as he reached for her hand and pulled her to the dance floor.

Danni gasped as Armstrong snaked his arm around her waist and pulled her to him. The moment took her by surprise and left her legs quivering with anticipation. The music was thick and sultry, and the other couples dancing cheek to cheek beside them were lost in the moment. Her alcohol high had diminished substantially, and she was suddenly taken aback by the nearness of the man. He was solid muscle and he smelled like heaven and Caribbean spices, she thought as she rested her head against his chest, unable to resist the temptation to lose herself in his arms. Her hands were looped casually around his neck, and she allowed her body to move easily with his. Maybe she hadn't sobered as much as she'd thought, she mused as her hips seemed to move with a mind of their own. Time seemed to stand still. There was an echo of silence that vibrated through her head, and the only sound she recognized was the beat of her heart as it pulsed like a drumline in her chest.

Chapter 8

The ride back to the hotel was peppered with laughter and anecdotes about Danni's two left feet and the number of times Armstrong had tripped from the club to an Uber. As the driver waited, he walked her to her door, wished her a good night and caught the ride to his own home. Neither had been in any condition to drive, and he arranged to pick up his vehicle the following morning before they were expected at his family dinner.

Now his head was throbbing, there wasn't an aspirin to be found in his medicine cabinet and he couldn't get that woman off his mind. There was no denying the level of comfort they'd found with each other. He had thoroughly enjoyed their time together, and just the mere thought of their spending time together again had him excited.

Armstrong had been a perfect gentleman, despite the battle that desire and need had waged in his southern quadrant. There weren't many women who actually took his breath away, and last night Danni had left him gasping for air more times than he cared to count. Admittedly, she had caught his attention and was holding on to it with two tight fists. But crossing that professional line went against the grain of everything he'd been taught and all he knew from past experience.

Together they had bigger fish to fry and work that required every ounce of their attention. He couldn't allow last night's diversion to deter them from what needed to be done. It wasn't how he worked, and he knew it wasn't how she operated, either.

He lifted his large frame from his king-size bed, kicking at the bedclothes that had landed in the middle of the carpeted floor. Despite the tossing and turning, he'd slept fairly well, the sweetest dreams trolling through his slumber. He chuckled softly as he thought about Danni and the fantasies that had tightened the muscles below his waist. He shook his head, thankful that only he and God knew his thoughts. Now he needed a large glass of ice water, the Sunday newspaper and an hour of prayer to put him back on the straight and narrow.

When Armstrong dialed Danni's cell phone number, he was already sitting in the hotel parking lot waiting for her to exit. She answered on the third ring.

"Hello?"

"Good afternoon! How are you doing?"

He sensed her smiling into the receiver as she answered. "I'm really good. How about yourself?"

"I'm good. Not nearly as hungover as I thought I would be."

"You did drink a lot last night."

"Says the woman who went shot for shot with me."

"But I don't have a hangover. In fact, I was up bright and early and went to the gym."

"That's impressive. I went to morning church services."

"Really? Where do you attend church?"

"My living room pew, pastored by the television evangelist of the moment."

"You really are a heathen!" she said with a warm laugh.

Armstrong laughed with her. "I'm outside when you're ready," he finally said.

There was a brief moment of silence, an awkward stillness that seemed to swell between their phone lines.

Danni gasped. "We're having dinner at your parents'!"

"You forgot!"

"Oh, cuss!" she said. The expression was one she used in lieu of actual profanity, and her enthusiastic use of the term had been fodder for much laughter the night before. "I did! What time is it?"

"It's one thirty, so you can't cancel. I'll wait for you to get ready."

"I'm showered and dressed. I just need to pull a comb through my hair and maybe put on some lipstick."

"Maybe?"

"Are you really going to give me a hard time about wearing makeup?"

"If you plan to show up looking like a fourth-grader, yes."

"I only look like a fourth-grader when I'm undercover. Give me ten minutes and I'll be right out," she said before she abruptly disconnected the call.

Those ten minutes turned into fifteen. When Danni

finally exited the building, Armstrong was standing outside his car, in conversation with another man. She paused, waiting for them to finish their chat. When the other guy walked off, disappearing down the road, she moved to where he stood.

A wide smile pulled across Armstrong's face. She was wearing a long-sleeved knit dress that hugged her nicely and black suede boots that stopped thigh-high. The heels gave her just enough lift to elongate her legs, making her seem taller than she actually was. Her hair hung down to her shoulders, loose waves framing her face. A hint of mascara and lip gloss were her makeup of choice. Looking very much like the adult she was, she now bore no resemblance to a grade-schooler. Much like her transformation the day before, she cleaned up well. So well that he found himself rethinking that line between business and pleasure that he'd sworn to never cross.

"Thank you," she said, her expression smug.

He looked confused. "What are you thanking me for?"

"You were just about to tell me how incredible I looked."

Armstrong laughed. "Now that was funny," he said, shaking his head from side to side.

He reached for the passenger door and pulled it open. "You're going to make us late, and my mother will not be happy."

Danni laughed as she slid into the passenger seat. "If what you said last night is true, your mother is going to be thrilled about your bringing a woman home for her to meet."

The smile on his face drooped slightly. "Excuse me? I said something last night about my mother?"

"You said a lot of things!" Danni teased.

He shook his head. "Things like what?"

Amusement danced out of the woman's eyes, and she laughed again, ignoring his question. "Shouldn't we be going?" she asked.

Armstrong paused before closing the door after her. Everything about the moment suddenly had him in his feelings. Something like joy swept through his spirit.

"By the way," he muttered after closing the car door, knowing she couldn't hear him. "You look amazing."

The home of Jerome and Judith Black was located in the heart of Chicago's historic Gold Coast neighborhood. It was situated on a large corner lot, the stone and brick architecture timeless. As he held her hand, Armstrong entered through the front door without knocking, the entrance having been left unlocked. A wealth of laughter echoed through the interior, dropping into a brief moment of silence as he called out in greeting.

"Hello! Anybody home?"

A warm voice responded from the rear of the home. "We're all in the family room, Armstrong!"

He took a deep breath and then turned to give her a look. "Are you ready for this? My family can be a bit overbearing, so don't say I didn't warn you."

Danni smiled. "As ready as I'll ever be. I think the better question is, are you ready?"

"Hell, no!" he exclaimed as he squeezed her fingers and then led her through the front foyer and past the formal living room.

From the moment she'd laid eyes on the solid wood and glass door with its ornate iron details, Danni was in awe of the home's beauty. Stepping through the entrance was like stepping into a whole other world, a busy Chicago lifestyle easily left behind for the comfort and quiet of the family retreat.

The decor imparted an Old World feel with walls papered in silk, sparkling chandeliers, ornate wood moldings and fireplaces meticulously carved in stone. The windows were draped in sumptuous fabrics, and every detail, from the coffered ceilings to the highly polished hardwood floors, had been meticulously selected.

Armstrong's mother met them in the short length of the hallway. She was a tall woman, nearly as tall as her son. She had picture-perfect features: high cheekbones, black eyes like dark ice and a buttermilk complexion that needed little if any makeup. She was elegantly dressed in black linen slacks and a pale peach sweater set that complemented her fair skin. Lush silver-gray hair fell in soft waves past her shoulders. A bright smile blessed her face. "Hello, my darling!" she said, reaching to kiss her son's cheek. "Thought I was going to have to call the troops to come look for you."

"It's all her fault," he said, cutting his eyes in Danni's direction. "I think this one might be high maintenance. It took her forever to get ready!"

"I know you did not just say that!" Danni exclaimed. Her eyes were wide, amusement dancing all over her face.

He shrugged. "Danielle Winstead, I'd like you to meet my mother, the Honorable Judith Harmon Black. Judge Black, this is Danni, the new detective I was telling you about."

Danni extended her hand, trying not to look surprised to discover he'd talked about her with his mother.

His mother laughed as she reached to wrap Danni in a warm embrace. "I'm a hugger, dear. It's a pleasure to meet you."

Danni laughed with her. "The pleasure is all mine, Judge Black."

"Please, call me Judith. We stand on little formality in this house. Come, let me introduce you to my other children."

The matriarch looped her arm through Danni's and pulled her along. "I can't begin to tell you how excited I was when Armstrong told me he was bringing a friend for a family dinner."

Danni tossed him a look over her shoulder as he followed behind them.

"Danni and I are just partners," Armstrong noted. "She's new in town, and I didn't think she should spend her day off alone. We're not friends like that."

"After working with you all week she might have wanted a break," Simone interjected as the trio moved into the living space.

"I know that's right!" Vaughan chimed from her seat in the corner.

Armstrong shook his head. He leaned toward his mother and whispered loudly, "Please tell them not to embarrass me."

"You need to worry about embarrassing yourself!" A deep baritone voice came from behind them. They turned as Jerome Black entered the room behind them. There was no missing the resemblance to his children. His sons had not only inherited their father's good looks but also his height and athletic frame. The patriarch was one distinguished man with salt-and-pepper hair and a full beard and mustache. At first glance he reminded Danni of Sean Connery in the movie *The Hunt for Red October* but with a complexion that was a rich, chocolate brown.

He moved to his wife's side and hugged her warmly,

then extended his hand toward his son. He stood in front of Danni, his eyes sweeping over her. "Now, who is this beautiful lady?"

Danni stepped forward to shake the man's hand. "Danielle Winstead, sir. It's an honor to meet you."

Armstrong's father held her hand between both of his, gently patting the top of her fingers with one as the other held the appendage firmly. "Detective, the honor is all mine. We're very lucky to have an officer of your caliber here to help us with this nasty trafficking business. Welcome to my home."

"Thank you, sir," she said, her eyes gleaming with joy as she finally released the warm breath she'd been holding.

Judith gestured them toward a seat. "Make yourself comfortable, sweetheart. I want you to feel at home here," she said. She gave her son a quick glance. "Introduce your friend, Armstrong."

He grimaced. "She is not my friend!" he quipped. "Not like that," he added, trying to clean up the comment.

"We heard you two looked quite friendly on the dance floor last night," Simone said. She and Vaughan exchanged a look and laughed.

"Word travels quickly, I see," Danni said, laughing with them.

"Especially when people are talking about their boss," Vaughan said. "Those women at that club love gossiping about their Detective Black."

Danni shot Armstrong a look. "You own that club?"

He shrugged. "Something like that."

She shook her head, much starting to make sense as she thought back to some of the comments and looks she'd gotten through the night.

"Chicago might have a population of two point seven million, but the police rank is a community unto itself. If you don't want everyone to know, don't tell a brother in blue. It's nice to meet you, Danni. I'm Mingus, Armstrong's older brother."

"Private investigator, right?" Danni asked.

The man nodded. "Yes, ma'am. At your service."

"And we're his sisters," one of the women added. "That's Simone, and I'm Vaughan."

"I'm Davis," the youngest in the family said. He gave a nod toward his sisters "And those two are more like Armstrong's personal bodyguards. Overprotective and sometimes mean!"

"That's *Alderman* Davis Black," Armstrong added.

"Our next mayor-elect," Vaughan teased.

"No time soon," Davis stated emphatically, clearly not agreeing with his siblings on his political endeavors.

"And, these are my brothers Ellington and Parker," Armstrong said as he pointed out one and then the other, concluding the formal introductions.

Ellington greeted her warmly. "We're glad you were able to join us, Danielle."

"Please, call me Danni." Her eyes danced around the room, excited to take everything in. They were truly a beautiful family, she thought, noting the resemblance between them. They were each tall, his sisters slim and long-legged like their mother. Complexions were warm, in varying shades of light brown, their biracial melding a thing of pure beauty. Their facial features were chiseled—sculpted cheekbones, picture-perfect noses, luscious lips and strong jawlines. Like Armstrong, his brothers had solid builds, broad chests, limbs solid as tree trunks and the same magnificent smiles that were instantly welcoming.

From where he stood on the other side of the room, Parker only nodded, gesturing with a slight salute. Danni smiled in response, suddenly self-conscious about his wariness.

Armstrong seemed to sense the shift in her mood as he moved to stand beside her. "Don't pay him any attention," he said as he dropped into the seat beside her. "He's always been the overly cautious kid in the family."

"He knows employee fraternization is strictly prohibited by the city," Simone interjected. "And you, dear brother, are always fraternizing with someone who could get us all sued."

The color drained from Danni's face. "It's not... I... We..." She was suddenly stammering, feeling like she couldn't form a coherent sentence.

Judith cleared her throat. "That will be enough. Simone, you need to leave your brothers alone, please."

"I didn't do anything," Simone said, a slight pout pulling at her lush lips.

"You never do anything," Vaughan said, "but you're always doing way too much!"

Simone snarled, her eyes rolling skyward.

"You all need to stop," Armstrong said casually. "You're scaring my partner."

Parker shook his head. "Forgive us, Danni. And I apologize if I made you uncomfortable."

"I understand," Danni said. "But really, Armstrong and I are not friends like that. We would never cross the line of our professional relationship."

"Armstrong will pull his toes right up to that line,

though. We do know that," Vaughan added. "You'll have to keep your eyes on him."

"Okay, that's enough of that," Jerome snapped. "You all play too much. Armstrong knows what's at stake. I trust that he will not embarrass my family name. The rest of you should. Now, no more business. We will have one afternoon without discussing the politics of this city. Is that understood?"

There was a collective stare that swept around the room, all of the siblings nodding but not saying anything as they looked from one to the other.

Judith suddenly laughed, her deep chuckle moving Danni to smile. "My family can be too damn serious, Danni! Pay them no never mind. So, how are you liking Chicago?" she asked.

"If it wasn't so cold I'd probably like it more! I'm from Georgia, and it was eighty-four degrees when I left."

"I'm moving to Atlanta," Vaughan said. "I hate the cold, and don't talk about snow!"

Danni smiled. "I've actually never seen snow. Not real snow."

"Hasn't it snowed in Atlanta before?" Simone said.

"It has," Danni answered, "but every time it did I've been on vacation or out of town."

"You're kidding us, right?" Simone said, shifting forward in her seat.

Danni shook her head. "Never. That would actually be the icing on some very sweet cake if I solved this case *and* it snowed before I have to head back home."

Laughter rang warmly in the room as they all began to pepper Danni with questions, curious to know more about her and her life in Atlanta. Armstrong sat back in his seat and took it all in. He could tell that his sisters liked her, despite their best efforts not to, and his mother found her equally intriguing. When the women discovered she was also a sorority sister, having pledged Alpha Kappa Alpha at Howard University, the unspoken bond was completely solidified. Before he knew it they were exchanging telephone numbers and making plans to go shopping together.

Hours later the family had eaten and eaten well. Judith had laid out a spread of seasoned beef roast and gravy, freshly baked popovers, steamed broccoli, sautéed carrots and pickled mushrooms. For dessert she'd served her famous pineapple upside-down cake. Laughter and conversation had been abundant, and Danni fell into the flow as if she'd been a part of the mesh since forever. After the meal the men had been relegated back to the family room and the big-screen television to watch the Dallas Cowboys play Minnesota. Danni had gone upstairs with his sisters, the women talking about whatever it was women talked about.

Judith pulled her son aside, demanding his presence in the kitchen to help her dry the dishes and prep a pot of hot coffee. Armstrong followed reluctantly, sensing a potential lecture coming that he was not in the mood for.

"Danni is very sweet," his mother said as she passed him a dry dish towel.

He nodded. "She is."

"So, what are your intentions with this young lady? Clearly, there is something going on between the two of you."

"We're just partners. Everyone is reading more into our relationship than there is. Last night we both just needed a break from the work. There was nothing to it."

His mother tilted her head slightly. "The fact that you're being so defensive might be concerning if I didn't know you as well as I do. You have always denied, denied, denied, until you had no other option but to face the truth."

Armstrong paused. "I wasn't being defensive and I wasn't denying anything."

"Yes. You were," she said matter-of-factly. "You like that young lady. There's nothing wrong with that. You like her more than you want to admit. And that's fine, too. But lying to yourself doesn't mean the rest of us will lie with you."

Armstrong took a moment to ponder his mother's comments. Women had never been a problem for him. They fell into his path like leaves from a tree in the fall. A dazzling array of beauty enjoyed for a brief period of time. Most had wanted more from him than he'd been willing to give. A few had understood that he had no expectations that a few nights of pure, unadulterated pleasure could not fulfill. He had not been ready to settle down, dedicated to his career first and nothing else second. He hadn't met any woman who'd motivated him to live his life differently. Most of the women in his past had understood that from the beginning. Yet, there had been a select few of Chicago's most eligible bachelorettes, for whom his family had had high hopes. Women who had barely been a blip on his radar. Keeping his feelings to himself had made things easier all around. Now there was Danni and he wasn't ready or willing to acknowledge what he was feeling.

"We're just partners," he repeated, not sure that there was anything else he could say.

Judith laughed. "You keep telling yourself that, son, and let's revisit this conversation in a few months."

"She'll be gone in a few months."

"Maybe she will. But if I were a gambling woman, I'd put my money on Ms. Winstead spending many, many more family dinners with us."

Chapter 9

Danni was already at work when Armstrong arrived. She was obviously eager to get started, and her enthusiasm shone all over her face. She was dressed down, jeans and a T-shirt that looked like she'd slept in her clothes, but her hair was pulled into a ponytail and her face had that freshly washed glow.

As he entered the conference room, she shot him a quick look as she stood rearranging the images taped to the whiteboard. He watched as she strung a line between the photos, connecting dots he didn't quite understand.

"Good morning! What's going on here?" he asked as he moved to her side to stare where she stared.

She gave him a warm smile, the light dancing in her eyes speaking volumes. They hadn't spoken since leaving his parents' home the night before, neither acknowledging anything that had been teased or insinuated about the two of them. The ride back to the hotel had been quiet. And comfortable. Each had fallen into their own thoughts. When they'd parted, wishing each other a good night, there had been a look between them that hinted of longing and concern and maybe even a little worry that everything between them had changed.

He had lost hours of sleep, tossing and turning as he thought about her and all that had happened. But mostly he thought about what needed to be accomplished and what would be required from them to make that happen. They now transitioned back to their professional relationship seamlessly.

"I've been going over this in my head, and I think I need to approach it differently. Obviously, we know who some of the players are—Pius, Ginger and that crew. Possibly the grandfather. But they haven't let me in on their business operations to know for sure, and they haven't exposed their hand. We know Josef Havel and his attorney are connected to Pius, but clearly he doesn't do business at the coffee shop, so I need to get a foot in the door of where they actually do business."

"And you have a plan for how to do that?"

She nodded. "A girl's hard up for money. The backstory is going to be that my cousin has abandoned me and I need cash and somewhere to stay and I need it fast."

There was a lengthy moment of hesitation as he considered her suggestion. "That means you're going to have to go deep cover. I don't know if I can keep you safe if something happens."

"I can keep myself safe, Detective."

"I'm sure you think you can, but you might be asked to do some things you aren't going to be able to avoid."

"I know how to play this, Armstrong," she said, the

lilt of his name rolling off her tongue. "It's like I've said before, I really just need you to trust me."

Their gazes locked, deep stares dancing so tightly that it took him by surprise. Armstrong dropped his eyes first, drawing a deep breath to still the quiver of heat that suddenly pulsed through each of his muscles. He drew his index finger around the collar of his shirt, loosening the silk necktie he wore. Despite wanting to rail against her suggestion, he furrowed his brow in resignation. He nodded. "You need to check in with me daily. I want regular updates."

Danni grinned. "I've already been upstairs. Those geek guys cloned my phone. You'll be able to track my whereabouts and see all the calls and messages I make. And I won't take off my wire," she said, gently fingering the jeweled cross that hung around her neck.

Armstrong took a deep breath. "If you don't make any headway by the end of the week, I'm pulling you out," he added.

"I may need two weeks," she countered.

"You're really pushing it," he answered. He suddenly reached out his hand and drew his index finger along the line of her profile. "Keep yourself safe, please."

Danni smiled sweetly, not needing to answer.

The usual crowd filled the small coffee shop, the list of regulars never seeming to change. Pie and Ginger sat in their regular spot in the far corner, only one bodyguard tagging along this time. Carlo was behind the counter, focused on whittling down the line of lunch customers. When Danni entered, she swept the room with her eyes, then eased herself to a table not far from where the trio sat in the back. She sat with her hands pushed deep into the pockets of her oversize jacket, her shoulders hunched forward. She lacked her usual exuberance, making herself look distraught and out of place. As she fidgeted in her seat, Ginger saw her first, taking notice a split second before Carlo. They both moved to her side at the same time. Ginger dropped into the seat beside her as Carlo stood protectively over them both.

"What's wrong?" Ginger asked, genuine concern ringing in her tone.

"Are you okay, Danni?" Carlo questioned as he pressed a warm hand to her shoulder.

Danni shook her head from side to side, tears falling from her eyes. "My cousin took off with her boyfriend. She hadn't paid the rent, and they padlocked the door. I don't have anywhere to stay, and I don't have any money."

"Call your parents," Carlo suggested. "They'll come get you, I'm sure."

She shook her head. "My parents are dead. I sort of lied. I don't have anyone except Juicy, and she got all in her feelings because her boyfriend kept staring at my ass."

"You do have a nice ass," Carlo said teasingly, a warped effort to make her smile.

Ginger rolled her eyes. "I hate men," she said. "All of you are pigs!"

"Some of us more than others," Carlo quipped. "But I like to think I'm one of the good guys."

"It's a good thing you don't get paid to think," Ginger muttered under her breath.

"I'm glad you're feeling very confident this afternoon," Carlo said, his eyes narrowing as he and Ginger exchanged a look.

The woman turned her attention back to Danni. "It's

all good. You can crash with me over at Pie's house until you can figure out what you need to do."

"I need to find a job," Danni said, still sobbing softly.

"We can make that happen, too," Ginger responded.

Carlo cleared his throat and squeezed her shoulder gently. "I always have tables that need busing and dishes that have to be washed."

Danni swiped the moisture from her eyes. She reached into her pocket and pulled out a rumpled dollar bill and a handful of change. "It's all I have," she said, "but I'll help wash dishes if I can get a cup of coffee and a sandwich."

"Put your change away. Your money's no good here."

"Thank you," Danni said, giving him a slight smile. "You've been so nice to me. I don't know how I'll ever be able to pay you back."

He winked his eye at her. "We'll worry about that later. Right now let me go get you something to eat." He suddenly leaned to kiss the top of her head, the gesture surprising her and Ginger, wonder registering across the other woman's face.

After Carlo had disappeared behind the counter, Ginger leaned in toward her. "Don't trust him. He's not your friend," she whispered softly.

Danni frowned. "I don't understand. He's been so nice."

The young woman shrugged. "Yeah, they're all nice. But I haven't met a man yet who hasn't had his own agenda. Especially him."

Danni turned to stare, Carlo's gaze meeting hers as he smiled, the depths of his expression gleaming from his eyes. Ginger's assessment of all men was one she'd heard many times before. Knowing what she knew, though, she wished she could tell the girl that there were indeed good men in the world and not all of them were as mean-spirited and as abusive as Pie. She suddenly found herself thinking about Armstrong, her eyes misting slightly.

"Just be careful, that's all I'm saying," Ginger concluded.

"What does Danni need to be careful about?" Carlo asked as he returned with two cups of coffee and a chicken salad sandwich on freshly baked bread. He rested the tray on the table as he focused a curious stare on Ginger.

"I was just giving her some friendly advice about these streets," Ginger said, her voice dropping an octave. "I don't want her hooking up with any creeps."

"Well, we're going to make sure that doesn't happen," he said. "She can stay with me."

Danni shook her head. "I can't do that. Really. I..." She paused, blowing a gust of air out of her mouth.

Carlo gestured toward Ginger. "Would you excuse us for a minute, Ginny? I'd like to talk to Danni alone, please."

Ginger gave her one last look before moving onto her feet and easing back to Pie's side. Danni watched as the two were suddenly huddled in conversation, Ginger and Pie both shooting quick glances in her direction. Carlo dropped into the seat Ginger had vacated, dropping a large hand against her forearm.

"So, let's be honest with each other for a moment."

"Okay."

"Just how old are you, Danni?"

Danni took a breath, her eyes skating across the man's face.

He commented again. "Don't think about it. Just answer. You say you're eighteen, but we know that's not true. So how old are you really?"

"I just turned seventeen," she said.

He nodded. "And your cousin? Was she real? If I were to ask one of my police officer customers to track her down, would they find her?"

Danni nodded, tears again rising in her eyes. "I ran away from my foster home. Juicy is the only family I have left, but she wasn't happy about my showing up on her doorstep. She let me stay, but then she started complaining that I needed to help with the bills and paying my way. Last month she hooked up with this guy who kept grabbing at me when she wasn't looking. She would let him stay, and it was bad! It just got worse when I told her." Danni blew a soft sigh, dropping her eyes to the floor as if she were recalling a bad memory. She swiped at her eyes with the back of her hand and continued. "I'm sorry I lied before, but I didn't know if you would call the cops on me or try to send me back to the foster system."

Carlo nodded. "I need to trust you, Danni, and I get that you didn't know me before. I also get not wanting to get caught back up into the system. But I hope you know that I'm your friend and I'm going to make sure you're okay."

Danni nodded and tried to force a smile onto her face. "I appreciate your offering to give me somewhere to stay, but I don't think that would be a good idea. Your girlfriend might get the wrong idea about us."

He laughed. "First, I don't have a girlfriend. Second, there is no idea for anyone to get. You need a friend, and I'm here to be one for you."

"I'm a virgin," Danni suddenly blurted out, her voice

a loud whisper. She stammered. "I don't… We… What would…"

Surprise wafted over Carlo's face, the comment clearly unexpected as she purposely avoided his stare.

"I wasn't expecting you to sleep with me, Danni. In fact, the exact opposite. I just want to help."

Her eyes were wide as she pondered whether or not to believe him. "Thank you," she finally whispered.

Carlo looked over his shoulder toward his brother and Ginger, who were both watching them intently. He turned back toward Danni. "I get it. You think you'll be more comfortable with Ginger because she's a woman and you think she's your friend. And that's fine. But I have to warn you that not everything that goes on in that house may be kosher, so you'll still need to watch your back. Don't let anyone pressure you into doing anything you're not comfortable with. My brother can be…well…just be careful," he concluded. "And I'm here if you need me."

"You're not mad?"

"Sweetheart, of course not," he said, his warm smile inspiring her own. "I could never be mad at you. I see big things in your future, Danni!"

Pie and Ginger were suddenly standing beside them. Carlo stood up, turning to look directly at Ginger. "I'm leaving Danni in your hands. Take care of her."

Ginger nodded. "She'll be fine."

"She better be," he said, the comment directed at his brother. He gave Danni one last wink and headed back to his business behind the counter.

Pie stared at her, his dark gaze so intense that it was almost frightening. Annoyance was painted over his face. Danni smiled at him, but he didn't smile back, instead turning and exiting the space abruptly.

"I have something I need to do, but I'll be back to get you before closing," Ginger said.

"I need to go get my things so I can meet you back here. I don't have a lot. Just one bag that my cousin's neighbor is holding for me."

"That'll work out fine, then."

"Are you sure it's okay for me to stay with you? Pie won't be mad?"

"Pie is always mad. Don't worry about it."

"Thanks, Ginny. I really do appreciate this."

Ginger stared at her briefly. "Don't thank me yet," she finally said, and then she, too, disappeared out the door.

As Danni threw clothes into a used duffel bag she'd found at Goodwill, Armstrong paced her hotel room floor. His brow was creased, and frustration ran like fine age lines throughout his face.

"Are you sure about this?" he asked for the umpteenth time, pausing with his hands clutching his sides.

"We're in. I'm very sure."

"And you're comfortable your cover story won't blow apart?"

"If someone decides to dig, it could always blow up on me. But all they're going to find is that I have no family here in Chicago. No cousin named Juicy."

Armstrong took a large breath, holding it deep in his lungs. "We'll be trailing you, but at any time if you feel like you need to get out of there, you know what to do."

Danni nodded. "Thank you. But I'll be fine."

His cell phone suddenly vibrated in his pocket. As he moved to answer it, Danni paused to watch him. He had come the minute she had called, listening intently as she laid out her plan to move in with Pie. He wasn't happy about it, but he'd been clearly impressed by her gumption. His concern for her safety was genuine and slightly overprotective. She hated to admit it, but she liked that he was worried about her, his reservations feeling like they had nothing to do with the case or his authority over her.

They suddenly locked eyes. He was clearly listening to someone on the other end, but his focus was on her, his stare so intense that her stomach rippled and then her knees buckled so that she had to sit down against the edge of the bed. Perspiration dampened her palms and trickled like the most minute stream between her small breasts. Her breath quickened, and it took a moment before she could catch herself, fighting not to let the emotion show.

Armstrong was still staring at her when he disconnected his call. The energy in his eyes had shifted drastically. "Josef Havel is dead," he said, his tone dry as he moved to the window and looked past the mini blinds to the parking lot below. "They found him hanging in his cell a few hours ago."

Danni's own gaze was wide. "His extradition was supposed to happen tomorrow. How could this happen?" she asked, the question more rhetorical than anything else.

"I don't think it's a good idea for you to…"

She interrupted his comment, knowing exactly what he was about to say. "I'm not changing my mind. I'm going through with this. Now more than ever. Havel was our only link to tie Pius to my sister's abduction and possibly all your open murder cases. I need to figure out how he plays into all of this now more than ever."

Rising from her seat, Danni eased her way over to stand beside him at the window. She hated to admit it, but the nearness of him actually took her breath away. Something was simmering between them, something that had been ignited the night he'd pulled her close on the dance floor. It burned hot and sizzled when they were in each other's presence. When they weren't, they could pretend it didn't exist, fighting not to fan the flames that would have burned otherwise. Eventually she was going to have to address the attraction she was feeling toward him, but for the moment she needed to push it down and continue to ignore it.

Once again he seemed to read her mind. "We need to talk," he started, seeming to search for the right words to put things into perspective. "There are some things I need to say to you."

Danni shook her head vehemently. "We do, but not now," she responded. "Please. I don't need any distractions. I really need to stay focused."

He inhaled deeply, only nodding his head in agreement.

Danni changed the topic as she continued to pack. "Have you found out anything else about Carlo?"

"Only that there isn't much to find out. Considering the family, he's almost too good to be true."

"Then maybe he is," Danni said softly.

Armstrong clearly didn't miss the edge in her tone. "Is there something you need to tell me?"

Something in his tone moved her to look directly at him before she answered. "He offered me a place to stay."

Armstrong's gaze narrowed ever so slightly as he stared back at her. "In exchange for…?"

She shrugged. "Nothing. He said he just wanted to be a friend."

"Did you believe him?"

"Actually, I did, then Ginger told me not to trust him. But she said it like I shouldn't trust any man because you're all dogs."

"You like this guy, don't you?"

Danni hesitated, sensing there was more to the question than she was wanting to answer. She shrugged. "He's always been very respectful. He hasn't given me any reason not to like him."

Armstrong paused before responding. "Trust your gut," he said finally. "If you think he's one of the good guys, then he probably is."

His phone suddenly rang a second time. "I need to answer this," he said as he pulled the device into his hand. As he answered the call, he stepped away from her to the other side of the room. Danni turned to stare out the window where he had stared, everything playing over again in her head.

Chapter 10

Danni thought she'd prepared herself for everything, but she truly was not prepared when she entered the single-family home that sat in the heart of Chicago's Southport Corridor. From the outside, the nondescript brick building looked like all the others in the upper-middle-class neighborhood: concrete stoop, small porches and aged architecture. There was a bicycle left unattended on the manicured lawn, and the gated fence around the property was identical to the neighbor's next door and down the street.

But the house was far from being an average family home. Pie disappeared up a flight of stairs as soon as the front door was closed behind them. Danni watched him as he took the steps in four swift leaps, and then she took in the rest of her surroundings. There were at least a dozen young women splayed out in the living room,

watching television. They looked unamused as a rerun of
the old television show *Friends* played loudly. The two
bodyguards sat in the kitchen, pulled up to the breakfast
table. Both gave her a nod as she passed through, and
Ginger gave her a quick tour of the downstairs.

The space that should have been a dining room housed
at least a dozen computers, and two young men who iden-
tified themselves as Pace and Adam were running point
on the activity crossing their screens. Wide-eyed, Danni
didn't miss the high-tech security system and dozens of
cameras that were capturing everything that went on inside the home and outside the front and back doors. Nor
did she miss the multitude of pornographic images being
uploaded on the computers, Pace and Adam regularly
scanning a multitude of photographs and loading other
images from flash drives girls would randomly drop into
a basket on the table.

She shot Ginger a look, her gaze questioning.

Ginger came to an abrupt halt. "So when you're here,
there are some rules you need to follow. First, don't piss
off Pie. Stay out of his way. Don't talk to him, don't try
to be his friend, don't go into his space—and his space
is wherever he is at the moment. Stay…out…of…his…
way," she repeated, emphasizing each word. "Second,
don't ask anyone here any questions. Mind your own
business and stay out of everyone else's. Everyone here
has their own problems, and they don't care about yours."

Danni nodded. "I'll stay out of the way. I promise."

"And lastly, you can come and go as you please. The
doors are rarely locked and if they are, there is always
someone up who can let you in. But don't ever tell anyone
about this place or bring anyone here. And if you have
any doubts, refer to rule number one. Don't piss Pie off!"

Ginger gestured for her to follow as she ascended the stairs. There were four bedrooms on the second floor, each set up like college dorm rooms with bunk beds on three walls. A second flight of steps led to a third level, and when Danni looked up the stairs, Ginger shook her head. "Upstairs is off-limits. Do you understand?"

"Yeah," Danni said, her head bobbing like it was unhinged.

Ginger led her into the back bedroom on the right. A girl who barely looked thirteen lay on a top bunk, never bothering to look up when the two entered the space. She was playing with a collection of dolls and talking to herself. Ginger pointed to a lower bunk. "You can sleep there. And remember what I said. Mind your own business."

Danni nodded. "Thanks, Ginger. I really appreciate this."

"Don't make me regret this."

"I won't. I promise."

The woman stole a quick glance at her wristwatch. "I'm working tonight, so I need to get ready. If you're hungry there's always food downstairs."

"They ordered pizza," the girl said, turning her frail body around to stare down at the two women. She stared at them with bright blue eyes and blond hair that hung in two ponytails down her back. "Adam ordered pies and sent someone to get them."

"Whatever," Ginger responded as she did an about-face and exited the space.

Danni smiled at the girl, tossing her hand up in a slight wave. "Hi. My name's Danni."

"They call me Angel, but my real name's Alissa. How long are you staying?"

Danni shrugged. "I'm not sure. Have you been here long?"

"Not too long. But it's cool here. No one really bothers you unless you have to work, and it's better than sleeping out on the streets."

"You slept out on the streets?"

"Yeah. Didn't you?"

"I was at my cousin's until she took off with her boyfriend."

"Sorry."

"No reason for you to apologize. It's not your fault," Danni answered. She tossed her duffel bag onto the thin mattress.

"I just remember what it's like when people you care about are gone and you don't have nobody. That's all."

"Don't you have any family?"

Angel didn't answer, her eyes widening slightly. "You shouldn't ask questions," she said, her voice dropping slightly. "The last girl that asked a lot of questions disappeared."

Danni tossed a glance toward the door as she took a step closer toward Angel. "What happened to her?" she whispered.

Angel shifted around to peer over the side of the bed. The young girl shrugged her narrow shoulders. "Pius took her away. Everyone says she's probably dead. Or worse."

"There's something worse than being dead?"

Angel whispered back. "Yeah," she said softly.

Danni took a deep breath. Clearly, her new friend wanted to share, but she knew if she pushed it might not serve either of them well. She gave Angel a big smile, allowing the subject to drop until she could revisit it safely.

Angel changed the subject, too. "They put your profile up yet?"

"My profile?"

"Yeah. All of us get a profile online. It's how we get work."

Just then another young woman came through the door. She narrowed her gaze on the two of them, but she didn't bother to speak.

Danni smiled. "Hi. I'm Danni."

Her stare narrowed even more as she looked Danni up and down.

"That's Marissa," Angel interjected.

"Shut up!" Marissa snapped. "How many times do we have to tell you to keep that trap of yours closed? Keep it up and you're going to piss off Pie."

"I didn't say anything," Angel snapped back. She rolled back to face the wall, waving a Barbie doll from side to side.

"You opened your mouth, so you said too much!"

"She didn't say anything," Danni said. "It's all good."

Marissa's mouth lifted in a slight snarl, but she didn't bother to respond. She shook her head and moved to exit the room. She called out over her shoulder, "There's food downstairs."

Angel squealed with delight as she scrambled off the top bunk, jumping down to the floor. She grabbed Danni's hand and pulled her along.

Armstrong hadn't planned on stopping by the coffee shop after leaving the jailhouse to review the report on Josef Havel's untimely death. He had planned to head home but instead found himself standing alone, staring at the menu. Carlo was sweeping the floors when he entered, acknowledging him with a quick nod of his head.

"What can I get for you, Detective?" he asked, pausing

as he rested his weight against the broom handle, both hands clutching the length of wood.

"Not quite sure," Armstrong answered. He took a quick look around, noting the one college student studying in the corner. "What time do you close?"

Carlo looked toward the clock on the wall. "About fifteen minutes ago."

"I'm sorry. I didn't realize it was so late. I'll get out of your way."

"It's not a problem, Detective Black. I'll probably be here for another hour or so. I'll be glad to get you something."

"Have we met before?" Armstrong asked, noting that the steel-gray sweat suit and Jordan sneakers he wore didn't identify him as a police officer.

"Not officially." Carlo moved toward him, pausing to rest his broom against the counter. "Carlo Mancuso," he said, extending his hand in greeting.

"Armstrong Black." The handshake was firm.

"Your reputation precedes you, Detective Black."

"I'm not sure that's a good thing."

"It is what it is."

Armstrong nodded. "Are you related to the Mancuso family from Michigan Avenue?"

Carlo's smile was slight. "My maternal grandfather was Benito Mancuso. My mother was his youngest daughter with wife number three."

"Benito! What a small world. My father and your grandfather were friends. I remember him well."

"I met your father once or twice, I think, but each time he was dining with Alexander Balducci."

There was a moment of pause as Armstrong eyed the man intently. "He and Mr. Balducci have history."

Carlo nodded ever so slightly. "That they do," he said. He smiled, the smug gesture causing the baby hairs at the back of Armstrong's neck to rise.

"So, how do you know the Balducci family?"

"My mother was married to Leonard Balducci."

Armstrong took a deep breath. "I'm sorry for your loss."

"No need to be. My mother died in an accident when I was four years old. Her family raised me. I really didn't know my stepfather like that."

The awkward shift in the conversation suddenly flooded through the space, vibrating in the silence that wafted between the two men.

Carlo changed the subject. "I have some chicken salad that's really good. Let me make you a plate," he said. "On the house."

"That's kind of you. Thank you."

Armstrong moved to sit where Danni often sat, the chair allowing him great views of the room, the door and the sidewalk outside. He watched as Carlo moved behind the counter and began to prep. Across the way the college student was still lost deep in the pages of a chemistry book. The young man suddenly rose with his coffee cup and walked to the counter for a refill. As he passed he gave Armstrong a nod, then quickly returned to his studies.

Minutes later Carlo returned with two plates in hand. He'd piled heaping servings of chicken salad atop a bed of lettuce. Sliced tomatoes and a wedge of French bread rested along one side of the dish, and strawberries and melon rested on the opposite side. "Do you mind if I join you?"

"Not at all. I'd appreciate the company."

Carlo rested one plate in front of Armstrong and the other across the table. He moved to the front door, engaged the lock and shut off the Open light. With a quick flip of a button, the motorized window blinds slowly rolled into place, cutting off the outside view. Before taking his seat, he disappeared into the back room and returned with two bottles of chilled beer. For the next hour the two talked sports, politics, business and family. They discovered they had a number of mutual acquaintances and much in common. Occasionally, the college student, a young man named Richard, interjected, expressing opinions that were indicative of his age. Carlo and Armstrong exchanged a look.

"That's why there is more wrong with the city than there is right," Carlo stated. "These kids today don't have a clue."

"Say it again!" Armstrong chimed.

"You two old heads just need to come out of the dark ages," Richard said with a deep laugh.

"Did he just call us old?" Armstrong questioned, throwing a glance toward Carlo.

"You better school him!" Carlo teased.

The laughter was abundant and easy, and when the meal was done, Armstrong understood what Danni saw in the man. Under different circumstances they might have been friends. Depending how things went with the case, and Danni, they could still be. Rising from his seat, he shook the man's hand.

"Thank you! Are you sure I don't owe you anything?"

Carlo smiled. "Maybe one day but not this one. I don't have a license to sell beer, so I couldn't charge you and not be breaking the law. I would not want to be downtown standing sideways while they take my picture."

Armstrong laughed. "My father often says, 'Obey all laws except the one you're breaking.'"

"Your father is a wise man," Carlo said as he unlocked the door. "You have a good night, Detective."

Armstrong gave Richard a slight salute, said his good-byes and disappeared out the door.

Two slices of pepperoni and one orange pop later, Danni felt like she'd fallen into some bizarre sorority house movie. She wasn't sure if it was a sick comedy or a horror film, but she knew there could be no happily-ever-after for many of the young women under Pius's roof.

She knew the statistics and had quoted them often. Each year countless women and children were sold for sex in America, many through classified sites that regularly faced litigation for the advertisements traffickers placed in their adults-only sections. Even the more popular social networking sites were now being used by traffickers to promote prostitution and solicit the sale of minors.

Seeing it up close and personal had actually moved her to tears. Everything in her had been ready to wave her gold badge and call in the troops, but she knew that doing so would send many of the girls fleeing into worse situations and just allow Pius to move his operation to another home in a different neighborhood. Shutting him down for good was going to require the patience of Job and a fortitude she wasn't quite sure she possessed.

It took no time at all for her to understand the lay of the land. Between what she knew from previous research and what the girls in the house shared, Danni was garnering a wealth of information. Dozens of online ads on those popular sites advertised sex disguised as innocent massages and platonic companionship. These code words allowed posts that seemed innocuous at best but actually promoted illegal transactions to take place: *bareback* for unprotected sex, *Greek*, *French* or *Roman* for anal, oral or group sex. Fees were called *roses* or *donations*, and the word *discreet* opened the door for illicit activities Danni couldn't begin to fathom.

Pius had mastered the art of selling sex. Each of the girls had an online profile that was uploaded to various sex sites to bait their perspective clients. The images ran the gamut from sweet to graphic. Some dates stayed online, the girls coquettishly teasing perverts over private channels in the comfort of their own homes. Others were booked for physical dates, the bodyguards driving them to secondary locations to provide sexual favors in exchange for payment made by cash, credit or bitcoin.

As a group, they considered themselves a family of sorts, and Pius was their caregiver. Danni heard horror stories of pimps who had prostituted and abused them until they'd been saved by the almighty Pie. In their young minds they lived well, better than others, and he cared for them. Care included a regime of required STD testing, birth control pills doled out at breakfast and the watchful eye of Pie invoking fear in all of them. Inasmuch as Danni found it all disturbing, one girl who couldn't fathom any more for her young life was one too many.

"I want to be like Ginny," Angel said as they all watched her leave for work.

Ginger had changed into a formfitting dress and love-me pumps that accentuated her mile-high legs. Another of the girls had pulled her hair into a high bouffant, and her makeup had been meticulous. She'd looked stunning and expensive.

Marissa rolled her eyes. "Why? She's still a whore just like the rest of us."

"Yeah, but she chooses and she gets dates with the wealthy guys. She has regulars and they're doctors and lawyers, and one of 'em is even a judge."

"She still gets her ass beat sometimes," a girl they called Diamond interjected. "I heard her judge is a freak. And he's crazy!"

"Plus, she has to service Pie," another girl said as she cringed. "That's nearly as bad as being sent to the tombs."

"The tombs?" Danni questioned, looking from one to the other.

"It's where they send the girls who become a problem. It's overseas somewhere, and we hear they keep them drugged and tied up there."

"Yeah," someone else said. "I only know one girl who came back, and she wasn't the same after. Now she's turning tricks for twenty dollars a pop just to stay high."

"After the tombs you either don't come back, you come back dead or you come back wishing you were dead," another interjected.

"Crystal came back," Angel said softly.

"And then she was gone," Diamond added. "I heard they found her body in a Dumpster. It was on the news."

"Shut up," Marissa snapped, looking from one to the other. "We have it good here. Any of you mess this up for me and I will kill you!"

"You shut up!" Angel barked. "Crystal was my friend."

Ginger suddenly hissed from the doorway. "Are you trying to get yourselves hurt? You know better," she said as she shot them all a look.

Pie suddenly stepped into the room behind her. His eyes shifted slowly, inspecting each of them one by one.

His stare was cold, and Danni felt Angel stiffen as she shifted her body closer. When his gaze rested on her, pausing a minute longer than necessary, she felt herself sit up straighter, her body tensing. No one said a thing, and then just as quickly he exited the room. Time stood still as they listened to his footsteps fading away to the upper level of the home.

"All of you shut up," Ginger finally snapped. "You know the rules! And you," she said, pointing at Angel. "You're walking on thin ice. Don't say I didn't warn you."

Girls came and went all hours of the night. Angel cried herself to sleep, muffling her sobs beneath her pillow and blankets. Ginger had scared her, and she'd barely spoken two words to Danni after they'd gone back to their room. It was well after midnight when Ginger and Pie disappeared again, not returning until daybreak. Danni hadn't rested well, anxious about what could happen if she closed her eyes and relaxed. Hours later, when she rose, the two were still sound asleep in their room on the top floor.

Slipping out of the house wasn't a problem, and when the car service Danni had summoned pulled up at the corner, no one knew, or cared, that she was gone.

"We have to stop meeting like this," Armstrong said, flashing her a bright smile from the driver's seat.

Danni smiled back. "Am I glad to see you."

"How's it going?" he asked as he shifted gears and pulled into traffic.

"We've got to get those girls out of there."

"You ready for us to raid the place?"

She shook her head. "Not yet. I need more information," she said as she detailed everything that had happened since her arrival. "The kid named Pace is very chatty. He likes to show off what he knows. He thinks he's brighter than everyone else. I also think he has a little crush on Ginger, so he's not a big fan of Pie's."

"So, you're telling me none of the girls are being held against their will?"

"None in that house. They can come and go as they please. They just exchange sexual favors for the privilege of staying."

"What happens if they want to leave?"

"That's the thing…none of them want to leave. They don't necessarily like the work, but most have been through worse and what Pius offers is the closest thing to family they know. They're protected. They eat well. There are occasional shopping sprees. Most only have to work a few hours a day, and in the house it's like a slumber party twenty-four/seven."

Danni jotted notes onto a lined notepad resting on the back seat as she continued. "I need you to see what you can find on a little girl named Alissa. Not sure of her last name, but she goes by the nickname Angel. And so that you know I'm earning my keep," she said as she wrote a series of numbers at the bottom of the top sheet of paper, "here are some of the IP addresses for their computers and a website link they're uploading profiles to."

"How'd you pull that off?"

"Photographic memory. I wandered into the computer room, being nosy, until I was thrown out. Everything I saw is written down here for you and the team."

"They have a computer room?"

"A dozen computers with their own network servers in the dining room. It's all here," she said, gesturing with the notepad. "And I drew you a layout of the house."

"Nice work, Detective."

"Not nice enough. I need to figure out where the tombs are and what gets you sent there. And the girls also knew Crystal. Apparently she came back from the tombs before Pius took her away."

"They said that?"

"They said *Pius* took her away, and then she was dead. That's what they said."

"Do you think they'll testify to that in a courtroom?"

"I'm not so sure about that," Danni said after a moment of pause. "They're scared of Pie. They might not be willing to testify against him. Hell, he scares me!"

"I'm sure you'll be able to convince them," Armstrong said.

Danni turned to stare out the window. "I sure hope so," she said.

For another good hour, the two strategized as Armstrong drove around the city, giving her a quasi-tour of the city. He pointed out his former high school, the YMCA where he often played basketball and his favorite doughnut shop. During the drive, they pondered resources that would help with their case, and the girls, when the time came. Armstrong promised to do some digging to discover what more he could about Pie and Ginger. Neither one of them mentioned Carlo.

Chapter 11

There was a brief moment before Armstrong had dropped her off around the corner from the coffee shop when Danni found herself wanting to tell him that she missed him. Missed his company. His laugh. The way he looked at her when he thought she wasn't looking. She had dismissed the thought as quickly as it had risen, but remnants still lingered. Every ounce of it was out of character for her. She rarely ever let herself get so emotionally entangled with a man, most especially a man she hadn't known long. But from day one, when she wasn't thinking about the case, she was thinking about Armstrong.

She pulled her jacket closed around her torso and stuck her hands deep into the pockets. The weather was turning, a cold chill vibrating through the early-morning air. Something about it felt ominous, and Danni found herself a little homesick for a little Georgia heat and sun. As she turned the corner toward the coffee shop, she saw Carlo and Ginger were standing outside. She paused, slowing her stroll as she eyed the two curiously.

Ginger's body language was telling as she stood with her shoulders rolled forward, her head hanging low. Every so often she would cut an eye toward the inside of the store, something like fear furrowing her brow. Carlo stood with his arms folded over his chest. His expression was cold, his eyes were narrowed and his jaw tight, his teeth clenched. It was obvious he wasn't happy about something. Danni watched the two of them until Pie suddenly jumped from the passenger seat of his car, his arms flailing as he spewed a lengthy list of expletives that the entire neighborhood could hear. The two men suddenly stood toe to toe in heated conversation, and then just like that the moment was over. Pie stomped back to his vehicle as Carlo turned and shook his index finger in Ginger's face, then pointed her after his brother. When the two pulled away in Pie's car, the tires screeching on the street, Carlo turned, spying her for the first time.

Danni watched as he took a deep breath to stall his anger, and then he forced a smile to his face. He waved his hand and called her name.

"Hey there!" Danni exclaimed, smiling back. She walked to his side, closing the distance between them. "Is everything okay?"

"Everything's good, but I was worried about you. Are you all right?"

She nodded. "I'm fine. Spent most of the morning pounding the pavement to find a job."

There was a split second of pause as he stared at her. "Ginger didn't know where you'd disappeared to."

"Is that why you were yelling at her?"

"I wasn't yelling at her. But I did let her know I wasn't happy that they didn't know where you were."

Danni shrugged her narrow shoulders. "She and Pie were still asleep when I left. I didn't want to bother them."

"It's all good," Carlo said. "Sometimes I just need to get my brother in check. Ginger is supposed to be watching out for him and…well…lately he's been out of control."

"He has a lot going on. With his business and all," she replied.

There was another lengthy pause as he pondered her statement. "Maybe," he finally said. "It still doesn't excuse him." He gave her another smile as he changed the subject. "So, can I interest you in a cup of coffee and a chocolate Danish? Fresh baked!"

Danni smiled as he held the door open for her. "I'd really like that."

Inside, the coffee shop was empty, not even college students there debating politics, their physics classes, the world's social evils or the purpose of dryer lint. As he moved behind the counter, Carlo made small talk about the weather, something he'd watched on television and his to-do list for the business. Danni only half heard what he was saying, still trying to make sense of what she'd witnessed. She had more questions than answers and, truth be told, was beginning to think she was getting nowhere with the case. The pretense of being seventeen was starting to take its toll on her, and she hadn't been undercover long enough to have it all make sense. The evidence thus far was circumstantial and barely enough to drag anyone in for questioning and definitely not enough to execute a warrant or arrest that would lead to Pius's prosecution and conviction. She needed more to prove he was the master of their operations and pulling everyone's strings, and more meant biting her tongue and pretending to close her eyes to things that turned her stomach and made her blood boil. She knew what her reasons were, but she couldn't begin to understand his.

A half dozen customers had come in needing to be served before Carlo was finally able to take a break. While she waited for him to join her, Danni pretended to be interested in the morning newspaper, using a dull pencil to circle prospective jobs. When Carlo finally sat down, he shook his head.

"I told you there's a job here for you. Why won't you let me help you?"

"You've been very nice. I just don't want to be a burden to you."

"It's only a job. An honest day's pay for an honest day's work," he said.

She gave him a slight smile. "May I ask you a question?"

He met her stare, his gaze curious, and he gestured for her to continue.

"Does what your brother does bother you? His business?"

"What business?"

"The prostitution and using young girls for internet porn."

He studied her intently. There was an awkward pause as he seemed to be searching for what to say. "I'm not sure what you think my brother's business is, but it's not what you might think it is."

"Have you ever been to his house? Seen the girls? The computers?"

"I'm not sure what you're talking about, Danni. Or what you think you saw. I know Pie and Ginger take in the occasional stray and help them out when they can.

Much like they took you in. I hardly think that's a business."

Danni shook her head. "I think it's more than that," she said softly.

He shrugged. "Well, I also know he might occasionally sell a little pot, but that doesn't make him some kind of crime lord, either." He chuckled softly. "Prostitution? Porn? Really? You've got quite the imagination, little girl!"

"I know what I saw," she responded.

He nodded. "Well, maybe I need to go see this for myself," he said. "And if he's really into those things, I will call the police on him myself."

"You would?"

"Of course. I could never condone that kind of behavior from Pie or anyone else!" he said emphatically.

"I don't want to get him into any trouble. Or make him mad," she said.

"Did he do something to you? Or try to make you do something you didn't want to do?"

Danni shook her head once again. "No. I just...well... some of the girls...they..."

Carlo held up a hand. "It's okay. I understand. You're just worried. And you should be. But trust me when I tell you most of these girls can take care of themselves. Ginger's like you, though. She went through her own hard time, so she wants to save the world, one runaway at a time."

He stood up abruptly. "I've got someone covering the shop tonight. Why don't I give you a ride home as soon as he gets here and you can show me what has you so concerned?"

Danni gave him her brightest smile. "Thank you," she said.

Carlo winked an eye at her. "No, thank you. I appreciate your looking out for Pie."

They'd become masters of small talk, chatting about everything from artistic impression to zabaglione, the custard-like dessert best served warm. It was all idle chatter to cover a loud silence neither was interested in falling into. Carlo talked and Danni listened, pausing to ask questions she already knew the answers to. It made the ride from the coffee shop to Pie's home less painful.

Danni took a deep breath as they pulled into an empty space in front of the home. The house was glowing, a light shining through the windows from every room. Danni couldn't begin to imagine why everything was suddenly so bright when the norm under that roof seemed to be dark and secretive. Carlo brushed a hand against her back, seeming to sense her sudden discomfort.

"You okay?" he asked, his brows raised in concern.

"I'm fine," Danni said with a slight nod. "I just…" She hesitated as she took a deep breath.

"It's going to be okay," he said. "Let's just go inside so I can see this criminal enterprise you were telling me about."

Danni wrapped her arms tightly around her torso. Carlo's tone was teasing, like he thought it was all a joke. She suddenly regretted having said anything. Clearly, what Carlo thought he knew about his brother wasn't what she knew. After asking the question, she hadn't expected him to be so lighthearted about it all, barely concerned that something might be amiss. Although she expected him to be surprised when he stepped inside, she wondered if he'd try to justify his brother's behavior or if he'd call the police like he'd said.

He pushed the door open without knocking or ringing the bell. He called out in greeting. "Hello! Pie? Ginger? Anyone home?"

Pie suddenly appeared from the dining room. "Hey," he said, looking from Carlo to her and back. "You staying for dinner?"

Carlo shot Danni a look and a smile. "Who cooked?"

"Mama Teresa. Grandfather is here, too." Pie sauntered past the two of them, barely glancing in her direction as he moved through the foyer toward the living room.

Danni was immediately taken by the quiet in the home and the smell of garlic and tomatoes that billowed from the kitchen. Gone were the usual rush of bodies in and out and the women lounging in wait to earn their keep. She cast her gaze up as Ginger came bounding down the stairs.

"Hey, what are you doing here?"

"I gave Danni a ride and thought I'd pop in to say hello. Didn't know we'd be here in time for dinner."

Ginger nodded, her flaming-red hair waving like she'd stepped out of a shampoo commercial. "How was your day, Danni? Did you find that job you were looking for?"

The two women locked eyes. Danni shrugged ever so slightly. "Still looking," she said softly.

"I'm sure you'll find something soon," Ginger replied, a hint of sarcasm in her voice. "You should go say hello to Mr. Balducci. But first, you need to change for dinner. I left a dress upstairs on the bed for you."

Carlo reached out his hand to trail his palm along her

arm. "Go change while I look around," he said, his voice dropping an octave.

Confusion wafted over Danni's face. She moved to the dining room and looked inside. The space had been transformed, the computers from that morning gone. The sizable oak table that sat in the center of the room suddenly had matching chairs, a tablecloth and a simple floral arrangement and had been set with heavy stoneware plates and silverware.

An older woman was beginning to set platters of food out to be served. She was small in stature and slightly hunched forward, her shoulders rounded from age. She wore black pants and a white tailored blouse with a ruffled collar, and pink bedroom slippers adorned her feet. She looked up as Danni moved toward her. Her smile was welcoming.

"You must be Danielle," the old woman said, a light cackle in her singsong tone.

"Yes, ma'am."

"I'm Teresa Balducci," she said as she swiped her hands against a printed apron tied around her waist. "But everyone calls me Mama."

Danni forced herself to smile back. "It's very nice to meet you," she said softly.

"Well, dinner's ready. Why don't you go wash up and get ready? I hope you're hungry!" she exclaimed. "I cooked lasagna!"

Carlo suddenly hurried past Danni, sweeping the matriarch up into his arms. He kissed her cheek as she giggled with glee.

"Put me down, boy!" she exclaimed as she patted him warmly against the back.

"I wasn't expecting to find you here," he said as he greeted the woman warmly.

"I had to come check on that brother of yours. There was nothing in the refrigerator, so you know I had to do something about that."

Carlo laughed warmly. "I came to check up on him, too. Glad I did. I wouldn't have wanted to miss out on your famous lasagna."

"Come see me more and you can have my cooking anytime you want."

Mama Teresa turned back to give Danni a look. She fanned her hand at the young woman. "Hurry up, now. We don't want the food to get cold," she said.

"I'll give you a hand," Ginger suddenly said from the doorway, locking gazes with Danni for the second time. "We don't want to keep Mr. B waiting."

Danni nodded as she followed Ginger out of the room. Behind her, Carlo and the woman they called Mama were still laughing warmly together as he caught her up on his doings.

As the two women bounded up the stairs, Danni whispered loudly, "Where did everybody go?"

Missing from the hallway and the other rooms were the bunk beds. Two twin beds now decorated the room where Danni had slept, her duffel bag resting at the foot of one. Nothing was as it had been when she'd left that morning.

"Where are Angel and the rest of the girls?" Danni asked as they moved into the space and Ginger closed the door.

Ginger suddenly slammed her hard against the wall, knocking the breath from her. Danni grabbed her shoulder, pressing her palm to the rising bruise she knew would bloom there.

"What the hell…!"

Ginger hissed between clenched teeth. "Shut up! I brought you here to help you. Now you got Pius looking at me like I'm crazy. I told you to mind your own business and don't ask questions, didn't I?"

"I didn't…"

"You did. You had the girls talking about things they shouldn't have been talking about. Like Pius wouldn't find out. He knows everything, you stupid fool, because he has eyes and ears everywhere! Now the grandfather's here, and that's never a good thing!" She threw her hands up in frustration. "So he moved everyone. I was able to keep Angel and them safe here. Now I don't know what's going to happen to them, and it's all your fault." Tears suddenly rained down over her cheeks. She turned, dropping down against the corner of the bed.

Danni stammered, her eyes skating back and forth as she tried to make sense of it all. "I'm sorry… I didn't…"

"That's right. You didn't think. You were too busy acting all superior, like you were better than the rest of us. Nosing around in everyone's business, asking questions about what we do instead of just minding your own damn business like I told you to do."

"I just wanted to understand," Danni whispered, fighting back her own tears.

"Well, understand this. Get yourself changed. Go downstairs and pretend like we're all one big happy family, and keep your damn mouth shut. Can you do that?"

Danni nodded. Ginger stood back up and moved to the dresser mirror to touch up her makeup.

"Pius won't hurt the other girls, will he?" Danni asked.

Ginger turned and eyed her with a narrow gaze. Her face was red with ire. She stared at Danni for a lengthy moment before she answered. "Pius will kill them and not think twice about it. Don't let him fool you. And the rest of his crazy family wouldn't blink an eye, not even that old lady. So, if you don't want to turn up dead or get me killed, too, shut up! And tomorrow you need to find someplace else to stay. You can't stay here."

The door suddenly swung open, Pie standing on the other side staring at them. Ginger took a deep breath. "We're coming, Pie," she said as she forced a smile to her face. "I just needed to fix my makeup."

"You look pretty," he said, the comment unexpected. Ginger nodded. "Thank you, Pie."

He gave Danni a glance before turning his focus back to Ginger. "Dinner's ready. He said come down now." And then he turned, moving swiftly back down the stairs.

Danni snatched the dress from the bed, pulling at her sweats at the same time. In the blink of an eye, she was changed, her hair pulled into a high ponytail, and Ginger had dusted her face with foundation and a light lip gloss.

"Remember what I said," Ginger hissed one last time. "Just keep your mouth shut and stay out of their business."

Alexander Balducci sat at the head of the table, Carlo in the seat on the opposite end. Pie sat beside his grandmother, who had already begun dishing food onto their plates. Danni and Ginger dropped into the two remaining chairs.

"Sorry we're late," Ginger said softly.

"I apologize," Danni offered. "It was all my fault."

Alexander nodded, his hands clasped together as his

elbows rested against the tabletop. "It's good to see you again, Ms. Porter."

"Thank you, sir," Danni answered.

"It's been a while since we were here at your table, Paul," Alexander said as he turned toward his grandson, calling Pie by his given name. "Carlo had some concerns that things might not have been well with you all here."

Pie shot Danni a look before he answered. Ginger's leg brushed against hers, the gesture meant to be a warning. Danni took a deep breath and held it.

"Everything's fine," Pie answered.

"And business is good?" his grandfather asked. "Nothing I need to be concerned about?"

Pie nodded. "Yes, sir, business is fine. You don't need to worry."

Alexander suddenly shifted his attention back to Danni. "Ms. Porter, I understand that you've been worried about some of Ginger's friends. Concerned about their well-being while they had been staying here?"

The moment was suddenly more uncomfortable than it had already been. Danni felt everyone staring at her as they waited for her to respond.

She exhaled the breath that she had been holding. "No, sir. I think I just misunderstood something one of the girls said."

"Which young lady was that?" he asked.

Danni shook her head. "I don't remember her name."

He paused, his gaze narrowing ever so slightly. "You were concerned about something this young woman said and now you can't remember her name?"

"No, sir. I can't remember her name. I've met a lot of girls recently." There was just the faintest hint of defiance in Danni's tone.

Alexander suddenly smiled. "Then I guess there's nothing for us to worry about," he said. He lifted his glass of wine to his lips and took a sip.

The conversation changed gears as the family caught up with each other's doings. Carlo commanded his grandfather's attention as he updated him with details about the coffee shop and a realty venture he was considering. Danni listened with only half an ear. She forced herself to finish the food on her plate, that lasagna like cardboard and dust in her mouth. She had no appetite. She couldn't stop thinking about what she may have done. She needed to get a message to Armstrong. They needed to find Angel and the other girls before it was too late. She was fairly certain that Alexander was controlling the strings that moved Pie. His grandson was nothing but a puppet doing his bidding. Now she just needed to prove it.

She pushed her plate aside. "May I be excused?" she asked, sliding into the role the family seemed to want her to play.

"That will be fine," Alexander answered. "I'm sure Mama could use your help washing up the dishes."

"Danni and I will take care of the dishes," Carlo said as he stood, beginning to gather the plates from the table. "Pie, why don't you go show Grandfather what you and Ginger have been working on?"

Rising from her own seat, Danni reached for the dishes Carlo missed and moved swiftly into the kitchen, dropping them all into the sink. She clutched the edge of the counter as she took a deep breath and then another, fighting to still her nerves.

"I tried to tell you, Danni," Carlo said as he moved into the room behind her. He dropped the pile of dishes he carried into the sink. "This wasn't where you needed to be. My family aren't all good people."

"Whatever," she muttered as she began to rinse the plates to set into the dishwasher.

"You're angry."

Danni shot him a look. "I just need to get my things and get out of here."

"Come stay with me," he said, pressing a hand to her forearm. "I told you I would take care of you. Let me!"

Danni leaned back against the counter, stepping away from his touch. She wrapped her arms tightly around her torso. She was on emotional overload and really needed a minute of peace and quiet to think. "I don't know," she said softly, meeting his stare.

"Well, you shouldn't stay here. Obviously, you don't feel safe."

"She'll be fine," Ginger said, suddenly appearing in the doorway. "Nothing is going to happen to her here."

"You sure about that?" Carlo snapped, a hint of anger in his tone.

"I'm positive." Ginger moved to Danni's side, the gesture feeling very protective. "She'll be fine."

"I agree," Alexander suddenly added, surprising them all as he joined in the conversation. "Danni will be just fine here. Won't you, Danni?"

She nodded. "Yes, sir."

"Good. Carlo, we need to have a conversation, son. Why don't you follow me back to the house?" he said, the comment clearly meant to be a command and not a request. "Pie can ride with you!"

Carlo nodded. "Whatever you need from me, sir." His eyes were still locked tightly on Danni's face as she returned the look he was giving her.

Alexander tapped his grandson on his back. "Wonderful!" He gave both women a bright smile. "Well, Ms. Porter, Ms. Taylor, it's been a pleasure. I look forward to seeing both of you ladies again very soon."

Knowing they'd been dismissed, Danni and Ginger both turned at the same time, moving out the door. Carlo called her name before she could disappear from view.

"Think about what I said, Danni. Please."

Danni hesitated and nodded as she forced her lips to bend into a slight smile.

"We can talk more tomorrow at the coffee shop," Carlo concluded.

"Good night," Danni said softly.

An hour later, the house was suddenly quiet. Danni peeked out the window and watched as the two cars pulled out of their parking spaces and disappeared down the street. Ginger must have been doing the same thing because it was barely a minute later before she knocked and opened the room door.

"I'm sorry," Danni said as they locked gazes. "I didn't mean for anything to happen to the girls."

Ginger dropped down onto the side of the bed. "I know you didn't mean it," she said. She heaved a deep sigh, her whole body seeming to deflate from the gesture.

"What's going to happen now?" Danni asked, dropping onto the bed beside her.

"Business will go on as usual. All of this—" she gestured with her hands "—was to prove how quickly they can make it go away if they want it to. They can pack and move business in minutes and make it like it never existed."

"And they did it because I was asking questions?"

"They did it because the girls were still talking, even when you weren't asking questions."

"How can I help? What can I do?"

"You're going to disappear, preferably voluntarily, and Pius will keep doing what he always does. I'm going to do whatever I need to do to keep Pie happy and Mr. Balducci off my ass until I can find my way out of this unholy mess." She blew another deep sigh.

"It doesn't have to be this way, Ginny. You can go to the police! You don't have to keep doing this. I'll go with you!"

"You really are trying to get us both killed," Ginny quipped. "Don't you know the Balducci family has the police in their pockets? How do you think they get away with half the business they do? We'd never get out of the station alive, and I don't know about you, but I really want to live to see another few years."

"Do you know who the bad cops are?"

"As far as I'm concerned, they're all bad. I know I can't trust any of them, and I'm not willing to take that risk."

"Do you know where they took the girls?" Danni asked.

A tear suddenly rained down Ginger's cheek. She nodded. "Most of them went to the house on Morgan Street, I think. They have places all over Chicago. But Pius said he was going to send Angel to the tombs for talking to you and the other girls. I tried to change his mind but…" Her voice trailed.

"Where are the tombs, Ginny?"

"She'll be getting on a plane soon if she hasn't already left."

"But where is it?"

"Europe someplace. I don't know! And I don't want to know! I've seen what they do to the girls there!"

"How? What have you seen?"

"They videotape the stuff they do to some of the girls because there's a market for it. I've seen the tapes, and it's not pretty. Some of the men…" Her voice trailed off as she tried to bite back the emotion.

"She'll come back, right?"

Ginger's tears flowed freely. "She's just a baby. She'll never survive the tombs. And if she does come back, she's going to spend the rest of her life wishing she was dead."

Danni felt her heart drop into the pit of her stomach. She broke out into a sweat, perspiration beading across her brow. Tears pressed hot against the back of her eyelids but she batted them away. She couldn't afford to let her own fear get the best of her. She had to stay on task. She wrapped her arm around the young woman's shoulder. "It's going to be okay. I really want to help. Tell me everything you know about the tombs, Ginger."

Ginger suddenly jumped to her feet. "Who are you? And why are you asking so many damn questions?"

"What?"

"Don't play me, Danni. If that's even your name. Who are you spying for?" Ginger's voice dropped to a low hiss, ire seeping from her eyes.

"I'm not…"

"You're working with somebody! Is it the cops? Or is it Mr. Balducci? Does he have you spying to test us? To see what we'll tell or who's talking?"

"No, I don't work for Balducci. Look, Ginger, I'm…"

Their conversation was suddenly interrupted, Pie calling Ginger's name from the floor below.

She cursed, narrowing her gaze on Danni. Her voice

dropped to a loud whisper, and she spat venom. "I don't know what your deal is, but if you want to live you need to get as far from the Balducci family as you can. All of them. None of them can be trusted. And if you betray them and they find out, there is nothing you're going to be able to do to keep them from coming after you."

Danni grabbed Ginger's arm. "I want to help you, Ginny!" she whispered back.

There was a moment between them as both paused. Ginger looked from Danni's hand around her arm to the woman's face. "I can't do anything for you anymore." She snatched herself from Danni's clutch and moved toward the door. She stole a quick glance out to the hallway, took a breath to calm her nerves, then shouted down the stairs, "I'm coming right down, Pie."

"We need to go now," he shouted back.

"Coming! I was just fixing my face!"

Ginger eased the door closed and moved swiftly back to Danni's side. She leaned in close to whisper in her ear, her cheek pressed against Danni's cheek. "They bought your little virgin routine. He thinks you need us with your little sob story about being hard up for money and needing someplace to lay your head. He bought it and he plans to work it for all it's worth. I don't know what's true and what's not, but you ask too many questions for your own good. It doesn't matter, though, because Pius is planning to auction you to the highest bidder, if he doesn't take you for himself first. There are men willing to pay big money for a pretty, young thing like you. All fresh and innocent and untouched. You are money in the bank for him, and he cares about his money more than he cares about anything, or anyone. Even you."

"He told you that?"

"He told me that you're to be at the coffee shop by eleven o'clock tomorrow. If you don't show, he's going to hold me responsible. Don't try to leave tonight. It'll look too suspicious. Roll out tomorrow morning like you've been doing. I can't help it if the runaway runs away to someplace else. So do me a favor, show up, say goodbye and get your ass out of Dodge before you can't get out!"

Ginger took a step back and gave her a look. Danni knew their conversation was done. She watched as the young woman turned on her heels and headed out the door.

She didn't know how long she'd been standing there. Downstairs, someone was watching television. She knew the bodyguards in black were there, and she'd heard Marissa talking to some girl she didn't recognize. There was also chatter that didn't register one way or the other with her. It was almost comforting to hear noise in the house again. She knew Ginger and Pie had left and come back, and for all she knew gone a second time. For the moment, though, she wasn't sure what to do or how next to proceed. She was scared. For the girls, for Ginger and herself. But the more she thought about it, the more she knew she couldn't run. No time soon, at least.

Chapter 12

The knocking on his front door pulled Armstrong from a deep sleep. He thought he'd been dreaming, but the soft *tap tap tap* became louder and more persistent. He flung his body forward and threw his legs off the side of the bed. Standing, he stretched his arms and legs up and out, then pulled on a pair of pants and hurried to the door. Throwing it open, he was surprised to find Danni standing on the other side.

"Danni, hey! What's wrong?"

Her eyes widened as she took in his bare chest. "I messed up," she muttered as she pushed her way past him. Moving to the center of the living room, she spun around to face him. Remnants of her tears streaked her face, and worry furrowed her brow.

"What happened?" Armstrong asked as he moved to her side. He gripped her elbow and tugged gently, pulling her down onto the sofa as he sat with her. "Did someone hurt you?"

She shook her head vehemently. "No," she said, "but Angel is in trouble. We need to find her." It took her less than ten minutes to explain everything that had happened in the last twenty-four hours. By the time she finished, she was crying again. She swiped at her tears with the back of her hands.

Armstrong nodded. "Are you sure you're okay?"

"Please don't mistake my tears for weakness. I'm frustrated and I'm angry. I'm angry as hell, and if anything happens to that little girl I don't know what I'll do."

He took a moment to contemplate her statement, sensing that her emotions went far deeper than simple anger. She was enraged, and fury rained down her cheeks with each tear. "I understand. We'll find her," he said as he stood up. "I need to make a quick call." He disappeared down the short length of hallway into a back room.

As Danni waited for Armstrong to return, she felt herself begin to relax, like she could breathe freely for the first time in a long while. It had been a long night, and she imagined it was going to be an even longer day. She hadn't rested well, half expecting Pie or one of his goons to come storming in to take her captive, but that didn't happen. A semblance of comfort had come when Marissa had shown up unexpectedly and had fallen into the other twin bed, snoring softly before her head settled against the pillow.

Rising with the sun, Danni had dressed quickly, grabbed her things and tried to sneak out of the house without being seen. Pie had been standing in his underwear, in front of the refrigerator, guzzling from the jug of orange juice. His presence had startled her. His speaking to her had sent her into shock.

"Where are you going?" he'd asked, his dry tone void of emotion.

No one else was awake, and she'd quickly contemplated an escape plan that didn't involve her pulling the gun from the holster strapped to her thigh.

"My cousin has a friend who has some money for me. I need to meet him before he goes to work. But I'll see you at the coffee shop later," she'd added.

Pie had stared at her, visibly pondering her response, assessing if he believed her or not. He'd finally nodded his head as if giving his approval. Without another word, he had dropped the empty container onto the counter and had eased his body past her, exiting back up the stairs. Danni had practically run from the home to a car, driven by one of their task force members, waiting in front for her.

By the time Armstrong returned, Danni had dozed off. The sight of her gave him pause. Even as she slept, he could see that her rest was disturbed, everything weighing heavy on her spirit. In that moment he would have given all he had to ease her burden and make things well for her. He reached for the cashmere blanket that rested on the arm of his sofa and laid it gently over her. Tiptoeing from the room, he eased back into his bedroom for a shower. She couldn't sleep long, but he hoped the few minutes of rest he could afford her would help.

Danni woke with a start. It took a moment for her to remember where she was and why she was there. Sitting upright, she shifted forward in her seat, stretching her limbs until she felt the bones in her back and neck crack. The muscles relaxed and the tension along her shoulders eased. She rose from her seat and was just about to call Armstrong's name when she heard the shower running from somewhere in the back of the home. She moved to his kitchen and the Keurig coffeepot. Puttering from one cabinet to another, she found a mug, sugar, creamer and a box of K-cup packs. In no time at all she'd brewed a cup of hot coffee and was savoring the intense flavor, delighted by the taste against her tongue. She lifted her slight frame onto one of the barstools and made herself comfortable.

Minutes later she realized she'd been staring down his hallway, anticipating his return. She hadn't meant to, but as she'd sat gazing off into space she realized his bedroom door was ajar and she was waiting patiently for him to come through it. She was suddenly taken aback when a very naked Armstrong passed by the open gap, his backside seemingly gesturing for her attention.

Danni gasped. Loudly. Her breath hitching in her chest as she inhaled swiftly. Armstrong was solid. Rock-hard muscle on top of muscle beneath skin that was as slick as silk. He was perfection personified, and for a split second Danni forgot every ounce of sense she was supposed to possess. She spun around in her seat and took a big gulp of her morning beverage. Her eyes closed as she struggled to contain her breathing. On top of everything else she had to contend with, seeing him naked was almost too much for her to bear.

She had finally stopped shaking when Armstrong called her name, moving in her direction. He was fully dressed, his requisite suit and tie adorning the hardened body she'd just gotten a quick peek at.

"Hey, how are you feeling?"

Danni nodded. "Much better. That power nap helped. Coffee has lifted me back up. Were you able to find out anything?"

"Alexander has a private jet that's scheduled to depart from Midway Airport. I've already requested a warrant for us to board and search. You little friend is named Alissa Merrill. She's a runaway. Her mother was hospitalized after the death of her father, and she was put into foster care. Not a good home, unfortunately. But her mother has been looking for her and there's an active missing persons case open on her, so let's pray we can get a happy ending out of this."

"We just have to find her."

Armstrong nodded. "We will."

"Did you find anything on Ginger?"

"Your girl Ginger is something else altogether. There's nothing on her. It's like she never existed. There is absolutely nothing about her that we can use as leverage one way or the other."

"She knows something's up. She thinks I'm spying for Balducci or someone else. I almost told her I was a cop, and then Pie interrupted our conversation."

"Did you think that was wise? Telling her the truth? Clearly, her loyalty is to Pius and the Balducci family. What if you had blown your cover and she told them? What would you have done then?"

"I'm not sure why, but I trust her. Ginger's smart. In that moment it was the only thing that made sense to me. I think if she knew she would help. I also think I can get Ginger to roll on the Balduccis, but we've got to be able to give her something in return."

"Something like…?"

"Witness protection, maybe? I think she just wants a new start."

He nodded. "Let me talk to my brother. Because this case crosses state lines and we've got federal backing, that might be doable."

For a split second Danni thought about telling him that Carlo had accused one of the Blacks of being dirty and Ginger had alleged the Balducci family had officers on the take. For a second, and then she changed her mind, opting to play that information close to the vest until she could determine what was true and what wasn't. She nodded. "Do you mind if I take a shower? I need to get to the coffee shop."

"I don't think that's a good idea."

"A shower?"

"No, your going back to the coffee shop. I think I should pull you out."

"That's not an option. If I don't show up, Pius is going to know Ginger told me what he said. I'm not going to risk her life. I can't."

"I'm going to put additional detail on you and your boy Pie. You need to contact me the minute your little meeting is done and finished and let me know what's going on."

"I will."

"Promise me, Danni." His stare was intense, his eyes locked tightly on her face.

"I promise, I will," she said softly. Danni jumped down from the stool and moved to get her duffel bag.

"There are towels in the closet at the end of the hallway. Just help yourself to whatever you need."

"Thank you," Danni said softly. She turned toward the hallway, making her way slowly in the direction of the master bedroom and bath.

"Hey," Armstrong called after her. "How did you know where I lived?"

Danni chuckled softly. "Officer Lankford was my driver this morning."

"Huh," Armstrong muttered. "I wonder how he knew."

She laughed. "I called your sister and she gave me the address. I made him bring me and drop me off."

"I'll need to talk to them about that."

"Don't bother. Your sister likes me, and I threatened to take Lankford's shield if he didn't comply."

"You don't have that kind of authority."

"He didn't know that," she said as she gave him her first full smile since arriving. "And I can be very convincing."

Armstrong smiled back as she made an about-face and disappeared into his bedroom, closing the door behind herself.

Everything about Armstrong's space was definitively masculine. Not one feminine touch decorated his home. His bedroom was painted a deep shade of charcoal gray. The drapes were black velvet with sheer white gossamer panels underneath. The furniture was contemporary, rich wood painted a sleek, glossy black and accented with silver drawer pulls. The king-size sleigh bed was black leather and boasted a massive headboard that was tufted and finished with silver tacks. A white, down-feather comforter adorned the bed, one side tossed askew where he had rested and risen.

Unable to resist, Danni moved to the bedside, her palm caressing the sheet where she imagined he had lain. She lifted the pillow to her face and inhaled his scent. His cologne was a dark amber with the faintest hint of citrus and jasmine. She took another deep breath before dropping it back against the bed, beginning to feel slightly like a stalker.

Moving into the bathroom, she was awed by its size. The space was larger than expected and exceptionally sparse. The marble counters were mottled in varying shades of gray with hints of white and black. There wasn't an ounce of clutter anywhere, everything likely stored neatly beneath the cabinets and in the many drawers.

She was instantly drawn to the massive whirlpool tub with the strategically placed jets. There were two pillowed headrests, and she couldn't help but wonder who might have had the pleasure of being in that tub with him. She shook the thoughts from her head as she moved to the oversize shower, stepping in to turn on the spray of water. As she waited for the water to warm she stripped out of the sweats she wore, dropping her dirty clothes to the floor. She unstrapped the holster pressed against her skin and rested her gun against the counter. The room was becoming nicely heated, just the faintest hint of shower mist filling the air.

Stepping into the shower, she relaxed, the flow of hot water immediately soothing. She pressed both hands to the tiled walls and allowed her body to simply sink into the luxury of feeling safe and protected. The pulsing massage of the showerheads was like a thousand fingers kneading her taut muscles. Minutes later the water had started to cool, and Danni knew she needed to get out and get dressed. Her moment of comfort and quiet was over.

Armstrong's own frustration was showing when Danni moved back into the other room. Showered and changed, she felt better, as if she'd been able to wash away a wealth of doubt and confusion. She felt revived and invigorated and ready to kick whatever asses needed kicking.

He was tense, his posture telling as he shouted at someone on the other end of the line to do their job. He met her gaze, watching as she moved toward him. When she reached her coat, resting her duffel bag on the floor as she pulled the garment on, he cupped his hand over the telephone receiver.

"They found Angel."

Danni's eyes widened. "Is she okay?"

He held up his index finger as he shouted another directive into the telephone. Following the conversation, Danni realized something was amiss, and her stomach was suddenly churning again. She tensed as she took a step toward him, her arms folding around her torso as she waited for him to finish his conversation.

"What happened?" she asked as he finally disconnected his call.

"She was unconscious when they found her on the plane. She was with a woman who said she was Angel's aunt and that Angel was under a doctor's care and on medication. Angel is in protective custody for questioning at Northwestern Memorial Hospital."

"I need to see her."

He nodded his understanding. "I'll make that happen as soon as it's feasible."

"Thank you." She took a breath, blowing relief past her full lips. "I need to go. It's almost eleven."

Armstrong reached a large hand out, his fingers toying with the charm around her neck. He stared into her eyes. "There will be a team out on the street and someone inside watching. If things go left and you get into trouble, you push this button—is that understood?"

"Yes, but it's going to be okay. I think I know how to play this. I plan to take Carlo up on his offer to move in with him." Danni dropped that bomb softly, knowing full well he wasn't going to take it well. It was why she hadn't mentioned it sooner.

Armstrong took a step forward. "Excuse me?"

"Carlo knows what his brother does. He's also closely connected to his grandfather. Maybe more than we even know. He's my way inside."

"That's not going to happen, Danni."

"Yes, it is. I think I can get him to let his guard down. Maybe even spill something he wouldn't normally share."

"Are you interested in this man?"

Danni's eyes widened slightly. "I'm not sure what you're trying to imply, but you need to check yourself. I'm here to do a job, and I'll do whatever I have to if it means bringing down Pius and the rest of his family."

"I wasn't trying to imply anything. I know that man is interested in you, and his wanting to *help* doesn't have anything to do with having a compassionate spirit."

"You need to trust me, Armstrong."

"I do trust you. It's him I don't trust!" His voice was raised, the comment coming sharply. His hand fell back to his side, his fists clenched tightly together.

There was a moment of hesitation as Danni resisted the urge to take another step toward him, wanting to feel his arms around her. The desire to be held was intense, and frustrating. Armstrong seemed to read her mind, battling his own wealth of emotion.

"I didn't mean to yell. I just don't want anything to

happen to you. I would feel bad." His whole face lifted
in a bright smile.

Danni laughed, her eyes rolling skyward. Just like
that, the tension between them eased. She pressed her
hand to the center of his chest, tapping lightly. "I will
call you as soon as I leave the coffee shop."

"You better, and that's an order, Detective."

Armstrong was still standing in the window of his
town house as he watched Danni's car pull into traffic
and disappear at the intersection. Trying to deal with
what he was feeling was harder than he would ever have
anticipated. But his concern for Danni extended well
past his responsibility as her partner. Danni had gotten
under his skin, and the way he wanted her was starting
to spread like a virus, unchecked and potentially lethal.
He didn't need to compromise his case because he was
falling for his partner. But truth be told, he wanted Danni
more than he could ever admit to her or anyone else. If
he was perfectly honest with himself, the thought of her
being with Carlo, for any reason, had him on edge.

Closing the window blinds, he moved back to the
kitchen counter and the cell phone he'd dropped against
the counter. He checked for any messages, but there were
none. He sauntered back to his bedroom, and the master bath. Danni's revolver still sat on the counter where
she'd left it. His heart skipped a beat and then two. He
knew her well enough to know she hadn't forgotten it, the
gun left there on purpose for him to find and hold on to.

Leaning against the counter, his mood shifted from
angry to worried and back again. Had he known she
was unarmed, there would have been no way he would
have allowed her back into that lion's den. But she had

known, and she'd gone anyway. After standing in reflection, he heaved a deep sigh and moved out of the space back to his kitchen. He trusted her and he knew enough that Danni didn't do anything without good reason. After double-checking that the stove was off and everything was back in place, he grabbed his keys and headed out the door. He had a meeting to ask Alexander Balducci a few questions, and he didn't want to be late.

Chapter 13

The smell of freshly baked cinnamon rolls and newly brewed Colombian coffee met Danni at the door of the coffee shop. Inside, Carlo was behind the counter in deep conversation with a customer. The tall blonde was giggling heartily, clearly enjoying whatever they were discussing. Pie and Ginger were seated at their usual spot in the back, the boys in black flanking them on either side. A half dozen customers sat around the room, each focused on their cell phones or laptops or lost in conversation with a companion. Nothing seemed amiss.

Danni moved to her usual table and sat down. As she pulled off her coat, Carlo spotted her and winked. She gave him a bright smile and a nod. Tossing a quick glance over her shoulder, she caught Ginger staring at her. The two women locked gazes, and it took very little for Danni to know that the other woman was not happy with her.

She took a deep breath and waited. It took no time at all before Ginger rose from her own seat, crossed the room and dropped down into the empty chair beside her.

"Hey," Danni said, her voice a loud whisper.

Ginger shot a quick glance around the room before she responded. "You find someplace to go? Because once you finish your coffee and you're done playing nice, I don't want to ever see you again."

Danni took another deep breath. "I can't run, Ginger. Not yet."

Ginger shook her head. "Then you're on your own. I can't help you, and I'm not going to run interference between you and Pius."

"I'm not asking you to. I just need you to let me help you."

Ginger smiled. "I've been doing this too long to need any help now. You just need to take care of yourself. *Cop.*"

They exchanged a look. Danni's gaze skated around the room, checking who might be within earshot of their conversation. "I don't know what..." she started.

Ginger held up a hand. "It's the only thing that makes sense," she said, her voice dropping two octaves. "But your secret's safe with me. Telling could get me killed, and I'm not interested in dying anytime soon."

"Will you talk to me, Ginger? I could use your help."

"No. I don't know anything, and I have even less to say. If you know what's good for you, you might want to not know anything, either."

"I'm planning to take Carlo up on his offer to stay at his place."

Ginger shook her head. "You really do want to get yourself hurt," she said.

"What do you mean?"

Ginger suddenly stood up. "Don't say I didn't warn you," she muttered, and then she stood up and moved back across the room.

As Ginger stepped away, Carlo suddenly replaced her, moving to Danni's side. He carried a tray with two cups of hot coffee and a plate of those cinnamon rolls that scented the air.

"Good morning!"

"Hi, Carlo."

He drew a warm hand across her shoulders as he eased into the seat on the other side of the table. "So, are you feeling better about things today?"

"I'm good. I shouldn't have said anything. I hope Pie's not mad at me."

"Don't you worry about Pie. So, did you think about my offer? Because it's still open. If you need someplace to stay, you are more than welcome to stay with me."

"I don't want to be any trouble."

Carlo reached his hand across the table and took hers. "You won't be a problem. I wouldn't have offered if I didn't want you there."

"I wouldn't need to stay long," Danni said. "Maybe a couple of weeks. Just until I can find a job and make some money to afford a room somewhere."

"I could always use your help here," Carlo added. "I don't pay much, but it would put a few dollars into your pockets."

"You'll get tired of me," she said with a slight smile. "If I'm here at work and then you go home and I'm there, I'm sure I'll wear out my welcome sooner than later."

"Don't you worry about that. What's on your agenda today?"

"I actually have an interview at one o'clock down at

the mall, and I was planning on putting in a few other applications when I was done."

Carlo nodded. "Well, when you're done, just come on back here and I will take you and your things over to my apartment."

"Will it be okay if I leave my duffel bag here?" She pointed at the oversize bag sitting at her feet.

"Not to worry," Carlo said. He stood up and reached for her case. "I'll just store this in the back room for you until you get back."

"Thank you," Danni said, "for everything."

"Everything is going to be fine," he said as he leaned to kiss the top of her head. "I promise."

An air of superiority echoed off the walls of the prestigious Union League Club of Chicago. It imbibed the essence of high society: the well-dressed elite, fine china and silver in the dining rooms, and the smell of old money. For 140-plus years the Chicago landscape had been idealized, compromised and defined within those walls. The decor was opulent with one of the most impressive private collections of fine art covering the walls. Situated on Jackson Boulevard, the social club was mere minutes from the Chicago Board of Trade building with a membership largely comprising high-profile professionals—investors, attorneys, physicians, politicians and most of the Black family.

The downtown refuge for the rich and powerful had been a staple in Armstrong's life since he'd been in his teens. His parents had been members for what seemed like forever, and as he neared maturity they often brought him and his siblings there to rub elbows with many of Chicago's young elite. As an adult he'd often sipped scotch in one of the club's many bars, the twenty-three-story structure boasting quite a few.

The private club was known to open doors, members influencing every aspect of the city. Philanthropy was essential to the club's mission statement, funding numerous charitable outlets. The Union League was known to champion causes such as racial equality, women's suffrage, labor reforms and civil rights. It was there, in the Presidents' Room, where past club leaders were honored, that Senator Dick Durbin convinced Barack Obama to run for the presidency of the United States.

Armstrong's parents had sponsored each of their children for admission into the enclave. Multiple references had been necessary, and after a review period, their memberships were approved by the Board of Directors. Now he maintained the privilege with a monthly check.

Alexander Balducci agreed to meet him in that space, allowed him to keep the appointment informal. He hoped for answers that wouldn't necessitate another warrant, with Balducci clamming up beneath the directives of his large team of attorneys. If that happened, he knew he would never get any answers and be forever entangled in bureaucratic paperwork. He was willing to forgo protocol to get what he needed.

He found the man sitting in the Wigwam Dining Room. He had already ordered an oversize steak with a baked potato and sautéed vegetables, washing down his meal with a shot of brandy and a beer chaser. Sitting at the table beside him was Armstrong's father. Jerome Black had his own plate of food, his meal partnered with a bottle of his favorite French wine. The 2004 Château La Fleur de Bouard was a rich Bordeaux, both expensive and pretentious. As much as his father loved it,

Armstrong despised it, never understanding his father's obsession with it.

Both men stood at the same time to shake hands with him.

"Good afternoon, son," Jerome said as he tapped his son on the back.

"Hey, Dad," Armstrong said as he gave his father a quick embrace.

"It's good to see you, Armstrong," Alexander Balducci interjected. "I think the last time I had the pleasure to sit down with you and your father was shortly after you graduated from college. Well, before all that bad business with my son."

"It has been a while, sir," Armstrong replied. "Under the circumstances, I appreciate your taking a moment out of your schedule to talk with me."

"Well, it's not often I get to spend time with the police superintendent and one of his detectives at the same time. I assume this has something to do with the warrant you executed on one of my aircrafts earlier today?"

Armstrong nodded as he pulled out a seat and sat down. "It does."

"So maybe you can tell me exactly what you and your people were hoping to find on my plane?"

"We had reason to believe that a young woman was being held against her will."

Alexander nodded his head slowly as he took a bite of his steak and then a sip of his beverage. "Well, I'm sure one of my attorneys told your office that we do not use that plane exclusively for my business. It's my understanding that a third party had rented it for that particular flight."

"Yes, they did."

"So there really isn't anything that I can tell you." He dropped his fork to his plate, the utensil clattering against the china. He sat back in his seat, clasping both of his hands together in his lap.

"Do you know a young woman named Alissa Merrill? Or a woman by the name of Lourdes Monteagudo?"

Alexander paused as if he were trying to put a face to either name. He finally shook his head. "No, sorry, neither rings a bell with me. I wish I could be of more help to you. Was this young woman being held against her will?"

Armstrong smiled. "We're still investigating."

"Well, I'd appreciate it if you kept my people informed. If someone is abusing their privilege and taking advantage of my generosity, I need to know."

"I will do that, Mr. Balducci."

Armstrong exchanged a look with his father. Jerome looked as if there was something he wanted to say, but he held his tongue. He always knew that at some point in time his father's longtime friendship with Alexander Balducci would prove to be problematic. The two men had been childhood friends, growing up together on Chicago's South Side until the Balducci family had moved to the western industrial suburb of Cicero. Both men had been away at school during the race riots of the mid-1960s, the violent protests widening the divide between the city's growing population. Time had eventually brought them back together, their relationship revived with a semblance of decorum and many respective boundaries. Jerome credited Alexander with introducing him to Armstrong's mother, and over the years, the memories of being boys and friends had allowed their relationship to evolve.

The death of his son Leonard had severely strained

the relationship. Despite his parents' efforts to shoulder much support to help the family through what was obviously a difficult time, their son killing Balducci's son had pooled a wealth of animosity between them. Then one day, it was if all had been forgiven, the two men moving past and forward together, their friendship having weathered a monumental storm. Armstrong had his father to thank for brokering this meeting, allowing him to do what he needed to do, his way.

Armstrong shifted the conversation. "I had the pleasure of meeting your grandson recently. We had a good time together. I look forward to getting to know him."

"My grandson?"

"Carlo."

Something Armstrong couldn't read washed over the old man's expression as he forced a slight smile to his face.

Armstrong continued. "We had dinner together at his coffee shop. I look forward to getting to know him better. Maybe he and I might be old friends like you two one day."

Alexander suddenly pushed his plate away as he stood up from the table. "I'll have to tell Carlo I ran into you."

"Please do. Give him my regards and tell him I'll be stopping by again sometime soon. Maybe the four of us can get together here at the club for dinner?"

Alexander smiled. "Maybe." He extended his arm toward Armstrong's father. "Jerome, I hate to eat and run, but I need to get across town for a meeting."

Jerome moved onto his feet as he shook the man's hand. "It's always good to catch up with you. We still playing racquetball later this week?"

"Wouldn't miss it. Kiss Judith for me, and let's all plan to have dinner together soon."

Both men watched as Alexander took his leave and exited the space. Armstrong met his father's gaze.

"Are you hungry, son?" He gestured for a waitress. "What would you like to eat?"

"No, thank you. I'm good," Armstrong answered as he waved the waitress away. "I appreciate your connecting me with Mr. Balducci."

"Did you get the answers you were looking for?"

Armstrong shrugged. "You know him better than most. Did he seem to get upset when I mentioned his grandson?"

Jerome took a deep breath. "Carlo is a sensitive subject for him."

"I don't understand."

Jerome reached for his wineglass and chugged its contents. He reached for the bottle that sat on the table and poured himself another. "Carlo is not Alexander's grandson. He's Alexander's son."

"His son?" Actual surprise crossed Armstrong's face. "I thought Leonard was his only child? Who's Carlo's mother?"

James shook his head. He glanced quickly around the room to ensure no one was within earshot of their conversation. "What I tell you is never to leave this table. It stays between us, is that understood?"

Armstrong nodded. "Yes, sir!"

"Camilla Balducci. Leonard's wife was Carlo's mother."

Armstrong's eyes widened as his father sipped again from his glass and resumed his story.

"Camilla was a student at the university and working part-time in one of Alexander's clubs. He was smitten with the young woman, even though she was young enough to be his daughter. Before you knew it, they were in a relationship. Alexander being Alexander, he soon became smitten with someone younger and prettier. But by then Camilla was pregnant with Carlo. He refused to marry her, and she refused to terminate the pregnancy. She had her baby and sent him away for her parents to raise so she could finish school. Then one day, out of the blue, Leonard comes back home and announces he's married. His new wife was Camilla, and she was pregnant with their son Paul. Alexander was furious, but there wasn't much he could do about it, although he tried. He demanded they annul the relationship, and that didn't happen. He tried to buy her off and couldn't. And then she had that car accident. They were able to save the baby, but she died. Leonard believed his father had something to do with her death, but there was nothing linking him to a crime. He and Leonard were never able to come back from that. It was why he had so much guilt when Leonard was killed."

Jerome paused, seeming to collect his thoughts before he spoke again. "Leonard did some pretty ruthless things to get back at his father for Camilla's dying. Partnering with the Mancuso family against him was just the tip of the iceberg. He had loved her, and it broke her heart when she died. He had to raise his son alone, and that child had a lot of special needs. He was in and out of the hospital, then there were some behavioral problems as he got older. It was a lot for one man to have to handle. Until the day he died he held his father responsible for all of it."

Jerome blew a soft sigh before he concluded his story.

"Alexander always knew what kind of man his son was. Even though he was hurt by what happened, he couldn't blame anyone but Leonard. It's why we were able to come back from your killing him and still maintain a friendship, of sorts, today."

Armstrong suddenly felt as if his father had been able to read his mind, sensing the questions that had been on his heart to ask but he couldn't.

"You said Paul had some behavioral problems?"

"Kid still does. Alexander likes to pretend there's nothing wrong with him, but he'll always require someone to help him out for the rest of his life. I imagine he's well in his late twenties by now, but mentally and emotionally he will forever be twelve years old. Alexander keeps a tight rein on him, though, because he's easily frustrated and prone to violence. He's also gullible and easily led. But there's not much he does that his grandfather doesn't know about."

"Does Carlo know Alexander is his father?"

"I don't know for certain, but I would imagine he probably does. When Leonard died, both boys moved in with Alexander and his mother. He says they've become very close. Then again, he might not know anything at all. It's not my business, so I've never asked, and Alexander has never volunteered the information."

Armstrong sat in silence for a moment as he reflected on everything his father had just told him. Suddenly, the pieces to his puzzle were beginning to make better sense.

The patriarch changed the subject. "So, how are things with you and that young woman your mother likes so much? Danni, isn't it?"

Armstrong smiled. Before he could answer, his father interjected. "And don't tell me you two are just working together. I might have been born at night, but I wasn't born last night."

The younger man felt his smile spread into a wide grin. "Danni is working hard, and I'm trying to support her to the best of my ability."

His father nodded. "I need to say this," he started as he shifted forward in his seat. "If I didn't, I would be remiss in my responsibilities as your father. And as your superior," he added. "Close this case and let that young woman go back to Atlanta. This has the potential to elevate your career, and you don't need any kind of impropriety to derail you. Nothing good can come from this little dalliance between you two."

"Really? Dalliance? Now you sound like Mom."

"Your mother is a brilliant woman. It's why I married her."

"Why does this feel like it's coming more from my superior than my father?"

Jerome slowly blew hot air out of his lungs. "Because as your superior *and* your father, I need to protect your reputation and our family name."

"Says the man whose relationship with one of Chicago's most notorious crime lords doesn't threaten his good name. You act like people don't think Balducci is still able to do his dirt because he's garnering favor from his favorite cop on the take."

Jerome bristled. "I have never allowed my friendship with Alexander to keep me from doing my job, and you know that."

"I do, but other people aren't so sure. So what, if I enter into a relationship with the woman who helped me solve a case, that makes the bust less tangible? I don't think so. I think as long as we get the bad guys, we'll still be the good guys."

"It casts doubt on your credibility. And hers. You don't think Internal Affairs isn't going to question how much time was invested in doing what you needed to do versus the time you spent playing footsie in your patrol car? You need to think about all these things."

"And you need to let me just do my job and live my life the way I need to." Attitude suddenly rose like morning mist between the two men.

Jerome wiped his mouth and hands with the white cloth napkin that rested in his lap. He flung the linen to the table as he stood back on his feet. "I think you need to remember who you're talking to. I'm your father, and you will never be so grown that I'll take any kind of disrespect from you."

"I wasn't…" Armstrong started.

His father stalled his denial. "Yes, you were. And I want you to remember what you just said to me. It is your life, but every choice you make has consequences. Be ready to deal with yours when they come. I don't have anything else to say on the subject."

Armstrong sunk deep into his seat as his father turned and moved through the dining room door and out of the building.

The waitress moved back to the table. "Is there anything I can get for you, Detective Black?"

"Not unless you can rewind time," he muttered.

"Excuse me?"

He shook his head. "Nothing, thank you," he said, and then he followed behind his father and exited the building.

* * *

Danni couldn't run from the coffee shop fast enough. She had felt awkward and uncomfortable from the moment she had stepped inside. Her conversation with Ginger had only aggravated her nerves, and Carlo being so nice served to further add to her anxiety. Jumping on the number fifty-two bus, she settled herself down on a seat in the back, then got off, walked a short distance to the nearest bus stop and waited. An elderly man who reeked of too much cologne and even more bad scotch gave her directions to downtown. He liked to talk, and she listened with half an ear as he told her about his wife and how she had danced her way into his heart. His story was sweet, and she realized that losing love had sent him on a downward spiral that now had him fighting demons to ease the hurt. When the number thirty-five bus pulled up, she wished him well and hopped aboard. She rode past eight stops to the Orange Line Station, transferred to a second bus and sat staring out the window as the city of Chicago floated past her. Homes and places that were totally unfamiliar to her barely captured her attention as she tried to make sense of what was happening and what she needed to do. She wasn't even sure if she would end up downtown, just that she had to keep moving so that she could figure out her next steps.

Her cell phone vibrated beneath her coat, and she knew without looking that it was Armstrong. "Hello?"

"Why are you on a bus? You okay?" the man questioned. There was no missing the concern in his voice.

"One of the customers told me it would take me downtown. I'm hard up for money, remember? And they all think I'm headed to the mall for a job interview."

"You didn't call me," he snapped, trying to contain his annoyance about that fact.

"I know. I'm sorry. I just needed a minute to myself to think."

There was an awkward span of quiet that billowed between them. Armstrong broke the silence. "How soon before you get downtown?"

"I don't think it'll be too much longer." She glanced outside the window, taking in the long line of traffic and the quickly changing architecture.

"Meet me at the Art Institute," he said. "I'll be waiting for you in the African collection with masks from Burkina Faso."

"How long will it take you to get there?" she asked.

"I'm already here," he concluded, and then he disconnected the phone.

Chapter 14

The Art Institute of Chicago was almost one million square feet of space to explore. The museum was a series of multiple buildings, four levels high, that were connected via the first floor only. A grand staircase front and center of the museum led patrons from one art exhibit to another. Armstrong made his way through the South Michigan Avenue entrance. He flashed his badge and waved a hand at guest services, then headed past the South Garden to the Arts of Africa exhibit.

The Art Institute's African collection was a diverse assemblage of tradition-based arts. It included masks and figural sculpture, beadwork, furniture, regalia and textiles from multiple African countries, its collection of African ceramics the largest in any American art museum. The museum was one of Armstrong's favorite places to just hang out and chill. One of the many benches that sat room center was situated directly in front of a collection of masks from the West African country of Burkina Faso. Finding it empty, Armstrong took a seat and made himself comfortable.

His conversation with his father had answered a multitude of questions that he hadn't begun to know where to find the answers. He hated that he and the family patriarch had parted ways angry with each other. He knew he owed his old man an apology for some of the things he'd said, but he also knew that he had needed to calm down and not let his emotions impact whatever else might have been said. He always welcomed his father's advice, but he hadn't anticipated his being so negative. And despite his frustrations, he understood that his father had been right and only interested in what was best for him and his career.

He extended his legs out in front of himself and crossed them at the ankle, clasping his hands on top of his head and leaning back slightly, studying the artistic impressions before him. Every piece in the museum's collection resonated with history. He often wondered who and what had inspired the wealth of creativity in each piece of artwork. Imagining the motivations of other people, in other places, during different time periods often moved him out of his head and allowed him the freedom to see his own issues with a renewed eye.

He was grateful for the quiet and a brief moment to put aside his concern and feelings for Danni so that he could piece together the puzzle of the Balducci clan and how that related to his case. Clearly, everything Carlo had told Danni was a lie. Unless he didn't know Alexander Balducci was his father. Figuring out if Carlo had been dishonest and why, and how it impacted his case, was going to require further digging. Danni was clearly on the inside and likely the only one who might be able to get those answers, if there were any to be found.

The hustle and bustle of South Michigan Avenue made Danni smile. As she paused at the entrance to the Art Institute, she took in the two large bronze lions, both bearing a heavy green patina. For a brief moment she felt like a tourist and then just as quickly she remembered she wasn't. After grabbing a brochure and map at the museum's front desk, she maneuvered her way through the Asian Art Gallery and the American Gallery, lingering longer than she probably should have.

She made a quick stop in the restroom, where she paused to study her reflection in the mirror. She had forgone her usual ponytail and had let her hair down. The soft waves skirted her face, the look flattering. A hint of blush tinted her cheeks, and she reapplied a coat of lip gloss. Despite knowing better, she found herself hoping that Armstrong would like how she looked and then kicked herself for caring.

When she reached the entrance to the Arts of Africa room, she came to an abrupt halt, spotting Armstrong on the other side of the room. He sat in conversation with a beautiful young woman who was clearly captivated by his attention. Both were laughing heartily, and for a split second jealousy wafted through the pit of Danni's stomach with a vengeance. She inhaled swiftly and held the air in her lungs to stall the wave of emotion.

She was just about to turn an about-face when Armstrong looked up and saw her. A wide grin pulled across his face, and he waved as he stood up. After extending his goodbyes, he left the woman sitting there staring after him as he made his way to her side.

"I was starting to worry about you," he said softly. He resisted the urge to wrap his arms around her and pull her against him. The desire was overwhelming, and he stopped short, just running a large hand against her arm and shoulder in a light caress instead.

"Sorry, I didn't mean to worry you. I got a little side-tracked looking at the artwork. I could spend days here!"

"I sometimes do. It's one of my favorite spots. I can actually relax here."

"You're not worried about someone seeing us together?"

He pondered her question briefly. "Obviously, everything's a risk, but the criminal element we're trying to catch are probably all asleep right now. They're like vampires. They only come out after dark. I think we'll be good for a moment."

She nodded her understanding. "I didn't mean to interrupt," she said as she gestured with her eyes toward the woman who was still staring.

"You didn't. She sat down and just wanted to talk about her trip to Africa. Apparently it was quite the experience. I was just being polite."

Danni smiled. "So how's your day going?"

"Well, if you don't count the disagreement I just had with my father, I guess it hasn't been too bad a day."

"What did you and your father disagree about?"

"You."

Confusion washed over Danni's expression. "Me?"

Armstrong took a deep breath. "It's a long story."

Danni stole a quick glance down to her wristwatch. "I've got time."

Armstrong's smile was slight as he shrugged his shoulders toward the ceiling. "Let's walk," he said, "while you tell me how it went this morning."

"Ginger knows I'm a cop. I didn't admit it, but she knows."

Taking the comment in, Armstrong paused in reflection. After a moment he said, "You're not safe, Danni. I don't think you can trust that she won't tell Pius, or his brother. Maybe even the grandfather. I think you're done."

Danni shook her head. "I trust her. I just…" She hesitated, unable to find the words to explain what instinctively felt right. Finally, she said, "I don't think she is going to say anything. I think if she were, she would have done so already. I need to stay undercover so that I can keep trying to get her to tell me what she knows. I can get through to her. I'm sure of it!"

"I had a meeting with Alexander Balducci earlier. Of course, he says he knows nothing about his plane being used to transport a minor out of the country. He claims it was being rented by a third party, and it was. It was rented by a shell company out of Atlanta. The team is trying now to figure out who owns the parent company. I don't doubt that it will point back to him at some point."

"Did he say anything else?"

"Not really. I did ask him about his grandson."

"I'm sure he didn't say anything at all about Pie."

"No, I asked him about Carlo."

Danni shot him a look. "Carlo? What about him?"

"I went by the coffee shop the other day," Armstrong

said, detailing the meeting he'd had with the other man. There was something in his admission that made Danni sense the visit hadn't been purely about business and much about her. She wasn't sure how to take that.

Danni listened, suddenly in her feelings and not knowing why. "Do you think Carlo has something to do with all this, too?"

"I don't think he's as clean as he seems, Danni." For a brief moment Armstrong considered telling Danni what he'd learned about Carlo. But only for a moment, and then he remembered he'd sworn to keep the information his father had shared between them. "I think we need to take a closer look at him. And I think you do, too, which is why you agreed to stay at his place."

Silence filled the space between them. They paused in front of a Kathleen Blackshear oil painting. Standing side by side, both stared, dropping into thought. He was right, and Danni knew she didn't need to say so. Despite Carlo's kindness, she instinctively knew he wasn't nearly as perfect as he may have seemed. Whether she said so out loud or not, she had questioned if he had warned Pie to move the girls. If he had triggered the alarm about her questions and concerns. Clearly he knew what his brother did or didn't do, and just as clearly, he was willing to close a blind eye to it all. She wasn't gullible enough to think that they were becoming fast friends or that Carlo wasn't as knee-deep in the family business as Pie was.

When Armstrong suddenly reached for her hand, entwining his fingers with hers, it surprised her slightly and then it didn't. His touch felt as natural as breathing. She squeezed her palm against his, and she held on tightly to him. Hand in hand they resumed their stroll, enjoying the few minutes they were able to have with each other.

Pausing to read the museum map, Danni tugged, pulling him along as she maneuvered her way down to the Thorne Miniature Rooms. There were sixty-plus miniature room designs in one space, and Danni felt like a kid in a candy shop from the excitement of it all. She'd had a love for dollhouses since she'd been a little girl and her parents had gifted her a Barbie playhouse for her sixth birthday. She'd enjoyed hours of shifting toy furniture and playthings from one room to the next.

The Thorne miniature collection consisted of big-girl playthings. Each model was fascinating and painstakingly precise. Danni would have loved to have spent hours there studying each one in detail. Savoring the few minutes she had, she moved slowly through the space to enjoy as many as she could.

Danni finally broke the quiet reverie they'd fallen into. "So, are you going to tell me why you and your father argued about me?"

Armstrong shot her a look. "Why don't we grab something to eat? We can talk about it after I feed you. Then you need to head back uptown if you're going to do this. You don't need Pie or Carlo getting any more suspicious than they might already be."

She nodded her agreement, and they headed toward the main stairwell up to the third level of the Modern wing to Terzo Piano. The hostess at the signature restaurant greeted him warmly.

"Armstrong! Welcome!"

"Hey, Lisa. How are you?"

The woman named Lisa was all teeth as she grinned brightly. "I'm well. I hope that you are?"

He nodded. "I am. By chance, do you have a quiet table in the back, near a window?"

The woman's bright blue eyes skated from him to Danni and back. "Of course. Give me a quick minute and I'll be able to seat you," she said.

"Thank you."

They waited as Lisa disappeared for a brief moment and then returned. She grabbed two menus from a shelf behind her and gestured for them to follow.

Within seconds of their being seated, a young man greeted them warmly. "Hi. My name's Todd and I'm going to be your server this afternoon. Can I get you something to drink?"

"I'll take water," Danni answered. "With lemon, please."

Todd nodded. "And for you, sir?"

"I'd like a glass of your chardonnay," Armstrong answered. "And can I order an appetizer for us to share while we study the menu?"

"Yes, sir, of course."

"We'll start with an order of your *salumi e formaggi*," he said.

Danni scanned the menu quickly, noting the appetizer plate that included cured meats, the chef's selection of cheese, mustard, jam, pickled vegetables and crostini. "What else is good?" she asked after Todd had disappeared to the kitchen to put in their appetizer order.

"It's all very good. Locally sourced, seasonal, organic. I haven't eaten anything here that I didn't like."

"What do you like a lot?"

He smiled. "I usually order the Third Floor Burger. It's my go-to meal when I'm here."

Danni nodded. "I think I'm going to try one of the pasta dishes."

Minutes later she had ordered the lemon pappardelle,

a mélange of summer corn and Italian cured pork called *guanciale*, red onion and charred ricotta *salata*—an Italian cheese made from goat's milk—tossed with the large, very broad flat pasta noodle similar to fettuccine. Armstrong had ordered his black Angus burger, the sandwich coming with thick-cut bacon, house-made pickles, tomato, lettuce, four-year cheddar cheese and aioli fries. When their meals arrived, Todd asking for the last time if there was anything else he could do for them, she swiped one of his fries, then sat back to enjoy the meal.

Their conversation was easy and casual, comfort found in not needing to discuss anything heavy. Both knew that would come soon enough. There was a nice dining crowd throughout the space and a delightful view of downtown Chicago from the oversize windows. Danni was staring, her mind a complete blank as she watched the scurry of people below and those in the office buildings across the way. She was startled when she turned, realizing he'd been staring at her.

"What? I don't have something on my face, do I?" She swiped at her mouth, tapping her cheek as if she might find something offensive.

He laughed, his head waving. "No, there's nothing on your face."

She smiled. "Then what is it? Why are you staring at me?"

"Actually, I was just thinking how beautiful you are."

Danni blushed, color heating her cheeks. The compliment was unexpected, and flattering. "Thank you," she said, her voice a soft whisper.

Armstrong continued. "My father says I need to send you back to Atlanta when this case is over, and I was trying to figure out how I might convince you to stay."

Danni gently rested the fork in her hand onto her plate. She sat back in her chair, folding her hands together in her lap. "You want me to stay? Here in Chicago?"

He blew a heavy sigh. "I like you, Danni. I really like you a lot. More than I probably should. And I want to get to know you better. That can't happen if you're in Atlanta and I'm here. And right now it's hard to make that happen when we need to be focused on this case."

Armstrong was still eyeing her intently as he spoke. She met his gaze and held it. His stare was so intense, Danni felt as if she might combust from the heat.

"You know this...this...this thing between us probably isn't good for either one of us, right?" she asked.

"So you agree that there's something here?"

"I know that I'm attracted to you. I also know that professionally, it's a conflict for both of us."

He grinned. "But you still want me, right?"

Danni chuckled softly. "What either of us might want is irrelevant. That still doesn't make it okay."

"I guess that all depends on who you ask. I think we could be very good together. And I imagine if we had met under different circumstances there wouldn't be any questions or doubt about that."

"But the circumstances we did meet under preclude us from even thinking about where we might be able to take a relationship. We have a job to do, and doing that job is our first responsibility."

"I agree, but what about after?"

Danni took a deep breath. For a split second she dropped her gaze down to the table, her eyes dancing back and forth as she reflected on his question. When she finally lifted her stare back to his, he had shifted forward in his seat, his expression anxious. His brows were lifted questioningly as he waited for her to answer.

"Once we nail Pius," Danni finally said, "I guess I'm going to have to think about staying here in Chicago for a while."

Armstrong nodded, a wealth of emotion shimmering in his eyes.

Lunch lasted for another good hour and then they walked, the time used to strategize what Danni needed to do and the information she needed to try to uncover once she went back to the coffee shop. He walked her across the street to Millennium Park, showing her the Crown Fountain and Cloud Gate. The stunning architecture, sculpture and landscape design across the twenty-four-acre property were breathtaking, and the late-afternoon stroll was a pleasant way to end their day.

"Why did you leave your service revolver on my bathroom counter?" Armstrong asked as they stood at the bus stop, waiting for her return ride.

"I can't risk keeping it strapped on me, and I was afraid one of the girls might go through my bag and find it. I knew it was safe with you."

"I don't like you not having your gun."

"I'll be fine. I have a black belt in karate and jujitsu. I know how to take care of myself!"

Armstrong nodded. "So you keep telling me. It doesn't mean I'm not going to worry about you, though."

Danni rocked back and forth on her heels. She didn't bother to respond. Deep down she was grateful that a man did care. For longer than she cared to admit, there hadn't been a man who did. She cut an eye in Armstrong's direction, stealing a look at him. He exuded swagger, and there was no missing the attention he garnered when he walked into a room. It moved her spirit that she had captured his attention without even trying, and she was holding tightly to it.

Armstrong interrupted her thoughts. "There's a protective detail already in front of the coffee shop and another that will follow you and your bus. There will be someone on you at all times. If you get into any trouble, you know what to do."

Danni nodded. "I'll contact you as soon as it's feasible. And please, if there is any change in Alissa's condition, find a way to let me know."

"I will. I promise."

Danni's attention shifted to the bus that had turned the corner and was making its way toward them. A wave of sadness suddenly rippled through her stomach.

"You good?" Armstrong asked, sensing the change in her mood.

She nodded, biting back the rise of emotion. "I'll be fine," she answered.

As the bus pulled up to the stop, he drew her hand into his and pulled it to his mouth, kissing the back of her fingers.

Danni gave him one last smile as she fell into line with the others boarding the bus. She tossed a look over her shoulder as he stood staring after her. The woman in front of her was pushing an infant in a stroller. A boy about eight years old and a little girl about five clung to each side of the carriage. The little girl looked back at Danni and smiled before hiding her face in her mother's skirt. The line stopped, an elderly woman closer to the front struggling with a multitude of bags to get inside.

She suddenly spun around, the man behind her eyeing her warily. "Excuse me," she said as she pushed past him and stepped aside. She called after Armstrong as she hurried back to where he stood.

"What's wrong?" he said as she came to a stop in front of him.

"Nothing," Danni said as she pressed both palms against his broad chest. "Nothing at all." She lifted herself up on her toes as her gaze locked with his. Her hands slid up his chest to the sides of his face. She gently cupped her palms against his cheeks, and then she pressed her lips to his.

Chapter 15

When Danni walked through the doors of the coffee shop, there was no missing the ire that painted Carlo's face. He was angry and it showed, the man clearly not caring about the display of emotion. He stood in the back of the shop, in heated conversation with Pie, the two going toe-to-toe. Ginger stood off to the side, and when she saw Danni come through the door she warned her off with a shake of her head.

Danni moved to her usual table and sat down, eyeing them all suspiciously.

"I say!" Pie snapped, spewing venom and spit with his words. "I say and you listen. Don't you forget that!"

Carlo snapped back and grabbed his brother by the throat. "Pie, I will snap your…" he started, and then he caught sight of her staring at the lot of them. He bit back the threat he was about to make, practically choking as he swallowed the words back down. He released the hold he had on Pie's throat and took a step back.

The look he gave her was unsettling. "Where have you been?" he snapped, rage still tinting his tone.

Danni widened her eyes, trying to project fear to the trio. Seeing what could prove to be an opportunity, she took it, rising slowly from her seat. She suddenly sprinted for the door and tore down the street, Carlo yelling her name. She rounded the corner and slowed just enough that he caught her, breathing heavily as he chased her down.

"Danni, stop! Please!" Carlo said as he grabbed her elbow to stall her trek.

Danni spun around, her stance defensive as she met his gaze. "Don't touch me!" she shouted. Loudly.

A tall brutish-looking man in City of Chicago work clothes suddenly rounded the corner behind them. "Everything okay here?"

Carlo nodded. "Fine. Everything's fine."

The undercover officer met Danni's eye. "You okay, little lady?"

Danni's gaze shifted from him to Carlo.

Carlo held up his hands as if he were surrendering. "I'm sorry, Danni. I promise, I'm not going to hurt you. I'm so sorry!" He leaned forward, resting his hands atop his thighs as he gasped for air, fighting to calm his nerves. He took two deep breaths and then a third. The entire time Danni watched him, ready to strike if things didn't go as she'd planned.

"I didn't mean to scare you. I was angry at Pie, and I took my frustration out on you. It won't happen again. I swear."

Danni said nothing, counting slowly in her head.

When she reached ten, she turned her eyes back to the man pretending to be a Good Samaritan. "I'm okay. Thank you."

The man paused for a brief moment, and then as quickly as he'd appeared, he turned and went back in the other direction. Danni stood like stone, still eyeing Carlo cautiously.

"I promise I will make this up to you, Danni. Please, trust me."

She shook her head. "You scared me. I'm not staying with a man who scares me."

"Let's go back to the coffee shop and talk about it," he said. "Please?"

She hesitated one last time, and then she gestured for him to lead the way. Carlo nodded and turned, tossing her a quick look over his shoulder.

As they rounded the corner, he said, "I was worried about you, Danni. It's the only reason I asked where you had been."

Her arms were wrapped tightly around her torso. "That wasn't asking," she said, a hint of attitude in her tone.

"You're right. It wasn't. And I apologize again for that." He held the door open for her and waited for her to walk through it. Danni pushed her way past Carlo and moved back to her table. She dropped back down into the seat she'd vacated earlier.

Inside the coffee shop, Pie and Ginger were gone. Jack, the guy who was working the evening shift, was standing behind the counter serving up a sandwich and soup to a customer. Everyone still there who'd witnessed her quick departure turned to stare, concern and curiosity blessing their expressions. "Jack, two coffees, please,"

Carlo said as he sat down across from her. "Are you hungry?" he asked.

Danni shook her head, her body still tense as she continued to hug herself.

Carlo took another deep breath. "What can I do to make this up to you, Danni? Because I want you to trust me."

She lifted her eyes to stare into his. They sat staring at each other for a lengthy moment. The smoldering look he was giving her suddenly turned her stomach. She tried not to let it show on her face. "Why were you and Pie fighting?" she finally asked, ignoring his question.

Carlo let his body relax back against the seat. He was still staring at her intently. "Pie came into the coffee shop earlier making demands. He sometimes forgets that he doesn't run my business. I was just about to remind him when you came in."

She took a moment to reflect on his comment before responding. "I'm sorry," she said, her voice dropping softly.

"What are you sorry for?"

"That you had to deal with that. I know how Pie can be. I wouldn't want him messing with my business, either. And I'm sorry I ran from you." She smiled ever so slightly.

"So we're good?" Carlo asked. "You forgive me?"

Danni's smile widened. "I guess I can give you a pass," she said. "This time."

"And where did you learn to run so fast?" he asked, his tone teasing. "I still can't catch my breath."

Danni just shrugged her shoulders, not bothering to answer.

Carlo grinned. "Let's get those coffees to go and take you home. On the way you can tell me about your day."

The West Hutchinson Street home was not at all what Danni expected. After visiting his grandfather's lavish homestead and Pie's sizable abode in its upscale neighborhood, she'd suspected that Carlo was living as substantially. The classic brick bungalow in the heart of Portage Park was twelve hundred square feet of original hardwoods, beautiful stained glass windows and wood moldings. There was one bedroom on the first floor, two bedrooms on the second and two full baths, both with claw-foot tubs. The original kitchen had classic white subway tile, and the whole house boasted new storm windows, a brand-new boiler and a roof that was barely five years old. There was also a basement with a padlock that immediately caught Danni's attention.

Carlo pointed up the flight of stairs to the second level. "You can have your choice of bedrooms. Either one upstairs is yours. I sleep in the master bedroom down here. And I put fresh linens on the beds for you before I left this morning."

Danni nodded. "I won't be in your way long."

"You are not in my way. It's going to be fine. Now, if you're hungry, I keep the refrigerator and pantry stocked. And if you want something special, just ask. I'll get it for you."

"You don't have to do that."

"I want you to feel at home here, Danni. Whatever you need."

"You really are too nice. I don't know how I'm going to repay you."

Carlo smiled. "Don't worry about that. Let's just focus on getting you on your feet."

Danni smiled. Her eyes flicked back and forth around the room, taking it all in. The decor was minimal, just the barest necessities. The colors were warm and neutral, and everything about the space felt comfortable. Under different circumstances, Danni might have actually liked being there. She suddenly felt conflicted, red flags parading in her midsection.

They were both standing nervously, the moment suddenly feeling awkward. Carlo carried her duffel bag to the bottom of the steps and rested it there. "Why don't you go on up and make yourself comfortable? I'll order us a pizza for dinner, and we can find us a movie on Netflix and chill."

Danni laughed. "Really, Carlo? *Netflix and chill?*"

He laughed with her. "It sounded cool when I was thinking it."

She nodded. "I like pepperoni."

"With extra cheese?"

"You and I might get along after all!"

Armstrong sipped his third cup of coffee as he pored through the folders strewn across the conference room table. He hadn't been able to sleep, tossing and turning for hours. Coming back to the office to work had felt like the surest thing for him to do, a welcome distraction from the thoughts racing through his head.

He would have been lying if he'd said the case was what was keeping him up. Because even though it occupied a very large part of his mind, what he couldn't stop thinking about was that kiss. And Danni. And the fact that Danni had kissed him and left him wanting more.

Trying to focus on work was supposed to make the wanting easier, but it was doing the exact opposite. One of the officers assigned to sit outside the coffee shop had called to report there had been an incident between Pie and Carlo, and then Danni and Carlo outside the coffee shop. The news had him on edge. Apparently, she had things under control. At least, that's what he hoped. Since she wasn't calling for help, all he could do was wait and worry while he tried to piece together the final pieces of their puzzle.

Danni sat upright in the center of the queen-size bed. Her knees were pulled up to her chest, her arms wrapped around her legs. The house was quiet, which was actually disconcerting after the constant commotion she'd grown accustomed to while staying with Ginger and Pie. After their pizza dinner, Carlo had made them Orange Crush ice cream floats for dessert. Then they had watched that Netflix movie, something starring Morgan Freeman and Gerard Butler trying to save the president. He seemed to enjoy the action, and she had dozed off and on throughout the entire film. They had talked about her possibly going back to school, and she'd told more lies about searching for a job to help pay her bills.

He'd called it a night earlier than anticipated, wishing her sweet dreams as he'd retreated to his own bedroom. She had gone upstairs to the room with a view of the front yard and street and had locked the door. Now she was still wide awake, trying to put it all into perspective.

Running from him earlier had made her seem vulnerable. His running after her had been a test of his resolve, to see if he still trusted her cover story. For the moment she felt confident that she hadn't been compromised. She was fairly certain that Ginger hadn't told them anything she might have suspected.

Danni wanted to call Armstrong but knew that wasn't an option. She couldn't risk the conversation being over-heard. Or that Carlo wouldn't check her phone to see whom she was communicating with. She had used the bus ride back to delete her call history and was glad that she had. As she'd unpacked her duffel bag, searching for a pair of sweatpants and a tank top to change into, it had been obvious that someone had already gone through her personal things. She wasn't sure whom to suspect of committing that infraction when she'd found her pos-sessions out of place, but she was also grateful that she hadn't had her gun in her bag. Trusting her instincts had served her well in that regard.

Danni tightened the hold she had around her legs, leaning her chin against her knees. Thinking about the case, and Carlo's possible role, kept her from focusing on the kiss she'd shared with Armstrong.

Kissing the man had been the most impulsive thing she had done in quite some time. But in that moment, it had felt like the most natural thing for her to do. And from the moment her lips met his, it had been every-thing. If she could have described it, Danni thought, the words would have been too sweet and much too pretty for anyone to believe. His full lips had been like soft, plush cushions against hers. The exchange had heated quickly. His tongue had been quick to search out hers, teasing the line of her teeth to push its way past her lips. He'd tasted of peppermint, remnants of a stick of gum he'd chewed minutes earlier. His tongue had danced against hers gently, his touch drawing the air from her lungs. She had welcomed him eagerly, excitement rising with a vengeance that had consumed them both. If time had allowed, she would have gladly lingered in his embrace, but the bus door had closed and she'd had to pull herself from his arms to chase after her ride.

A sudden ripple of heat feeling like a volcanic eruption intent on implosion moved her up and out of the bed. Danni eased her way down the stairs, needing ice-cold water to help calm her nerves. She found a glass in an upper cabinet and water in a plastic pitcher in the fridge and also found a bag of Pepperidge Farm cookies. She leaned across the butcher-block counter, her thoughts shifting back to the case and away from the heat that was her partner.

Despite the reservations she and Armstrong both had about the man, she wanted Carlo to be one of the good guys. He always said the right things, and on the surface he seemed to be upstanding. She liked him, and even after that display of anger there was something about him, something she couldn't quite put her finger on, that made her want to trust that his gestures of kindness were genuine. It might have been nothing more than wishful thinking, but it was something.

The door to the basement swinging open startled her. And him. She saw from his expression that Carlo hadn't expected to find her standing there in his kitchen.

"Danni, hey! What are you doing up?"

She smiled sweetly. "Sorry, I got thirsty and then I saw these," she said, gesturing with the half-eaten cookie in her hand.

He laughed. "Makes sense to me."

"Why are you up?" she questioned curiously. "I thought you'd be sound asleep."

"I had some paperwork I needed to do." He moved to

close the basement door, securing the lock and depositing the key into his pocket. He sauntered to the counter and reached for his own cookie.

Danni nodded. She gestured toward the door with her glass. "Is that where you keep the bodies?"

Carlo looked from her to the basement door and back. Danni laughed to ease the sudden tension that seemed to billow up out of nowhere.

"It was a joke, Carlo!"

He laughed with her, his head shaking from side to side. "Sorry, I'm more tired than I thought. But no, there are no bodies down there. Not today, anyway," he said with a wide smile. "It's just my office. I keep it locked because Pie has a key to the house and he has been known to come over and rummage through things. It keeps me from coming home to a mess that I have to clean up. It also keeps us from coming to blows with each other like today, because if he screws up my office I would have to hurt him. I keep things very organized down there."

"You'll have to show me one day."

"Anytime," Carlo answered. "Anytime."

"Why are you being so nice to me?" Danni suddenly asked.

"Do I have to have a reason?"

She shrugged. "Something is motivating you."

He took a deep breath. "I suppose there is. But there's nothing sinister about it if that's what you're thinking."

"I don't know what to think. That's why I asked. Most men usually aren't so nice unless they want something."

"You already made it quite clear that's something you don't have to give."

"Like that has ever stopped a man before."

"I'm not that kind of man, Danni. I don't want any

woman who doesn't want me. And I don't want a woman who's more like a little sister to me than anything else."

Danni stood staring at him, nothing coming to her to say. "I should head to bed," she said softly.

Carlo smiled. "Good night, Danni. I'll see you in the morning."

It had been a few days since Danni had moved in with Carlo. The two had fallen into a quasi-comfortable routine with each other. She didn't have the luxury of coming and going as she pleased, because unlike his brother, Carlo seemed intent on knowing where she was at all times. He woke her each morning, insisting she ride with him to the coffee shop after they shared a quick breakfast of toast and cereal. At the coffee shop she'd become quite proficient at serving up coffee and wiping down tables. Working the register and becoming acquainted with the regular customers was quickly becoming second nature. She worked an easy six-to-eight-hour shift each day until Carlo was ready for her to ride home with him. And then nothing. Home was movies, board games, casual conversation, fast food for dinner and then bed. No one in his family visited, nor did he talk about any of them eagerly. He also hadn't offered her a key, which meant he always needed to be there to let her inside if she left. Under different circumstances she would have asked why.

Twice, she'd lied and said she had errands to run, and twice, one of Pie's goons in black had tailed her, leaving her with no other option than to run to the store and dip into a restroom to check in with Armstrong and the team before heading right back to the coffee shop. It was unnerving, and Danni said so. She and Ginger shared a corner table. The coffee shop was empty, the space quiet.

Outside it was pouring down rain, a bad storm keeping people away. Pie and Carlo had disappeared to run an errand, leaving Ginger to keep an eye on her. Both women relished the few minutes they had to themselves, without the men hovering over them.

"I need you to talk to me, Ginger," Danni persisted. She cut an eye toward the door.

The young woman shook her head. "You really are a dozen shades of stupid!" Ginger quipped, her own gaze following Danni's.

"Why? Because I want to help you?"

"Because you don't have a clue what you've gotten yourself into."

"So you keep saying, so why don't you help me understand? If you talk I can protect you, Ginger."

Ginger laughed. "Says the cop who walked right into the lion's den! You can't even protect yourself, and you don't even know it yet."

"What does that mean?"

Ginger leaned across the table, the gesture feeling conspiratorial. Danni leaned with her, meeting her halfway.

"Look, the last time you tried to help, I lost three girls back to the streets and Pie won't let them come back. Then cops popped Angel and her handler. Pius hasn't let that go yet. He lost money. Big money. All the girls are paying for that now. I can't risk things blowing up and getting worse for them. I can't. You might not believe me, but I care about them. I'm trying to protect them the best way I can."

"Then help them get out of this life."

"To do what? You'll ship most of them back to foster care, where they're from. They age out, no job, no education, and they're right back here on these streets with no one to protect them. It's a vicious cycle, and it's not going to stop because you want to be a Good Samaritan."

"It's not about anyone being a Good Samaritan. It's about doing my job, Ginny!"

"Your *job* will get people killed, and I don't plan to be one of them. I've been surviving this damn game since I was eight years old. I plan to keep surviving." A tear rained down Ginger's cheek. She swiped it away with the back of her hand as she took a deep breath.

"You deserve better," Danni said softly. "All of the girls do. Pius needs to be stopped."

Ginger shook her head slowly. "Don't you know that every time one guy like him goes away, there's always another ready to take his place? It's never going to stop as long as men rule this world. Pius is able to do what he does because of all the men with money who keep him in business. Men who don't care about anything except themselves."

"Not all men are like that."

"Well, all the ones I've met are. Judges, lawyers, teachers, politicians...all of them. Even some of our own damn fathers." Ginger's bottom lip quivered as she struggled to hold back her tears. She sat back in her seat, a look of defeat on her face.

"How did you get in this life?"

Ginger took a deep breath. She crossed her arms over her chest, extending her legs out as she crossed her legs at the ankles. "Same sad story. Molested by my favorite uncles before I was six. Then my father sold me to some guy he knew when I was seven. That guy sold me to a lot of other men. I was fifteen when I met Pie. He had his own problems, but he was nice to me. He liked me. It didn't take rocket science to figure out that my life could be different if I attached myself to his little red wagon, so I did. As long as I keep him happy, then I stay on his grandfather's good side, because he's even scarier than Pius could ever be. That's who you need to be going after."

"Then help me make a case against him! Everything you know that you could tell me will help!"

There was a lengthy pause as Ginger fell into her own thoughts. When she spoke there was an air of finality in her tone. "Before Pie I didn't have anyone to help me and I wasn't given a whole lot of choices. I just did what I was told and took whatever got thrown at me. I've met too many girls just like me. Same sad-ass story. But once I realized I had Pie's ear, I've been working hard ever since to give those girls options. To maybe make things just a little bit better. So understand me when I tell you that I...can't...help you!"

"That's why all the girls could come and go from the house without anyone bothering them."

Ginger nodded. "They work the way they want to work. We all do. Sure, it isn't all on the up-and-up, but they rarely have to do something they aren't willing to do. They work their own way if they want to stay. But they have to work to keep Pius off our asses." She took a deep breath before she finished. "You want to take those choices from them. Your way risks putting them back into the hands of men even worse than Pius."

"I'm going to take them down, Ginger. With or without you. But with you would be so much easier."

Ginger stood up. "Take them down first. Put them behind bars and I'll see what I can do."

"You'll testify against them?"

"Take them down *first*. Then we'll see!"

Danni nodded. "Can you at least point me in the right direction?"

The other woman stared at her, the intensity of her gaze compelling.

"Please," Danni said, eyeing the girl just as intently. "Please!"

Ginger rolled her eyes skyward. "Pius hasn't been able to get his hands on Angel, and that's a really good thing. The police told him she took off from the hospital and they don't know where she went. If you, or one of your associates, should find her, you should ask her about the doctor."

"The doctor?"

Just then the door to the café swung open. A young couple came hurrying into the space, shaking water from their plastic raincoats. They waved and greeted the two women warmly.

Ginger stood up. "Yeah," she said. "But you need to promise me one thing," she said, her voice dropping to a whisper.

Danni nodded. "What's that?"

"*If*, and that's a really big *if*. *If* Angel tells you, you're going to need to protect her because they will come for her when they find out."

Ginger turned from her. Her smile widened, her expression shifting moods. "Coffee's on the house," she said to the husband and wife as she moved behind the counter. "You two earned it coming out in this weather!"

Rising from her seat, Danni feigned her own bright smile and followed. "You should try the coffee cake. It's to die for!"

Chapter 16

Angel was eating Jell-O and watching an old episode of *The Fresh Prince of Bel-Air* when the officer guarding her door allowed Danni inside. Monitors clicked and beeped, and tubes ran from them to various parts of her body. There was an IV hook with a bag of saline attached, and both of her arms were heavily bandaged. When the little girl looked up, there was a moment of hesitation and then she broke out into the widest smile.

"Danni!" She sat forward, her excitement spilling out of her eyes like water. "What are you doing here?"

"Hey, Angel!" Danni said as she moved to the side of the bed and pulled the girl into a deep hug. "How are you doing?"

Angel shrugged, her head waving from side to side. "They say my heart's bad. Something to do with the drugs Pius and them gave me. They messed me up and now I'm on a donor list for a new one. The doctors say if they hadn't found me when they did, that the drugs would probably have killed me."

"I'm so sorry, Angel."

"No, it's all good. My mother was looking for me, and she's found me and I don't have to…well…you know. I'm officially retired." She grinned brightly.

"I'm happy for you, Angel. I really am."

Consternation suddenly folded the girl's face in a deep frown. "How did you find me? And why did they let you in? Did Pius send you?" Fear suddenly blessed her expression, and had she not been hooked up to the monitors that were tracking her vital signs, Danni imagined she would have taken off in a fast sprint.

Danni shook her head vehemently. "No, Pius doesn't know I'm here. No one does, and they can't ever find out. If they did, it would blow my cover."

Angel's brow furrowed, a question mark piercing her stare. "Your cover? I don't understand."

Danni took a deep breath as she dropped a warm hand against Angel's knee. "I'm a police detective. I've been undercover trying to find something on Pius and his business. We know he's been trafficking young girls across state lines. We also know he murdered your friend Crystal, but we don't have enough evidence to prove it and put him away. It's why I came to see you. I need you to tell me everything you know so we can get him. I need your help."

"You? You're a cop?"

Danni nodded. "Yes, I am."

Angel slowly eased back against the pillows that supported her slight frame. She pulled at the white sheets and cotton blanket, pulling them up under her chin. Fear lingered in her eyes. "I don't feel well. I think I need to rest now."

Danni persisted. "He was going to kill you, Angel. He was sending you away because he wanted to make you disappear. We need to stop him from doing that to another girl. We need to save the next Crystal before he can hurt her. You don't have to be afraid, Angel. I'll do whatever it takes to protect you."

Tears welled in Angel's eyes, deep pools of water tainting her view. She shook her head, no words needed to voice her refusal.

Danni blew a soft sigh. "Can you at least tell me about the doctor?"

Angel's eyes widened, her fear suddenly dancing with surprise. "How do you know about..."

"A mutual friend of ours thought you might be able to tell me about him."

A wave of silence swept between them as Angel pondered her comment. The girl's gaze swung back to the television, a cartoon figure having replaced the young Will Smith. Danni allowed her a moment to sit with her thoughts. She looked worn, like she'd done a marathon after never having run prior. Gone was the vibrancy that had engulfed her spirit when they'd first met. When she played with dolls when she thought no one was looking. Her glow had diminished substantially, the young woman a semblance of who she'd been just weeks earlier when she'd been willing to decry what had happened to someone she considered her friend.

"You need to leave," Angel suddenly snapped. "I can't help you. If they find out..."

"Please!" Danni begged. "Please, Angel!"

The two stared at each other as Danni continued to

plead her case. "A man we know who worked for Pius kidnapped my sister. I think he was going to take her to the tombs, but she got away. But there was a woman with her who didn't make it. They found her dead just like they found your friend Crystal. I want to make that stop. I don't want anyone else to suffer. And whatever you tell me will stay between us. Pius will never find out."

"He always finds out."

"We will protect you, Angel. And you'll be able to go back home with your mom and be happy. I swear!"

"You were nice to me. Sometimes the other girls would be really mean. But not you." Angel paused as if she were still trying to determine what she should do. She finally blew a heated breath of stale air past her chapped lips. She sat back upright, leaning toward Danni as if what she had to say might be overheard by someone who shouldn't be privy to the information.

"He's not a real doctor. Not like the ones here in the hospital. They just call him the doctor because he fixes all the paperwork. He gets passports and travel documents for the girls and does stuff with the banks for Pius."

"Do you know his real name?"

Angel shook her head. "No. Pius called him by a nickname once, but I can't remember what it was. But that was like the first time I met him. After that I had to call him Daddy whenever we were together."

"How often is this doctor around?"

"He only comes when they're getting ready to send someone away. Like right after an auction."

"An auction?"

"Sometimes new girls come in and they get auctioned off to really rich guys. *Really* rich guys! If they have to leave the country, the doctor will fix their papers. We all thought you were going to be auctioned."

"You did?"

She nodded. "Yeah," she said, not bothering to give any additional explanation.

"What else can you tell me about the doctor?"

"He used to be a police officer, too. I don't think he is anymore, though. And he's a really big guy. Like-a-bear big."

"If you saw him again, would you know him?"

Angel nodded. "Yeah. Pius would make me party with him whenever he did a job for him. Sometimes he would talk about when he was a cop. He liked talking about some club he worked for, too. He thought it was funny that he had worked on both sides of the law and no one knew."

Danni nodded. "Is there anything else you can tell me about him?"

Angel lifted her right hand ever so slightly. "He only has two fingers and a thumb. A drug dealer shot him in the hand. That's why he isn't a cop anymore. He likes to point it at you like it's a gun or something. He's weird."

Danni felt the remnants of her breakfast churn in her stomach. Her voice dropped an octave. "Did you ever hear Pius call this doctor person Tank?"

Angel hesitated, trying to recall what she remembered. "Yeah," she finally said. "I think that's what Pius called him once. Oh!" she suddenly exclaimed. "One other thing!"

"Yes?"

"He keeps copies. He said it makes him happy to look back on all the lives he impacted and know he did a good deed for all those poor girls. He also said it might be his get-out-of-jail-free card one day if things went left."

Danni nodded. "Do you know where he keeps them?"

Angel said, "There's a shed behind his house. There are photos, videos, tape recordings and all kinds of stuff under a floorboard."

"How do you know all this, Angel? Why did he share so much with you?"

The little girl smiled. "When you go out on dates, there's one sure way to make sure you get home safe and sound. You keep your mouth shut and your legs open. Then you collect your money and run. But Ginger always told us that if we keep our mouths shut and listen, men will talk. That it makes them feel important and they always talk about things that will be useful later. He liked to talk."

Danni smiled. "Ginger is a smart girl."

Angel shrugged her narrow shoulders. "Ginger protected us. She did whatever she could to keep us safe. Even when we didn't listen to her rules."

Danni hugged the girl one last time. "Thank you! You've been a big help."

"Danni? Can I ask you something?"

"Of course! Anything."

"If you can make Pius go to jail, what's going to happen to Ginger and the girls?"

"I hope we can get them back to their families. Or find someplace safe for them."

Angel smiled. "Good. That would be good."

"Can I ask you one last thing?" Danni queried. "When this goes to trial, will you testify about everything you know?"

There was a moment of pause as Angel's eyes shifted

back toward the television for a brief moment. Danni waited, understanding the magnitude of her request.

Angel finally shifted her gaze back. She nodded. "Yeah! Whatever you need if it will help the girls."

Danni and Angel had talked for another thirty minutes as Danni had explained all that would happen and what would be expected of her. When she exited the room, Armstrong was sitting patiently in the hospital lounge. She was only mildly surprised to see him there, and grateful. He rose from his seat as she approached, and although she wanted to walk into his arms to be held, she resisted the temptation.

"Did she give you anything?" he asked, his stance all business although something more personal gleamed in his eyes.

Danni nodded. "We need an arrest warrant and we also need to give her a photo lineup to pick out one of Pius's associates. One of the team also needs to come down and formally videotape her statement. Her mother will be here so that she has her guardian present."

"Did she give up Pius?"

"No, someone else. Tank. The doorman at your club," Danni said as she filled him in on what she had just learned.

Armstrong dropped back down into his seat. Surprise registered across his face. "And you're sure it's Tank?"

"I'm not sure about anything, but how many former cops with two fingers missing, who like to play cowboy with their hands, do you know?" There was a hint of sarcasm in her tone as she slid into the seat beside him.

Something like rage washed over Armstrong's spirit. He struggled not to let it show, too many eyes watching the two of them as they sat together. He shook his head, muttering between clenched teeth, "I never liked that guy."

"But he works for you."

"He and my brother were partners when they both started with the police force. There were rumors that he didn't always play by the right rules, and he's a notorious womanizer. He lost his hand during a bad drug bust backing up Parker. At the time, giving him a job was the least I could do."

She nodded her understanding. "Let's pick him up. If Angel identifies him, let's try to leverage that to get him to tell us what he knows about Pius. And get warrants for his house, the back shed and his car. We don't want any of this thrown out on a technicality, so let's make sure we cover everything."

"I will pick the son of a bitch up personally. Do you have time to ride with me to the station?"

Danni stole a quick glance to the clock on the wall. "Not much. I need to meet Carlo back at the café before he closes."

"I don't like that he's practically holding you hostage, Danni."

"It's not like that. Not really."

"Could have fooled me," he snapped.

Danni took a deep breath and held it, staring Armstrong in his eyes as he stared back. She was reluctant to tell him about the concerns she had about her host. Although she hadn't found anything linking Carlo to his brother or grandfather or one shred of evidence that showed him actively involved in their family business, he had begun to worry her.

There had been a shift in his attitude since she'd taken

up residence in his home. Carlo had become demanding and short-tempered with her, and she had enough training to know that she was being groomed for something. She didn't quite know yet what that something was. Just that she had to pretend and play along. He liked her docile and obedient, and despite her inclination to fight back, she didn't, allowing him the perception that she was doing as she was told. She knew that if she shared that with Armstrong, it would be a problem between them. An argument that she didn't have the energy for. Because she needed to stay focused. They had bigger fish to fry, and Carlo acting like an ass wasn't one of them.

She blinked, breaking the hold they had on each other. "One problem at a time, Detective," she said, her voice low. "One problem at a time."

The ride to the station was quick. And quiet. The conversation between them was minimal. Danni sat in the passenger seat and listened as Armstrong placed the necessary calls to start things rolling. Angel's statement was the first real break they'd had in the case, and her talking could only get them a step closer to their primary target.

At the station they confirmed the warrants were signed and put the team in place to execute them. An officer and videographer headed back to the hospital to get Angel's official statement, and Armstrong suited up to arrest Tank.

Danni watched as he snapped on his protective vest. "Do you think he'll be a problem?" she asked.

"I don't, but I'm not going to take any unnecessary chances."

"Just be careful, please."

"We will. The team is tight. We'll go in and pull

him out before anyone realizes what's going down." He snapped his holster in place and secured his weapon. "I'm still not comfortable with your going back in unarmed. Once Pius hears about Tank, things could get iffy. You don't know what Carlo might do if he's involved."

"*If* he's involved, and I'm still not sure that he is. I'll be fine. I need to get into that basement, though."

"And you think you can make that happen tonight?"

"Tonight, or maybe tomorrow. But I'm going to see what's down there that's so secretive."

Armstrong nodded. "You know the drill. If you need help, we're right outside your door."

Danni smiled. Armstrong took a step toward her, closing the gap between them. Heat rose thick and full between them. His gently clutched her arm, his fingers teasing the bend of her elbow. She inhaled swiftly, his touch warming like the sweetest breeze.

"Good work today, Detective," he said softly.

Danni nodded. "Thank you."

With a deep breath, Armstrong leaned and pressed a damp kiss to her forehead. His lips lingered longer than necessary, and then he gently caressed her cheek with his own as he whispered into her ear. "Please, don't do anything to get yourself hurt. It would break my heart if anything happened to you now." As he pulled away, their gazes locked and held. Nothing else needing to be said, he turned and exited the room, heading out to do his job.

Danni wasn't expecting to find Pie at the coffee shop when she arrived. He stood at the counter with his arms crossed over his chest. He and Carlo seemed to be in casual conversation, nothing amiss other than the brother's presence. She greeted them both cheerily.

"Hi, Pie! Hey, Carlo!"

Pie gave her a nod but didn't bother to speak.

Carlo winked an eye at her. "Hello, beautiful! How'd that interview go?"

Danni shrugged, her smile still wide. "Keep your fingers crossed. It's in the housekeeping department at the hospital, and they pay really, really well."

"Northwestern Memorial? You spoke to Donna Daniels?"

Her eyes narrowed ever so slightly. "Yeah, Northwestern, but I interviewed with a woman named Macy," she said, not at all surprised that he knew where she'd gone. She wasn't foolish enough to think that she wasn't being followed. He'd become overly possessive, and she'd come to trust, with a fair amount of certainty, that one of Pie's goons was always trailing behind her on his orders, Carlo's or both. What she'd also become proficient at was losing them when they least expected it. Earlier, at the hospital, slipping into the stairwell, out the front door and back inside had allowed her to lose them somewhere between East Huron Street and Banks Court. It was only when she was certain they'd lost her scent that she'd returned to have her conversation with Angel. Both men now looked stupid, sitting in the back, waiting for their next assignment.

Carlo nodded, smiling slightly. "Macy?" he repeated.

Angel reached into her pocket and pulled out a business card. "Lila Macy," she said as she passed it to him. She watched as he read the contents, noting the name and number of the hospital's human resources department. When he was done, he dropped it into his own pocket, not returning it to her.

"You ready to head home?" he questioned.

"Yes, sir," she answered, her eyes dropping to the floor beneath her feet. "Whenever you're ready."

"You're a lucky girl, Danni," Carlo said as he came from behind the counter. "Some girls aren't as lucky as you to have a roof over your head and someone to take care of you."

Danni smiled and nodded. "Thank you," she said.

He continued, and as he did, Danni repeated his new mantra in her head, having finally lost count of the number of times she'd heard the admonishment.

"You need to be grateful, Danni. And you show your appreciation by being dutiful."

Danni resisted the urge to roll her eyes, her lashes blinking rapidly instead. "Yes, sir," she answered.

"Are you grateful, Danni?" he asked.

"Yes!"

"Yes, what?"

"Yes, sir!"

"And you know how lucky you are, right?"

"Yes, sir!"

Carlo smiled. He wrapped an arm around her shoulder and hugged her. "That's my good girl!"

Good girl, my ass! Danni thought to herself as she smiled back.

Chapter 17

Armstrong and two armed officers entered Peace Row, moving swiftly down the narrow corridors to the bright red door. Tank was seated on a black wooden stool, and he lifted his hand in greeting.

"Hey, boss! I was just about to call you," he said as he waved his cell phone in the air.

"What's up, big man?" Armstrong asked as he moved to his employee's side, the two officers flanking behind him.

"Neighbor just called and said there's a commotion going on at my house. I need to head home to see what's going on."

"That's going to have to wait, Tank. Right now I need you to come down to the station."

Tank's face dropped, his happy-go-lucky smile twisting into a downward frown. "What's this about?"

"Marshall Bryant, you're under arrest on the suspicion of sex trafficking, rape of a minor and fraud. You have the right to remain silent. Anything you say can and will be used against you in a court of law. You have a right to an attorney. If you cannot afford an attorney, one will be appointed for you."

Tank snapped, "I know my rights."

"Turn around and put your hands behind your back."

Tank pulled his large body up, tensing as he looked from one man to the other. His jaw was tight, and he clenched hard fists at his sides.

Armstrong braced himself and shook his head. "Don't. We have an eyewitness, a victim, and right now we're executing a search warrant on your property. I imagine we're going to find a wealth of information hidden away in that shed of yours. Don't add resisting arrest and assaulting a police officer to the lengthy list of charges already piling up."

Suddenly looking more like a small Humvee, Tank seemed to deflate as he slowly turned, pulling his wrists to the small of his back. The officer on Armstrong's right snapped a pair of metal handcuffs on the man. Armstrong gave his associates a nod, and the duo led Tank out of the building to a waiting police car.

Armstrong took a moment to pause. Despite his personal dislike for Tank, the man was still a brother, the uniform having bonded them for a lifetime. Tank had also taken a bullet for his brother, and that, too, had bought him a level of loyalty from Armstrong and his family. It burdened him that Tank's wayward choices had put him in this position. The warrants and arrest had also triggered an Internal Affairs investigation that none of them needed to deal with. His moment of reflection was interrupted by Parker strolling in his direction.

"Was Marshall Bryant Mirandized?" Parker asked, not even bothering to say hello.

Armstrong nodded. "Yes, sir, Lieutenant. Everything's been by the book."

"And you trust that this is a good bust?"

"One hundred percent. Detective Winstead has been working hard for this intel and is still undercover, hoping that we can nail the man we believe has been running this entire operation. She trusts her source, so I do, too."

There was just a brief moment between the brothers, a silent exchange between them that solidified the moment. Neither needed to say a word to express what they were both thinking. Armstrong's cell phone suddenly vibrated in his pocket. He stole a quick glance down at the device. After reading the text on the screen, he sent a message back. He shifted his attention back to his brother.

"They've found something at Tank's place. I need to head over there before I go back to the station. Do you want to ride with me?"

"Yeah," Parker said with a nod.

Danni cleaned up the last of the dirty dishes from what had been an uneventful dinner. Pie had stayed for the pan-fried steaks, buttered green beans and baked potatoes she'd prepared. The two men had talked football, family and politics with Carlo doing most of the talking while she and his brother listened. She hadn't been allowed to join the conversation. Pie hadn't been interested, looking bored throughout the meal.

She'd asked about Ginger, the young woman noticeably absent, and Carlo had told her Ginger was out of town on business. Pie didn't bother to tell her anything, glaring in her direction instead. She'd become concerned until his phone rang, Ginger checking in and letting him know she was headed back home, her mission completed.

When they were finished, the two men had disappeared down into the basement of the small home. Danni didn't think anything of it. Pie was a regular visitor, always disappearing down to the basement, sometimes with his brother, sometimes alone, most times for many hours. It defied the lie he'd told her about not wanting Pie down there disturbing his office.

She had started down the steps after them but had been admonished to clean up the kitchen instead. Carlo's tone had been dry and curt, the order indicative of an attitude she found increasingly abhorrent. The dynamics of their friendship had shifted to something she didn't like. He'd become overly critical, exceptionally demanding and viciously mean. The more he pushed his will on her, the more Danni found herself wanting to push back. This game he was playing was becoming darker with each passing hour, and she was past the point of needing to put the brakes on him. Suddenly she didn't know Carlo as well as she thought she did, and that had her doubting her own instincts.

Just as Danni dried her hands on a dish towel, the back doorbell rang. The kitchen curtain was parted just enough that Danni recognized attorney Leslie Harper standing anxiously outside. She dropped low, her heartbeat suddenly racing. From the floor below, Carlo called her name. With stealthy quickness, Danni scooted out of the kitchen and hurried up the stairs. She stood like stone, listening, her mind racing with contingency plans.

The doorbell rang a second time, the woman outside

leaning heavily on the buzzer. Something had her anxious, and she clearly wasn't leaving before being heard. Danni listened as Carlo and Pie both came bounding up the stairs from the basement. Carlo called her name a second time, annoyance ringing in his voice. Someone pulled open the door, and Leslie's shrill voice rang through the space.

"I've been calling you," she snapped. "We have a real problem."

There was a thick pause, the air fraught with tension, and then Carlo called Danni's name from the bottom of the stairwell.

She didn't answer, moving slowly backward into the bathroom. When she heard him hit the bottom step, she eased the door closed and leaned against it as she quietly engaged the lock. She waited and listened, heard him moving down the hall into her bedroom. There were a long two minutes of quiet, and then she heard him move back, his steps coming to an abrupt stop. She coughed, sensing Carlo was standing on the other side of the door, his ear pressed to the wood structure listening for her.

"Danni?"

"I'm in the bathroom," she called back.

"Everything okay?" Carlo asked.

"Just a little sour stomach," Danni answered. "I'm going to be a minute."

"Let me know if you need anything," Carlo responded.

His footsteps were heavy against the floorboards as he hurried back downstairs. She moved closer to the door and eased it open just enough that she could still hear them below.

Pie was cursing, profanity spewing like water from a faucet. Clearly, he wasn't happy about something.

"Your grandfather says you should lock everything down. He also wants you both at his house until we know what we're dealing with. I'm headed to the police station now, but I won't be able to see him until after he's been officially booked. I'll know more then."

Pie muttered something under his breath and cursed one more time. Carlo mumbled as well as he responded with what sounded like a few choice words of his own. The sound of high heels clicked against the tiled floor, and then the back door opened and slammed closed. Danni stood where she was until she heard a car rev and pull out of the driveway onto the street. She blew a soft sigh, sensing that Leslie Harper had left and only the brothers remained downstairs.

Sliding back into the bathroom, Danni closed the door. She flushed the commode and then turned on the water and washed her hands. When she finally reopened the door, Carlo was standing midflight, waiting for her to exit.

"I have to run an errand. Do not leave this house," he commanded.

"Why can't I…" she started.

He snapped. "Don't argue with me. Just do what I tell you to do!"

Carlo took the remaining steps in two quick leaps. He rushed toward her, and Danni took a step back, her stance ready in case he struck out. Pie suddenly called his name, yelling up the stairs for his attention.

"Let's go," Pie shouted. "Now!"

Carlo closed his eyes and took a deep breath. "Sorry, something's happened with my grandfather, and Pie and I need to go to his house."

"Is he going to be okay? Do you want me to go with you?" Danni questioned, feigning concern.

Carlo shook his head. "No. It'll be fine. And I didn't mean to yell. I just don't want anything happening to you, and you know these streets aren't safe at night. I don't want to have to worry about you. Can you please just stay inside until I get back?" He gave her a weak smile, the gesture feeling very disingenuous.

Danni hesitated, and then she nodded.

Carlo gave her another smile, and then he hurried back downstairs to Pie, the two men racing out the door.

Danni moved down the stairs and watched from the front window as they climbed into Carlo's car. When they were out of sight, she hurried back up the stairs to get her phone. She had left it on the dresser with her purse. She wanted to call and give Armstrong and the team the heads-up that the family was on the move, spooked by events they had no control over. She knew with a fair degree of certainty that he had made his arrest, Tank behind bars. Now that Pius knew, too, she was quickly running out of time. She moved down the hallway to the bedroom, and then she came to an abrupt halt in the doorway. The dresser top was empty, both her purse and her phone gone.

The task force and a forensic team were tossing Tank's home from top to bottom. Police officers stood guard on the street in front of the brick house, and the neighbors stood as close as they could to the yellow police tape to be nosy.

One of Armstrong's detectives waved him to the shed at the back end of the small lot. Four officers stood inside, bagging and tagging the contents they were pulling from under the false floor. There was a small desk in the corner with a computer and printer, and the walls were papered with images of young girls and women half-dressed or naked and posed seductively for the camera.

Armstrong shot Parker a quick look over his shoulder. "What do we have?" he asked, his booming voice announcing their arrival.

"Detective! Lieutenant!" One of the officers greeted them both with a nod. "We hit the jackpot, sirs. We've got video and pictures. And names. He kept records."

Armstrong took the folder the man was handing him. Inside were pictures of their last victim, Crystal Moore. There was the copy of a fake passport that had been made for her and pictures of her dead body. Everything Angel had told them was true. He sighed as he passed the folder back to the man.

"We thought you'd want to see this," a second officer sitting at the computer said.

Armstrong moved behind the man, staring where he pointed on the screen.

"Bryant had an urgent email come in just as we got started." The officer clicked on the incoming mail folder and then the message at the top of the list. The sender was unknown.

Armstrong read the message once and then a second time. He clicked on the attachments and felt his breath hitch in his chest. "Are you sure he didn't see this?" he asked.

The officer nodded. "He's got no message forwarding, and I was sitting right here when it came through. I was the first and only person to open it. I called you the minute I saw it."

Armstrong stepped aside and pulled his cell phone

from his pocket. He dialed and put the device to his ear. Parker stepped around him to see what it was his brother had just looked at. On the screen were multiple photos of Danni.

Danni's police detail was parked too far down the street to see her waving for their attention from the upstairs window. "Oh, cuss," she muttered as she struggled to raise one of the bedroom windows, which were all sealed tight. Decorative wrought iron gates adorned the outside of each, making the home feel like a fortress.

Carlo had locked her in, the front and back doors requiring a key to enter or exit. There was no house phone, and he had effectively cut her off from all communications with the outside. She blew a deep sigh, her hands clutching the lean line of her hips. She stood in thought for a brief moment, then hurried back down to the home's main level. In the kitchen she considered her options, debating with herself if it was time for her to be scared, or not.

She suddenly noticed the padlock resting on the counter. The door to the basement had been pushed shut, but Carlo had forgotten to secure the lock. Danni moved quickly, checking the driveway first before bounding down the wooden steps to the level below.

The room was dim, the glow from a row of computers giving off the only light. Danni moved back up the steps for the switch on the wall, and she flicked on the single light bulb that hung from the ceiling. The space felt damp, the concrete walls unusually cool. The barest hint of mildew scented the air. A row of cabinets lined one wall with four computers on a countertop below. Data flicked off and on the monitors, information rolling across the screens. There was a large file cabinet in one corner, a utility sink and, on the other side of the room, a metal cot with a flimsy mattress and blanket. A pair of handcuffs was linked to the foot of the bed frame.

Danni moved to the file cabinet. There were only a few folders inside, most of the documents pertaining to the coffee shop. There was one folder she found particularly interesting. It held the deeds to some thirty homes and properties in the Chicago area, all filed in Carlo Mancuso's name, including the house Pie and Ginger lived in and the one on Morgan Street that Danni remembered Ginger saying the girls had been moved to. After reviewing and retaining the addresses of each, she placed the documents back where she had found them. She crossed back over to the other side of the room and opened each of the cabinets. There was nothing there but cleaning products, some hand towels, a tool kit and a host of assorted sundries. She shifted her attention down to the computers.

Much like the data room that had been at Pie's house, each computer was following websites that hosted the profiles of girls and women being bought and sold. There was a constantly rotating menu of sexual proclivities for a buyer to choose from. Danni was computer literate enough to know that unlike what she'd discovered at Pie's house, these websites were being hosted on the dark web, space where data existed on overlay networks that required specific software, configurations or authorization to access. Due to the high level of encryption, it was difficult for law enforcement to trace and monitor illegal operations. Websites couldn't track geolocation or the IP addresses of their users. As well, the users were not able to get that information about the host. This enabled dark net users to talk, blog and share files confidentially without the fear of being caught. This anonymity allowed for criminal activity such as illegal trades and media exchange for pedophiles and terrorists. After a quick study of the files and screens, Danni realized it was where Pius conducted a significant portion of his business.

Danni tapped the enter button on the last computer. The screen had been dark, and it loaded quickly. Surprise washed over her expression when her image suddenly filled the screen. The header read Own Her Cherry! She clicked on the content and discovered the web page was for an auction site. There was a photo of her at the coffee shop, Ginger sitting beside her in the background. She was laughing and there was a glow in her face, her youthful expression belying her age and experience. There was also a picture of her at the Balducci party, dancing with a circle of girls. All of them looked like they were celebrating at a high school dance. The last image was of her sound asleep in the bed upstairs. She was wearing a pair of running shorts and a tank top. The bedclothes had fallen to the floor, and she was sprawled on her back. One arm was curled above her head, the other draped across her waist. Her legs were open, one bent at the knee, the other dangling off the edge of the bed. There was a moment of consternation and then rage when she realized her privacy had been violated. She tried desperately to recall when she might have fallen asleep with the door unlocked but couldn't remember. She turned her attention back to the auction page.

Bidding for her had already started, the price up to $650,000. It jumped up another fifty thousand as she sat there. She blinked rapidly, trying to comprehend how any man would want to pay that kind of money for anything, least of all her. But there were only two hours left, bids were still coming and the timer was counting down. Delivery was promised within forty-eight hours of payment. Danni started to shake, fear finally taking hold.

Armstrong checked in again with Danni's police detail. They confirmed that Danni had not left the Mancuso house but that Carlo and his brother had been gone for almost an hour. A check of Danni's cellular location showed that her phone was currently at the home of Alexander Balducci. He was beginning to worry, but he knew Danni was smarter than most people gave her credit for. She was also a force to be reckoned with, and he doubted that she would have run into any trouble and not tried to signal them for help. He'd sent a second unit to Balducci's home, just in case.

The entire team had been called into the station, and they were going through the wealth of paperwork they'd confiscated from Tank's home. The more they dug into the chasm of dirt, the more the pieces of a very large puzzle began to fall into place. Armstrong asked for warrants to bring the family, Pie and Carlo specifically, in for questioning. He also planned to grab Ginger but would leave her for Danni to vet once she was back in house.

His investigation of Carlo had uncovered information he hadn't yet been able to share with Danni. The man's name on deeds to multiple properties around town had moved Armstrong to escalate the request for search warrants up the law enforcement pipeline, to secure the proper signatures without their needing to provide additional proof. The IP addresses and websites she'd initially given them had been linked to a number of those homes. He knew that he couldn't execute a search warrant on one home and not trigger the other criminals to shut down the system and run. They all had to be hit simultaneously. He wasn't willing to risk their cleaning things up and disappearing. That was not how he planned for them to go down.

One officer had been assigned to monitor the underground auction of Danni. Twelve perverts were bidding ferociously for the privilege of stealing her innocence. The nature of the auction made it virtually impossible to track down any of their locations. But it was clear that they each had deep pockets and, from the comments, a discerning taste for the very young and pretty. Comments were distasteful and scary, no one shy about sharing their plans for Danni if they were to get their hands on her. Armstrong knew the timing was going to be crucial. He had just over an hour before the auction would end. He needed to hear from Danni before then or he fully intended to go in, guns blazing. Until then he was going to trust that all was well and that she was still able to do her job. With a deep sigh, he grabbed the Crystal Moore folder and headed toward the interrogation room.

Danni hadn't heard the door open or close, sounds above muffled by the concrete insulation in the room below. Startled, she jumped, turning abruptly when Ginger called her name. Ginger stood in the middle of the stairway looking at her. Her eyes were wide, something like fear crossing her face. She tossed a quick look over her shoulder as she hurried down the last few steps.

Moving swiftly to Danni's side, she grabbed her by the arm. "Are you stupid? He will kill you if he finds you down here!" Ginger hissed from between clenched teeth.

Danni took two steps back toward the computer and

tapped the keyboard for the screen to light. "I doubt it," she snapped back, pointing toward the screen. "I'm worth one million dollars right now, and it looks like that number is growing. I seriously doubt he'll throw that away just to kill me for being nosy."

Ginger shook her head. "Where are they? Pie told me to pick him up here."

"Carlo said something happened to their grandfather. They went to his house. Did you know he was planning to auction me off?"

"You were warned. I told you to leave."

"We busted the doctor. I'm sure they've found his stash by now. Angel's already given us a statement. She's going to testify in exchange for immunity and protection. But you know how Pius is connected to all of this. I really need you to come forward, Ginger. Your testimony would help us put him away for good."

Ginger shook her head. Tears suddenly filled her eyes. "You really don't get it, do you?"

"Get what? Help me understand!"

"Say they do all go to jail, and then what? Do you really think you can keep him from killing me, or worse, sending me to some freak who gets off torturing me? Because I don't trust that you can. And what happens after that? Will I end up back on the streets turning cheap tricks just to survive? Because I don't have anything! This life might be crap, but it's been the best thing I've ever known. You're asking me to throw all of that away, for what?"

"For the chance to make your dreams come true. For an opportunity to do better. To know what it's like to not be a slab of meat for men to pass around and use!"

"Aaargh!" Ginger screamed, shaking her fists in frustration. "You're a fool to think it would be that easy!"

"I never said it was going to be easy. I said that we could make it happen. And I promise that I will do everything in my power to help you. But you have to help me, and we're running out of time."

Ginger stood staring at her. She clenched and unclenched her hands, trying to ease the tension that flooded her body. She took a deep breath and held it, the wheels in her head spinning rapidly.

Danni reached a hand out, resting it gently against her shoulder. "Do this for you, Ginny. And for the other girls. They look up to you. They know how hard you work to protect them. Even Angel said that. You can be an example for them to emulate. Show them this life doesn't have to be their future! You owe that to yourself and to them."

Ginger finally blew out that breath she'd been holding. "I'm scared," she said, her voice dropping to a loud whisper.

"I know. You have every right to be afraid. But I need you to trust me. Let me and my team help you. Please!"

Ginger took another deep breath as she tossed the length of her red hair over her shoulder. "We need to get out of here," she said. "As soon as I know they can't get to us, I'll tell you everything I know. But we need to go now!"

Danni nodded, reaching out to squeeze the girl's hands between her own. "Thank you."

"Don't thank me yet," Ginger said as she turned and headed up the stairs.

Danni followed closely on her heels. She had just reached the top landing when Pie suddenly appeared out of nowhere. Rage painted his expression, and he lashed out, backhanding Ginger without warning. The girl cried out from the blow, her scream echoing loudly through the evening air. A second strike sent her reeling, falling backward down the steps as she lost her balance.

Danni fell with her, unable to catch herself as Ginger slammed into her, bowling her over. The moment was surreal, feeling like they were moving in slow motion. She struggled to get a foothold, her petite frame taking the brunt of the trauma as she slid, *thump, thump, thump,* down the steps. Her body cushioned Ginger's fall, and they both landed hard at the bottom of the steps. Danni's head hit the concrete floor with a resounding thud, and everything around her suddenly went black.

As Armstrong rounded the corner, Parker stood at the door waiting for him. He met the look his brother was giving him with one of his own.

"You good?" Parker asked as he took two steps toward him.

"Who's asking?" Armstrong answered.

"Just showing a little brotherly concern."

"Then no, I'm not good. I'm worried about my girl, and I feel like punching the crap out of someone right now."

Parker smiled. "Your girl?"

Armstrong shrugged. "I kind of like the idea of having one. That one in particular."

Parker slapped him against his back. "Then let's get this over with so you can go get *your girl*. I also don't need this case to end with an incident involving one of our visiting task force members."

"You're joining me?"

"Just as an observer. This interrogation is all on you, and I expect it to be by the book."

"Isn't it always?" Armstrong responded with a nod.

He walked swiftly into the interrogation room. His brother followed him. Parker moved to stand in the corner, leaning against the wall with his arms crossed. He didn't speak. Armstrong tossed him one last look, then slapped the file folder against the metal-topped table as he dropped into a seat. Tank looked up from picking at the skin along his thumb, his mouth dropping open when he recognized what was in the man's hands.

"Counselor." Armstrong greeted Leslie Harper politely. She sat at Tank's side, twisting an ink pen between both her hands. She looked less polished and very unnerved, like it had been a long day of everything going wrong that could.

"Detective Black." She paused as if she was waiting for him to start, then decided she needed to speak her piece first. "This is truly an outrage. My client…"

Armstrong cut her off. "Your client has been linked to a sex trafficking ring responsible for the murders of multiple young women. A warrant was executed on his property, and we found more than enough evidence to put him away for the rest of his life."

The woman shot Tank a look. Her eyes widened, the information not what she'd been expecting. "You found evidence?"

Armstrong continued. "Yes. Documenting his involvement and keeping souvenirs appears to have been one of Mr. Bryant's favorite pastimes."

Tank grunted, his eyes rolling skyward. He and Armstrong locked gazes, and then he dropped his to the floor. He didn't bother to respond.

Armstrong opened the folder that rested on the table. He pulled the image of Crystal Moore's dead body from inside and pushed it toward the man.

Tank's gaze shifted from the photo to Armstrong's face. "I know what you're thinking, but I didn't kill her."

"Maybe you didn't pull the trigger, but you know who did. So why don't you save us all a lot of trouble and just tell us what you know?"

"My client doesn't…"

Armstrong snapped. "Your client is a rapist and a child molester and we have his own documented proof. Video, pictures, dates and times. We also have an eyewitness statement. There is enough irrefutable evidence that will easily get him a life sentence. But if he cooperates, maybe, and that's a slim maybe, the DA will be willing to give him a deal that will get him out of jail before his grandchildren graduate college. How old is little Bailey now? Two? Three?"

"What are you offering?" Leslie asked.

"I guess that all depends on your client's cooperation. He needs to give us Pius. We know he pulled the trigger. We just need him to confirm it and testify against him."

"You really want to get me killed, don't you?" Tank interjected. "Do you know what you're asking? Who Pius is connected to?"

"Do you know what's going to happen when you hit the prison yard and the other inmates discover you're an ex-cop with a penchant for little girls?"

Tank twisted his hands together anxiously. "And if I testify, you'll give me protection?"

Leslie held out her hand, cutting her eyes toward her client. "We really should discuss…"

"I need to look out for me," Tank snapped.

"We need to talk about this," the woman snapped back.

Tank shook his head. "Nah! We really don't. I'm not your priority, and I'm not going down for his kills. That's not going to happen. Pius can kiss my ass. I never liked him anyway."

Leslie visibly bristled, her face turning a vibrant shade of red. Clearly, the conversation was not going as she intended. "My client would seem to be under duress right now. He and I are going to need some time to…"

"No, bitch! You're fired," Tank snapped. He looked at Armstrong. "I need another attorney."

Armstrong's gaze shifted from one to the other. There was an awkward silence that fell around the room. Parker cleared his throat, drawing everyone's attention. He shifted his weight from side to side, then headed in the direction of the door.

Tank called his name.

Parker stopped short. He turned to meet the other man's stare. "Yeah?"

"Sorry, partner. Had to do what I had to do," Tank said, addressing the man directly.

Armstrong exchanged a look with his brother. Understanding swept between them as he silently acknowledged the hurt in his sibling's eyes. Discovering the truth about someone he'd called friend had been a serious gut punch, one that he would probably feel for months to come. Parker didn't bother to respond, quietly exiting the room.

"I think we're done here," Armstrong said to Leslie. He stood and gestured her toward the door.

"Mr. Bryant and I need a few more minutes…"

"Mr. Bryant, does Attorney Harper still represent your interests?"

Tank shot the woman a look. "No."

"You have the right to an attorney. Do you want to exercise that right?"

"No. I'm ready to make a statement. What do you want to know?"

Danni lay with her eyes closed. Despite her best efforts she couldn't open them, her head pounding and the room feeling like it was spinning. Everything hurt, and she was afraid she would move and find something broken. She took a deep breath and then another, fighting to regain her composure. In the distance she heard footsteps and loud voices, but she was unable to distinguish who was yelling at whom or even what they were arguing about.

Ginger had made it to her feet. A hand was pressed to the side of her face, and her legs were shaking as she braced herself against the wall. She called Danni's name and nudged her with her foot. "Get up! You need…to get…up!" she stammered softly. "Please…get up!"

Danni tried to nod, opening her eyes just enough to see that she was still in the basement. Still sprawled out on the floor at the bottom of the steps. She heard herself moan, sounding like a wounded animal. The noise was deeply disturbing.

Ginger reached down to help her. Warm hands pulled her upright, helping her to lean against the concrete wall. "You're bleeding," the young woman said, concern ringing in her voice. "We need to get you some help. Do you think you can get up?"

The door to the basement suddenly swung open, light shining down over them. Danni squeezed her eyes closed and then open as she struggled to focus her gaze. Her ears were ringing, the shrill drone in her head slowly beginning to subside. She pressed a hand to the back of her head, her fingers sliding across a wide gash. Bright red blood dampened her palm. She took another deep breath.

Pie's feet were heavy against the wooden steps as he moved down toward the two women. He reached a tentative hand out toward Ginger, his fingertips lightly grazing the rising bruise on her face. He suddenly began to rock back and forth, cursing under his breath. "Damn, damn, damn, damn, damn..." he muttered over and over again as he slapped himself in the forehead.

Ginger slapped his hand away. She snapped, her own rage rising with a vengeance. "Pie, I've told you to stop doing that. And if you hit me again I swear I will..."

Pie snapped in response. "Shut up!"

The redhead said between clenched teeth, "Do not tell me to shut up. I am not..."

Carlo suddenly appeared at the top of the stairs, his hands on his hips. He stared at the lot of them but said nothing. Ginger and Pie cut an eye at him and then each other, their conversation coming to an abrupt halt.

"What do you two think you're doing?" Carlo yelled.

Ginger inhaled swiftly. She was about to answer when Carlo's phone rang. He turned abruptly to answer the call, disappearing from view. The yelling started again, the conversation more profanity and cursing than anything else.

Pie started rocking back and forth, moving up and down between three steps. His behavior was reminiscent of a petulant child throwing a tantrum.

Ginger shook her head. "It's okay, Pie. Everything is okay. No one is upset with you. But Danni's hurt. You need to help me, Pie."

Pie hovered above them. He shook his head. "Pius

is pissed off. Really pissed off," he snapped harshly. "I told you she was going to be a problem! Now he's mad!"

Ginger tossed Danni a look, a wave of desperation washing over her expression. She shook her head. "Well, I didn't do anything," she said, turning back to face Pie. "She was already down here when I arrived."

Pie snapped a second time. "Don't tell me. Tell Pius!"

"Just help me get her up, Pie."

He muttered under his breath as he moved to the bottom step, where Danni still rested. He suddenly reached down and swept her up into his arms. Moving to the cot, he dropped her, the gesture less than caring. Danni moaned again, but before she could react he snapped the handcuff around her wrist, securing her by one arm to the bed.

"That's not necessary, Pie," Ginger said. She moved to one of the wall cabinets and pulled out a clean towel. Returning to Danni's side, she pressed it to the back of her head. She eased her gently down until she was lying comfortably against the cot.

Pie shot his friend a look. He turned, gesturing for her to follow after him. Ginger leaned to whisper into Danni's ear. "I'll be back," she said softly. "I'll try to get help as soon as I can."

Danni listened as their footsteps echoed across the concrete floor and back up the stairs. She opened her eyes, blinking until she could finally see clearly. Her gaze skated back and forth as her mind raced to put the pieces into place. Pie wasn't short for Pius. Pie wasn't the one pulling all the strings. Pie wasn't capable of pulling any strings at all. She'd gotten it wrong.

Chapter 18

Danni tugged at the handcuffs, assessing her next move. The shouting and screaming upstairs had stopped and things had gone silent. She was certain they were all still up there, and she called out, hopeful that Ginger might come back down. She debated whether or not to trigger her alarm, but she wasn't ready for that yet. She wasn't in any imminent danger, and she still needed to tie Pius to his crimes. Despite the throbbing in the back of her head, she knew she could hold out for a little while longer. Maybe make one last play that would benefit them all. She yelled out a second time.

The basement door suddenly swung open. Carlo paused at the entrance, then slowly made his way down the short flight of stairs. They were both watching each other warily. He moved to the computers, checking each one, then plugged a USB drive into each, watching as the hard drives began to purge their data. He paused at the last computer, nodding enthusiastically. On the screen the auction had ended and Danni's image was flashing with a banner across it that read Sold.

He tossed her a quick glance, his expression smug. "You just made me one point three million dollars, Danni! I think that's well worth having to put up with your being a nuisance."

Danni laughed. "Is that all? I was certain it was going to be at least one point five million. Did you tell them I cook and tap-dance, too? That might have made the difference."

Irritated by her sarcasm, he narrowed his gaze. "You'd do well to be a little more subservient and a lot less mouthy. Your new owner likes his little girl to be obedient and quiet. Obedient and quiet means a lot less pain."

"Actually, Pius, I'm thinking he's not going to be happy when you're unable to deliver his product."

"Oh, I'll deliver you. In fact, we're going to get you cleaned up, medicate you to make the trip more comfortable and send you on your way. And I'm going to even give him credit toward his next buy since you had to go and damage the merchandise. How's that head of yours, by the way?"

Danni shrugged. He didn't need to know that she had a major headache. She was fairly certain he wouldn't particularly care. But a handful of aspirin would have been a godsend right then, she thought. Carlo turned back to the computer, and she winced from the pain, grateful for the opportunity to not let him see her distressed. After the last computer had shut down, he turned his attention back to her.

Danni shifted forward, eyeing him intently. "So it's

been you all this time. You let me think your brother was Pius."

"I didn't let you do anything. You did that all on your own. You're not as smart as you thought you were, little girl."

"Neither are you, because I'm nobody's little girl."

"Oh, you're somebody's, and he has paid handsomely for you. His name is Hobart, but you're probably going to call him Daddy. I hear he's quite the barbarian when it comes to his girls. He likes them to hurt. In fact, I'm told they hurt so much that they never last long. It's why he keeps buying them fresh and new."

"And the girls you hurt? I hear they don't last long with you, either. They either get sent to the tombs or you kill them. Like Angel's friend Crystal. They say you took her away and then she ended up dead in a Dumpster. I guess that makes you a barbarian, too."

He paused, reflecting on her comment. Then he shrugged again. "Crystal was a casualty of doing business. Damaged goods that needed to be weeded out from the quality merchandise."

"So it's true. What the girls said about you? That you killed her and those other girls who didn't do what you wanted?"

"I did what needed to be done. And what needed to be done was to ensure I got my money when I was supposed to get my money. Now, we are finished with this conversation. Ginger's coming down to get you ready. And you will do what she says, because if you don't, I will hurt *her*. I will make sure she's the next pretty face found in a Dumpster, and it'll be all your fault. Is that understood?"

Danni nodded. "I hear you loud and clear," she said.

"Does your grandfather support your little business venture?"

Carlo bristled. "You ask a lot of questions. That's why you're here now," he said, his tone snarky.

Danni persisted. "Does Mr. Balducci even know?"

He moved swiftly in her direction, coming to an abrupt stop in front of her. His jaw was tight. "My grandfather is none of your business. And what he does or doesn't know is mine."

A slow grin spread across her face. "He doesn't know! He would have shut you down if he did. And he would never have let you get so sloppy."

Carlo drew back his hand as if to strike her. Pie suddenly called his name, stalling his arm in midmotion.

Danni took a deep breath. "Mustn't damage the goods, Pius! One point three million dollars, remember? My new daddy might not like any bruises on my face."

He stared at her, rage shifting about in his eyes. He tossed a look over his shoulder and shouted up the stairs. "What is it, Pie? What now?"

"I need my medicine, and Ginny says we have to go get it. And Grandfather is on the phone. He keeps calling!"

"There's medicine in my room, Pie! Tell Ginger to look in my room!"

The man took swift breaths to calm his nerves. He stepped back, his arm falling down to his side. He closed his eyes for a brief moment, an internal battle on his face as he struggled with what to do next. When he opened them, Danni was still eyeing him intently.

He reached his hand out, and Danni drew back abruptly.

"I just want to check your head," he said as he slowly extended his hand a second time. "If you're going to need stitches, I need to know. I'll have to call someone. Now, we can do this the easy way and you can cooperate, or the hard way, which means you won't know what happens until after it's over and you've been shipped to your new home. Your choice!"

After a moment of hesitation, Danni slowly leaned forward and allowed him to inspect the gash in the back of her scalp.

"That is not pretty," Carlo said, frustration adding to his other range of emotions. He pulled a key from his pocket and unlocked her wrist from the handcuff. "Upstairs," he said, pointing his index finger.

"You know what else isn't pretty?" Danni asked.

He eyed her curiously. "What?"

"Men who act like dicks!" she exclaimed, and then Danni slammed a hard knee into his groin that doubled him over in pain that she was sure had him seeing stars. As he fell forward, she swept his legs out from beneath him and followed with a steel-toed boot against his chin when he hit the ground. The concrete was unforgiving, and she imagined it hurt as much as her head.

Armstrong and additional tactical units were only minutes away when Danni's electronic device sounded the alarm. A wave of panic punched him hard, practically doubling him from the anxiety of not knowing what was going on. He clutched the steering wheel a little tighter as the team already in place updated him.

The Balducci brothers were barricaded inside the home with a light security team posted at each door. He had no doubts Pius had already gotten word that his entire empire was imploding around him. Warrants had been executed on all of his properties, his stable of underage prostitutes now in protective custody. The sex trade in Chi-Town had taken a direct hit, and he was going to ensure there would be no recovery for them anytime soon. Pius's open retail lines were shut down, and it was only a matter of time before they'd be able to shut down his underground operations, as well.

Tank had fingered him for all the open murder cases, with the exception of one, and if what they were reporting was correct, Danni had audio recordings of Carlo "Pius" Mancuso Balducci confessing to those multiple murders. Taking him into custody was the last thing they needed to do. That and making sure Danni was finally safe and sound.

When Armstrong pulled into the driveway, his team had already breached the house. He moved swiftly across the lawn to the front door. Stepping inside, he found Danni standing room center, one hand on her hip, the other clutching the back of a chair that Pie sat in. The young man was rocking back and forth, slapping himself as Ginger tried to calm him down. He and Danni locked eyes, and relief flooded his spirit.

He moved to her side, his gaze sweeping over her, around the room and back to her. She gave him a slight smile and a quick nod. "You good, Detective?" he asked, his eyes fixed tightly on her.

"I'm always good when we get our bad guys," she said, a slight smile pulling across her face.

He gestured with his head toward Pie, questions blessing his expression.

"Meltdown," she said, her voice dropping. "Apparently he's off his meds. They're going to transfer him to county hospital after we book him."

"I can get him calm," Ginger interjected. "And I need to call his grandfather."

"You need to make sure the medics check your injuries. They should probably take you to the hospital so someone can look at that bruise on your face."

Ginger shook her head. "I'm good. Really," she said. "I've taken worse punches."

Danni rolled her eyes skyward, she and Armstrong exchanging a look.

"I really need to take care of Pie right now," Ginger concluded, shifting her attention back to the man.

Danni nodded as Ginger went back to cooing and whispering in Pie's ear, her arms wrapped tightly around him.

Both Danni and Armstrong turned as an officer led Carlo up from the basement. He still looked dazed. His face twisted with anger when he saw her, and he moved as if to lunge.

Armstrong slid two paces to the side as he stepped between them. He seemed even taller as he side-eyed Carlo, the look he gave daring him to try something. He shook his head slowly at the man.

"Has he been read his rights?" Armstrong asked.

The other officer nodded. "Yes, sir." His hand was hooked around Carlo's elbow, and he motioned for him to move.

Armstrong turned his attention back toward Danni. "Good work, Detective."

Carlo bristled, stopping in his tracks. He spun back around, wide-eyed with confusion. "Detective? What...?"

Danni took a deep breath. "Detective Danielle Winstead. I'm with the Atlanta Police Department."

"Working with Chicago PD. She's been undercover

with our special task force," Armstrong interjected. "And she just took you and your entire operation down."

Danni gestured toward the uniformed officer. "Have a medic check him out after you book him. He took a nasty fall."

"Yes, ma'am."

"And here I thought I was going to have the honors," Armstrong said as they marched Pius out the door and put him in a patrol car.

"Of what?"

"Punching that bastard out!"

Danni smiled as the two exchanged a look. She clutched the side of the chair a little tighter. Turning her attention toward Ginger, she stood watching the young woman, her concern for Pie, who'd finally stopped rocking and was playing a video game on his phone, feeling quite genuine.

Armstrong stepped closer to her. He pressed his back against the chair, his arms crossed over his chest as they stood practically arm to arm. His voice dropped so only she could hear him.

"He has some serious psychological deficits stemming from an accident at birth. He'd been oxygen-deprived during the delivery and suffered some minor brain damage. I discovered that his grandfather has been trying to hide it—private school, tutors, personal escorts—" he gestured toward Ginger as he continued "—that kind of thing. His anger issues as he's gotten older have made that harder, though. Not sure yet if we'll book him. It looks like Pius used his nephew's deficiencies for his own personal gain. Once we get their statements, we'll probably release him to his grandfather until we decide what to do."

"His nephew…?"

He looked at her with a raised brow. "I'll explain it later," he said.

Danni nodded. Before she could reply, Officer Lankford moved toward them.

"Detectives? You were looking for me?"

Armstrong nodded. "I need you to escort Mr. Balducci and his companion down to the station. Stay with them both until Detective Winstead and I get there."

"Yes, sir!"

Danni gestured for Ginger's attention. "You and Pie go with this officer. I'll be right behind you. Everything is going to be okay."

Ginger hesitated. Her apprehension felt thick and tangible, like a winter blanket wrapped around them.

Danni read her mind, understanding sweeping between them. "It's okay. I trust him. You'll be safe."

Ginger finally nodded. "If you're sure."

"I am," Danni said.

She finally nodded. "Thank you."

The couple watched as Ginger coaxed Pie out of his seat. He stood upright, a snarl on his face as he shot Danni one last look and followed behind Ginger.

The duo stood side by side as they watched the team carry all the computers in the home to the police van parked on the street. They made no effort to move as officers rolled out the file cabinet and its contents and some paperwork and files from Carlo's bedroom.

Something they both had been missing washed over them. There was an easy energy that swept between them, extremely comfortable and slightly decadent. They took advantage of the moment to settle back into the luxury of it.

"You know I missed you, right?" Armstrong's voice was low, the whisper just loud enough for her to hear.

"I missed you, too."

"You had me worried there for a minute. I was just about to send in the troops."

Danni smiled the faintest smile. "I told you not to worry."

"That you did. Doesn't mean I listened." He gave her a smile back, the warmth of it flooding her spirit.

They stood in the quiet for another few minutes. Danni shifted her body closer to his, resting her weight against his side. The gesture was slight and probably only he noticed, his arms still folded tightly across his broad chest.

"I should probably get to the station so I can debrief Ginger," Danni finally said.

"You need a ride?" Armstrong asked, turning to face her.

"You should probably stay here until they're done. I can get one of the patrol cars to drop me off," she said as she finally released the hold she had on that upholstered wing chair. "But I think I need…" she started, and then just like that she blacked out, never finishing the sentence as she dropped to the carpeted floor.

Armstrong was pacing the floor at Northwestern Memorial Hospital. The emergency room was packed, the late-night cases running the gamut from women in labor to gunshot victims hanging on by a thread. The pace was fast and hectic, personnel running back and forth, people yelling and crying and the air singed with heated tempers and frustration. The wealth of it only served to feed his anxiety.

A doctor had been examining Danni for almost forty-five minutes, and he was getting nervous that something was seriously wrong. She had been transferred by ambulance after a medical team was unable to revive her. It was only after she'd passed out that he realized she'd been hurt. He was kicking himself for not having noticed it sooner.

He sauntered back to the nurse's station, the waiting room beginning to frazzle his nerves. The nurse on duty gave him a look, clearly tired of seeing his pretty face.

"I don't have any news for you yet, Detective. I promise," she gushed, "as soon as the doctor comes out you will be the first person I make him come see. You have my word."

"Sorry," Armstrong said, flooded with contrition. "I don't mean to be a nuisance."

The older woman smiled at him. It was obvious that she had been doing her job for many years. She nodded her graying head, the original jet-black strands peppered with ice-white threads. "You're worried, and I understand. I wish I had more news for you."

"Thank you anyway," he said. He hesitated, dreading the thought of going back to the public waiting room.

The nurse seemed to read his mind. She rose from her seat, placing the pen she'd been writing with on the countertop. "Why don't I take you to the surgical lounge? It's quieter there and you'll probably be more comfortable."

Armstrong nodded. "Thank you."

She chatted him up as they maneuvered down the hall and came to the surgical waiting area. The room was empty, no one occupying the pale blue space. The walls were adorned with local artwork, and there was a large, flat-screen television playing on one wall. The furniture was relatively new and comfortable, the whole room designed for calm and tranquility.

He thanked the nurse profusely before she turned to go back to her station. Moving into the far corner, he took a seat and pulled his phone from his pocket. He took advantage of the quiet and called to check in with all of his teams to ensure everyone was on task. As expected, Alexander Balducci had lawyered up his grandson, as well as the boy's companion, Ginger garnering protection under the family umbrella. Legally, they were allowed to hold the two for seventy-two hours before charges had to be filed. Armstrong made a judgment call, releasing both into Alexander's custody with the admonishment that neither was to leave town. Carlo wasn't quite so lucky, his father leaving him to fend for himself. He was behind bars, and Armstrong knew that wasn't likely to change anytime soon.

A breaking news banner suddenly flashed on the television screen, drawing his attention. He sat forward in his seat and listened as local newscasters announced that arrests had been made in a multistate sex trafficking operation. They noted that local law enforcement working in conjunction with federal investigators had shut down a child prostitution ring and solved the murders of a number of young women and girls. There had also been an arrest of a local business owner with known ties to a renowned crime family. They promised that further details were forthcoming. Apparently the mayor and the police chief were planning a news conference the next morning. There was media footage of one of the homes and some of the girls being brought out in handcuffs, their faces shielded.

Dr. Paul Reilly suddenly entered the room, moving swiftly. He extended his hand in greeting. "Armstrong, it's good to see you again, although I hate that we keep running into each other like this."

"It's good to see you, too, Paul. How is she?" Armstrong asked as the two men shook hands.

"Detective Winstead is one tough cookie. We gave her twelve stitches to close the laceration in the back of her head. And, she has a mild concussion. We would like to keep her here overnight, but she refuses to stay. She really needs to just rest. Her headache is going to persist for a day or two. Also, she might experience some nausea, dizziness and blurred vision. That will all go away as long as she takes it easy and doesn't get hit in the head again. I also don't recommend that she be alone for the next forty-eight hours. If the headache gets worse or there's any slurring in her speech, loss of consciousness or seizures, then you need to get her back here to the hospital as soon as possible."

Armstrong nodded. "When can I see her?"

"I'll walk you back to her room."

"Thanks, Paul," Armstrong said as he shook the man's hand a second time. "I really appreciate you."

"Just doing my job. How's that sister of yours doing?" the doctor asked.

Armstrong laughed. "Simone is still as mean as ever."

Dr. Reilly laughed with him. "I want to call and invite her to dinner, but I'm scared."

He nodded his understanding. His sister had a reputation for chewing men up and spitting them out without a moment of hesitation. Simone and the good doctor had dated very briefly before Dr. Reilly had left the country to do some mission work in Africa. His leaving hadn't sat well with Simone, nor had his return inspired her to reconnect with the man.

"It's like I warned you before, bro," Armstrong said, "you need to tread cautiously with that one. She even scares me!"

The two men laughed again.

"Well, duty calls," Dr. Reilly said as the beeper on his hip vibrated. "If Detective Winstead experiences any problems, don't hesitate to contact me. You have my private number."

"Thanks, Paul!"

Armstrong took a breath as his friend moved swiftly down the hall. He hesitated for a split second and then knocked on the door and waited for permission to enter.

"Come in," Danni called out.

Armstrong did, pushing the door open easily. "Hey!"

"Hey!" she answered, smiling at the sight of him.

"I hear you're refusing medical care."

"I received medical care. I'm refusing to sit in this hospital all night long. I have work to do." She had dressed and was sitting on the edge of the hospital bed, waiting for someone to bring her discharge papers.

He moved to her side, inspecting the large bandage that covered the back of her skull. Shaking his head, he cupped his hand beneath her chin and lifted her face to his. He kissed her gently, his lips brushing lightly against hers.

"Well, I'm taking you home to get some rest," he said when he finally pulled himself from her.

"But we still have work…" she started.

He shook his head. "Everything is under control," he said as he updated her.

"Are we sure Ginger is safe?"

"I spoke to Mr. Balducci myself. She's fine and he is bringing her down to the station tomorrow himself for us to talk to."

"I don't feel good about that," Danni said, concern furrowing her brow.

"I wasn't sure what was going to happen with you, so I made a judgment call. I didn't want to hold her in a cell all night, and I don't think she's going to run. He gave me his word that she would be safe, and I trust that, despite everything else I know about him."

Danni nodded, having no choice but to trust his decision.

Armstrong dropped down onto the bed beside her. "I'm a little pissed at you. Why didn't you say something about being hurt? You were worried about Ginger and Pie getting medical help, but not yourself."

Danni blew a soft sigh. "I really thought I was okay."

"Well, clearly you weren't. It's a good thing it wasn't worse."

"So, how long are you going to fuss at me?"

"This isn't fussing. Stick around and I'm sure you'll see fussing."

"I'm happy that you care," Danni said with a wry smile.

Armstrong pulled her into his arms and held her. Danni allowed herself to relax, resting her head against his broad chest. She closed her eyes and inhaled him. Joy swelled full and thick between them. They settled against each other as they waited, nothing else needing to be said. When the nurse returned with her discharge papers, he was still holding tightly to her, Danni having dozed off.

Chapter 19

Danni woke in Armstrong's bed. It was still dark out, the rising sun hours from reaching its full potential. The door was open, and she could hear him snoring softly in the other room. She remembered his insisting that she stay with him. He had retrieved her belongings and checked her out of her hotel room. Despite her protests, he had refused to take no for an answer, insisting it was doctor's orders.

Although she didn't say so, she was grateful. Being near him had put her at ease, and she realized just how unnerved she had been with Carlo and that lot. She blew a soft sigh as she thought about everything, putting the details into perspective.

Despite her initial hopes that he was one of the good guys, she truly hadn't been all that surprised to discover Carlo was involved. She hadn't pegged him for masterminding everything, thinking instead that he was a willing bystander, turning a blind eye and a deaf ear to what he knew was going on.

She and Armstrong had talked for a good long while before he had tucked her into his bed, kissing her gently as she'd fallen off to sleep. He'd shared the secret with her about the Balducci family lineage, swearing her to secrecy. Both surmised that had been the reason behind Carlo's motivation for doing what he had done. A part of him had wanted to carry on the family's illegal enterprises to build his reputation and perhaps impress the father who had yet to claim him as his son. Watching Alexander continually fawning over and protecting Pie had been a thorn in his side that he couldn't overcome.

She was excited to hear that the district attorney's office was willing to offer Ginger witness protection and an immunity deal; she just hoped by the time she talked with her, the young woman would still be willing to share everything she knew.

There was still the issue of some man named Hobart having transferred $1.3 million in bitcoin to Pius to claim her, but federal investigators had already taken up that search and were confident his days of buying virgins were done and finished.

Rising from the bed, Danni moved into the bathroom. Stripping out of her clothes, she examined herself in the full-length mirror. She was nicely bruised, black-and-blue marks covering her back and buttocks. Although she was sore, she wasn't in any major pain, and that headache had finally subsided. The bandage around her head wasn't cute, she thought, but cute was sometimes overrated.

Suddenly desperate for a hot shower, she turned on the water and stepped under the spray, mindful not to get her head wet. Some twenty minutes later, she felt renewed and invigorated. Her teeth were brushed and her face was washed. Wrapping herself in an oversize towel, she moved from the bathroom into the bedroom.

Searching her bags and finding her toiletries, she moisturized herself from head to toe. A light spritz of her favorite perfume had her feeling semi-normal again. She slipped on a pair of lace panties and an oversize T-shirt. A silk scarf wrapped around her head had her looking fairly stylish and less like a patient.

She sat down at the bedside, a host of things racing through her head. Armstrong Black dominated her thoughts. Everything about the man moved her spirit. Love had always felt like a foreign concept, but the idea of falling in love with Armstrong felt like the most natural thing in the world for her to do. Pondering the idea of staying in Chicago to pursue a relationship felt right in so many ways. She couldn't begin to explain how she suddenly felt like destiny was calling her name. Loudly. Whether or not she would pay attention still remained to be seen.

She rose from her seat and slowly eased her way into the living room, where he was sleeping soundly. His sofa pulled out into a bed, and he lay sprawled across the thin mattress, a sheet tangled at his feet. He was bare chested, wearing only a pair of navy blue boxers. His limbs were like tree trunks, thick and solid. His skin was a vat of warm, creamy milk chocolate, silky smooth and glossy. Both arms were curled over his head, and his mouth was open ever so slightly. It seemed as if he were resting well, his entire body relaxed. He slept peacefully. He was truly beautiful. She sat down beside him, watching the rise and fall of his chest as he breathed. He snored softly, a slight whistle on the exhale of each warm breath. The sound both amused and comforted her.

Danni stretched out her legs and crawled into the bed beside him. She eased her body against his. Armstrong woke with a slight start, but quickly recognized that she was there. He wrapped his arms around her and pulled her close.

"Are you okay?" he asked, his voice a loud whisper. "How is your head?"

Cradled in the curve of his arm, Danni nodded. "I'm good," she answered. "I just needed to be near you."

He gave her a gentle squeeze and shifted his body against her as he placed a damp kiss against her forehead. Danni eased her body up and over his. She pressed her palms against the mattress at his side, and her legs stretched over his body so that one knee was on each side of his hips. She captured his mouth, kissing him eagerly, her lips dancing easily with his lips. The beginnings of an erection searched between her parted legs. The hold he had on her tightened as he gasped, surprise registered in the swift gust of air.

Danni winced, a hint of pain shooting through her.

"Sorry! Baby, I'm so sorry. I didn't mean to hurt you," he said as he snatched his hands from her.

She shook her head. "Just not so tight. I'm a little more banged up than I realized."

Armstrong nodded as he resumed his ministrations, his hands gently caressing her, sliding beneath her T-shirt so that his fingers heated her skin. He stroked her back and hips and her buttocks, each pass of his hands raising the heat level between them. They lay like that for a good long while, just allowing themselves to revel in the warmth of each other's bodies. He took a deep breath and twitched for attention. In response, Danni chuckled softly, rotating her pelvis against him teasingly.

"You know what you're doing to me, right?" Armstrong whispered.

She gave him a seductive smile. "I know. I'm doing it on purpose."

"As long as we're on the same page."

"I certainly hope so. I know you're a little slow."

He laughed. "I'm going to let you have that for now because I'm a little challenged and you're not letting me think straight."

"Oh, you seem pretty straight to me," she said teasingly as she rotated her hips in the other direction.

Armstrong allowed himself to wallow in the sensations her touch was eliciting from his body. He was hard and throbbing, and with her pelvis like a magnet, drawing him toward the heat, all he wanted was to feel himself pulsing deep in her core. He trailed his fingers down across her backside, and she twitched, reminding him that he couldn't grab her ass the way he wanted.

"I don't want to hurt you," he whispered. "I'm going to follow your lead."

"You do that," she said. Danni kissed him hungrily, her mouth dancing sweetly with his.

Tongues tangled, searching, teasing, tasting. Hands glided, caressing, stroking, touching. Skin kissed skin, her whole body covering his. Her breasts were ripe oranges against his chest, and he marveled at how amazing she felt in his arms. He resisted the urge to pump his hips up into her crotch.

"Condom?" Danni whispered as she nearly brought him to orgasm, grinding intensely against him.

He nodded, rolling so that she lay back against the mattress. He moved into the bedroom, returning before she could blink. As he crossed the room, he stepped out of his boxers, returning to her in full glory. He tore at the wrapper with his teeth, pulling the prophylactic into his hand.

"Let me," Danni said as she took it from him. She was wide-eyed as she took him into her hands, stroking him slowly.

"I'm not going to last if you keep doing that," he muttered, his breathing labored.

Danni continued to pump her hands along his length a few more times before she sheathed him.

She pushed him back against the pillows. "This way," she whispered as she straddled him again easily. "I don't think I can lie on my back."

He nodded as he moved his palm down the back of one leg and up the other. He snaked his hand beneath her panties and stroked her backside. She was hot, a light layer of perspiration rising against her skin. He dipped his hand lower, teasing the entrance to her most private place, and was rewarded with slick moisture coating his fingers. She was wet and wanting, desire surging with a vengeance. He suddenly snatched her panties from her, ripping the silk fabric from her body, the garment discarded to the floor.

The gesture was intense and urgent, and Danni answered his demand. Rising slightly, she settled herself against him, the head of his erection teasing her labia. And then she plunged her body against his, taking him in deeply until her pelvis locked tightly against his. She rode him slowly at first as he massaged her breasts, teasing her nipples between his thumb and forefinger. The buds hardened like rock candy, and he lifted himself up to take one and then the other into his mouth. He suckled like he was drowning and desperate, savoring the taste of her as she slammed herself up and down against him.

The intensity of the moment was corporeal. Heat was thick and abundant. He met her stroke for stroke, heaving his hips up and down, as she rotated round and round, over and over again. He convulsed, his body saying what his head and mouth couldn't. A scream stuck in his throat, and he gulped air, fueling the sensations sweeping through his body. His orgasm hit hard, the volcanic eruption spewing with a vengeance, and then Danni fell into bliss with him, murmuring his name over and over again as if she were in prayer. When she finally collapsed above him, her body was spent, every nerve ending and muscle vibrating with sheer, unadulterated pleasure.

She couldn't begin to fathom going back to a life without him. She couldn't deny that this thing between them was more than either of them could have ever imagined. It was love. Beautiful, intoxicating, affirming, necessary and possessing. She loved him. She had fallen in love with him. A tear rolled past her dark lashes, and she struggled not to cry the ugly cry as understanding swept through her, sealing her fate and the eternity she yearned for. She wanted Armstrong Black, and she wanted to be with him for the rest of her life.

Armstrong shifted beneath her, his arms coming back around to hold her. He whispered, the words blowing like the sweetest breeze past his full lips. "I love you, Danni! I love you very much!"

They were like giggly grade-schoolers as they sat together over a breakfast of scrambled eggs, turkey bacon and toast. They'd gotten little sleep, their night together spent doing everything but sleeping. If she hadn't been sore before, Danni thought, she was definitely feeling very uncomfortable this morning. She swallowed two of the hospital-issued pain pills with orange juice.

In the wee hours of the morning they had made tentative plans. She would move to Chicago, but she would get her own apartment that she probably would sleep in only once or twice. They would date, but wouldn't go public just yet. They would tell his family immediately; hers could wait until whenever she felt like giving up the information. He got sex on Mondays, Wednesdays and Fridays. She got sex on Tuesdays, Thursdays and Saturdays, and sex on Sundays was up for grabs. She would find a nice Baptist church for Sunday services, and he would join her. Sunday dinner with his parents was mandatory. Hopefully she would find a job with the Chicago Police Department, and he promised to put in a good word for her with his brother and father. Their plans were tentative, and they were excited about each and every one of them.

Danni reached for his necktie and pulled him to her. She kissed his lips, then pressed her cheek to his. "I'd take you back to bed, but we need to get a move on it," she said as she let him go and gently straightened the paisley-printed neckwear.

"*I* need to get a move on it," he said, smiling at her. "*You're* supposed to be resting."

She winked an eye at him. "We'll compromise. We'll both get us a nap together later."

Armstrong laughed. "Why does that sound like we won't be napping?"

"Because you, Detective, have a dirty mind. Now, let's get you to that press conference before your brother is mad at both of us!"

* * *

As promised, Ginger and Pie both showed up at ten o'clock, accompanied by Alexander and a team of attorneys. Pie and his grandfather were escorted to one interrogation room and Ginger to another. Attorneys followed them both.

Danni knew before she asked the first question that Ginger had changed her mind, or it had been changed for her. Each of her questions was answered by the young woman's legal counsel, a lanky man with Elvis Presley hair in a very expensive suit. When it became apparent that she wasn't going to get any answers, she laid her pen down and turned off the tape recorder.

"Counselor, may I speak to your client privately? Off the record," she asked. Her gaze was focused on Ginger, who stared back at her with equal temerity.

"I don't think…" the man started before Ginger raised a hand to stall his comment.

"It's fine," she said. "Please leave us alone."

"I would advise you against…"

"It'll be fine," Ginger repeated, leveling him with a hard stare.

The two women waited until the door was closed tightly behind the man. Danni stood and flipped the switch to disengage the two-way mirror, cutting off their view from anyone standing on the other side.

"He got to you, didn't he?" she asked as she sat back down. "Did he threaten you, Ginny?"

"Who? Pius?"

"No. Alexander Balducci. Because if he did I will arrest him for witness tampering."

Ginger blew a soft sigh. "It's not what you think," she said.

"Then what is it?"

Ginger leaned back in her seat. "It's Paul," she said, calling Pie by his government name. "When we first met he was so innocent. And sweet. I was working for Pius. He started out helping me. Like he helped you. I moved in with him just like you did. He was really nice at first. Then he changed. But I learned how to play the game, and the more money I made him, the better it was for me. He wanted to, but he never got rid of me because he couldn't. Pie took a liking to me, and I used that to my advantage. As long as I made Pie happy and he wanted me around, there was nothing Pius could do about it. Mr. Balducci wouldn't have it." She took a deep breath before she continued.

"Pius didn't want to lose the money I was making him, so he started grooming Pie. Convincing him he was some kind of bad boy in charge and pimping me and the other girls was a good thing. With his temper, Pius knew the girls were afraid of him. He lashed out when he felt threatened or Pius pushed him. He looked up to Pius and he was always trying to impress him, emulating what he saw him do. But when it was just the two of us, he was really good, and he can be very sweet.

"Mr. Balducci has offered me the opportunity to stay with Pie. We're moving into the house with him and his mother. He says I'll be able to go to school if I want and Pius can't make me turn tricks anymore. I'll get an allowance and it'll be different. And he says if I ever want to leave, I can do that, too."

Danni took a deep breath, holding it briefly before she blew a heavy sigh. "And you believe him?"

"I do, because he knows one of my best friends, someone I trust, is a badass police woman and she won't let him hurt me."

"So you're not going to testify against Pius?"

"Oh, yes I will!" Ginger exclaimed. "I promised you I'd give you a statement, and I will keep that promise. I will do whatever it takes to send Pius to hell for the rest of his life. But I can't say anything against Pie. I won't testify against him, and you needed to understand why. I made that promise to his grandfather."

Danni nodded. "I'm proud of you, Ginny. You're an amazing young woman."

"I'm a survivor first. Always, no matter what."

"I guess we should call your attorney back in and I'll revise my questions?"

Ginger grinned. "That works for me, cop!"

Danni gave Ginger a hug before the young woman turned and exited the building hand in hand with Pie. There was something in her eyes, a sense of relief that seemed to flood her spirit, and her smile was light and joyous. She watched as the couple took off in her car and Mr. Balducci took off in the back of a limousine.

Armstrong moved to her side. Her arms were crossed over her chest as she cut an eye in his direction. "You good?"

She nodded. "I'm good. How about you?"

"It's always good when we get the bad guys."

"What's going to happen to Pie? He's not actually squeaky clean in all of this."

"Luckily we don't have to make that decision. We'll present all of our evidence to the district attorney and let them decide Pie's fate. I'm thinking they're going to cut him a deal in exchange for a guilty plea and no jail time."

"I can live with that."

"Me, too. What about Ginger?"

"That girl will be just fine. I have no doubts that by the time this is all done and finished, she will be holding an executive position in Balducci's organization. What's the update on Angel?"

"Angel and her mother have been moved into protective custody, but I don't think they have anything to worry about."

"Better safe than sorry."

"I agree. You've done good, Detective. Everyone's impressed with what you were able to accomplish."

"Thank you," she said, eyeing him a second time. "Sir."

Armstrong gestured with his head. "We have a meeting to attend. Lieutenant Black would like to speak with us."

"Lieutenant Black?"

He nodded and then he laughed heartily.

There was a round of applause for them as Danni and Armstrong moved through police headquarters on West Harrison Street. Making their way to the corner office with the view, the accolades were plentiful, high fives, slaps on the back and congratulations ringing through the afternoon air.

The couple exchanged a quick look as Armstrong knocked, waiting for permission to enter. Both were surprised when Armstrong's father pulled the door open and welcomed them both inside. Danni was suddenly nervous, her stomach turning flips like her intestines were part of a circus show.

She took a deep breath as Parker waved them both inside. They stood at attention until he gestured for them to relax.

"Please, take a seat," he said, gesturing for them both to sit on the sofa. His father turned one of the wingback chairs around to face them and dropped into it. Parker took the other. "I wanted to take a moment to commend you both. This was a big win for law enforcement, and you have done us proud."

"Thank you, Lieutenant," Armstrong said.

"Thank you, sir," Danni echoed.

Parker turned his attention toward Danni. "Detective Winstead, we understand you might be considering staying in Chicago? Is that true?"

Danni cut a quick eye toward Armstrong. His expression was blank as he stared straight ahead at his brother. She took a breath before she answered. "Yes, sir. It's something I'm considering."

Parker nodded. "Then I can assume you might be looking for employment?"

She nodded. "I would be."

"Well, the Chicago Police Department would like to offer you a position with us. We could use a detective of your caliber in our ranks."

A smile pulled at Danni's lips. "Thank you, sir. That's very kind of you."

"You'll need to meet with our human resources officer for specifics. They'll prepare a formal offer for you to consider."

"Yes, sir. I'll do that."

Armstrong's father cleared his throat. "You both understand that under the circumstances any offer will come with some restrictions. In light of your *relationship*, you two will no longer be able to work side by side.

We were thinking, Detective Winstead, that since you have a strong background in vice that you will do well in our Narcotics Unit."

Danni nodded. "Thank you, Superintendent Black. I understand."

Armstrong's father stood up. He extended his hand toward his son. Armstrong rose to meet him, the two shaking hands. "I'm very proud of you, son."

"Thank you."

Jerome winked an eye at Danni. "I expect we'll see you at family dinner on Sunday, Detective?"

Danni smiled. "Yes, sir. Thank you, sir."

The patriarch gave them all one last nod and moved out the door, closing it firmly behind him. Armstrong and Parker exchanged a look. The two men shook hands and bumped shoulders. Parker extended his hand to shake Danni's.

"You've impressed me, Detective. I want you to know we didn't offer you this opportunity lightly. You've earned your spot here."

"I really appreciate that, sir."

Parker leaned back against his desk, crossing his arms over his chest. "So, have you two picked out a date yet?"

Danni shot Armstrong a look. "Excuse me?"

"I was just asking. For a friend. Our mother, actually. She's nosy like that."

The trio laughed. Armstrong reached out and pulled Danni into his arms. He kissed her, the brazen gesture moving Parker to shake his head.

"Sorry," Armstrong said to his brother. "I couldn't resist."

"I'm going to pretend like I didn't just see that and

you two will refrain from doing that again while you're on duty. Is that understood?"

"Yes, sir!" the two chimed simultaneously.

Parker moved back behind his desk. "Detective Black, you are hereby ordered to take vacation. I understand you have some forty-plus days saved up, and I imagine Detective Winstead is going to need some help moving."

"Is that an order, Lieutenant?"

"It is and it came directly from the top."

Armstrong looked at his brother with a raised brow, curiosity rising. "From Dad?"

Parker shook his head. "No. Mom!" He picked up a stack of files from his desk and moved toward the door. "I'll be away from my desk for the next ten minutes or so. Be gone when I return," he said as he made his exit. He paused, his hand on the doorknob. "Congratulations again, Danni, and welcome to the family."

When they were alone, Danni stepped into his arms, moving her body against Armstrong's. "You've been talking about me!"

He nodded. "We agreed that I could tell my family."

"Why do I get the impression that you had that conversation sometime before we made that decision?"

"Probably because I did. I had to tell someone I loved you. I couldn't tell you! And I do tell my brothers pretty much everything."

Danni pressed a kiss to his lips. "I love you, Armstrong Black. You have made me the happiest woman in the whole wide world!"

He grinned. "Baby, I'm good like that!"

* * * * *